The Rebel Christian Publishing

Kindle Vella ASIN: B09YG6BLYZ

ISBN (eBook): 9781957290126

ISBN (Print): 9781957290133

This is a work of fiction. Any references to historical events, real people, or real places are used fictitiously. Names, characters, and places are products of the author's imagination. Inclusion of or reference to any Christian elements or themes are used in a fictitious manner and are not meant to be perceived or interpreted as an act of disrespect against such a wonderful and beautiful faith.

Cover image provided by Shutterstock

Artist: Momentum Ronnarong

The Rebel Christian Publishing LLC

350 Northern Blvd STE 324 – 1390

Albany, NY 12204

Visit us: http://www.therebelchristian.com/

Email us: rebel@therebelchristian.com

This book was originally published as an episodic story on the Kindle Vella platform. It has been modified and formatted for your enjoyment. Original author's notes can be found at the very end of the book. Please enjoy **Withered Rose** and take the time to leave your thoughts and opinion in a review on Amazon, Goodreads, and Bookbub. Thank you!

Series Order:

Withered Rose

Clipping Thorns

Starting Over (Fall 2022)

Other Books by Valicity Elaine:

Patches

The 'I' Word

I AM MAN series:

I AM MAN

I AM LOST

I AM BROKEN

I AM FREE

I AM COMPLETE

Cross Academy series:

Cross Academy

The Howler's Cry

The Nine Births of Carnage (Fall 2022)

The Testament Relics (coming soon)

Cross Academy: Book V (coming soon)

To Jesus Christ

Withered Rose

Book I

By Valicity Elaine

A Rebel Christian Publishing Book

Diamonds are just pretty shackles...

—*Christina Jäger*

A note from the author

*** <u>Warning</u> ***

This is a work of Christian fiction. There are no scenes of sex, no foul language, and no gore. However, the story does follow a young woman trying to escape the **mafia**. Rosa's environment is not warm and welcoming, but that only serves to strengthen her dependence on God.

That being said, readers may find some content to be sensitive/triggering, such as abuse, gang violence, etc.

Our protagonists are married, so I did not shy away from depicting their encounters. However, I am still a Christian author, and I do believe there are certain lines that should not be crossed in Christian fiction.

But just to be safe, **this book is best enjoyed by mature Christian readers ages 17+**

Please continue at your own discretion.

Chapter One

Minnie likes her tea sweet. I remember this at the last second and toss another three sugar cubes into the pot before I stir and set it aside. She's not a picky girl, but she can be fussy when it comes to her tea. I want to get this right because tonight is important, and it'd be a real shame if I ruined things by serving it bitter.

I load the tray on the counter with appetizers, grab three glasses and fill them with ice, carefully place a tiny bowl of lemon wedges in the corner, and carry the load out to the dining room. Minnie is sitting at the table with her mother, Melissa. She's smiling—which is a good thing—and when her eyes meet mine, they fill with joy as she lets out an excited laugh.

"Rose!" she says, hopping down from her chair and running toward me.

"Careful!" I try to balance the tray as she gives me a hug

and then snatches a deviled egg from the serving platter.

She laughs. "Did you make all this yourself?"

"I did," I grunt, carrying the food to the table. Minnie follows me, snatching another deviled egg from the tray before plopping into her chair and sighing.

"I'm so hungry!"

"Dinner will be ready soon," I tell her, passing out the glasses filled with ice. "Have some tea and appetizers until then." The teapot is still warm to the touch, but I'm too nervous to notice it burning against my fingers as I shakily pour. "When is Arthur getting here?" I ask as casually as I can.

Arthur is Minnie's older brother and the man I've been crushing on for the last six months. Things between us aren't serious at all, but he's the first man who's made me wish they were. I shouldn't even be thinking about dating—especially since I'm technically homeless right now, but Arthur isn't the sort of man who cares about that. He knows my situation and he's never seemed to mind. He was there when his mother took me in. He was there when I showed up on the steps of her church, dazed and covered in blood. He's seen me at my worst, and he's never treated me differently because of it.

Arthur is a good man. Good enough to make me want to take my chances with him. Even though getting attached to people is the last thing I should be doing. But it's already too late with Minnie and Melissa. I've been living here with them since I arrived in this little town of Norman, New Jersey. Melissa could have turned me away, she could have handed me over to the cops—or worse, sent me back to where I came from, but she didn't. She opened her home and heart to me; I couldn't help but open my heart to her in turn.

"He should be here soon." Minnie gives me a sly smile and I know I've been caught. She's only twelve-years-old, thirteen years younger than Arthur, but she's smart for her age. Smart enough to know when I'm prodding for information on her brother.

Over the last six months, I've learned that it's Minnie who has Arthur's heart and it's Minnie I've got to win over if I want him to share his heart with me. His mother is a darling, too, but Melissa's too busy running a string of homeless shelters to get overly involved in her son's love life. I don't think she's even noticed my little crush yet. Thank God.

"Are you excited he's coming over?" Minnie asks, squeezing the juice from her lemon wedge into her glass and then stirring with a spoon.

Arthur doesn't live here with his mother and sister, he moved out when he passed the entrance exams for the Norman Police Department. That was one month before I showed up—I sleep in his old room. Since he's a cop, he's busy most of the time and only comes over for dinner every now and then. Unless I see him at church on Sundays, we don't get to speak very often so this dinner means a lot to me, and Minnie can tell. She's known about my feelings probably longer than I have, but, mercifully, she's never said anything to him about it.

"I'm excited to see if he's got any news about a new job for me," I reply to Minnie, keeping my eyes on my glass of iced tea. I squeeze my own lemon wedge into the drink and then stir and sip. I grimace. It's cloyingly sweet but Minnie hasn't complained so I suppose it's good enough for her.

She grins at me across the table, crossing her legs like a lady and tossing a dark curl over her thin shoulder. Minnie is a mirror image of Arthur, just younger and feminine. Dark brown skin and thick hair, full lips paired with a round nose. She's been begging Melissa to let her get her nose pierced for the last month, but her mother won't budge on the issue.

"I'm sure Arthur's got great news," Melissa says, frowning at her iced tea. I guess she doesn't like hers as sweet as her daughter does. "I've been hearing whispers that the station is looking for secretaries."

I force myself to smile at the job offer. It isn't what I want to do for the rest of my life, but I threw my life away when I ran off and wound up here, so I'm going to smile and take whatever I can get. I'm blessed to have an opportunity like this in the first place. I have no resume, no education, and no experience, but Arthur's been putting in a good word for me at the station, hoping the influence of a fresh new officer stretches further than the occasional discount at the coffee shop up the street.

"Are you ready to start working?" Minnie asks, munching on a celery stick.

I nod slowly. I've never worked a day in my life, but I've got to start soon. I can't keep living off Melissa like this, and I need to start saving up money so I can get my own place.

"Don't be nervous." Melissa pats my hand and I realize

I've been holding my breath.

I exhale shakily. "I'm sorry. This is all still new to me."

"The first year of recovery usually is," she tells me, leaning close so I can see the lines of her face bunch together as she smiles warmly.

Recovery. Melissa thinks I'm a battered prostitute running from my pimp. I never told her that was the case, but she runs multiple shelters through her women's ministry, so she's used to taking in ladies in that sort of situation. Battered wives, daughters running away from abusive parents, prostitutes trying to find a new life.

I suppose when I banged on the doors of Trinity Baptist Church six months ago, I probably looked like any one of the ladies she's worked with before. I was barefoot, half deranged, covered in blood, and wearing clothes that were torn nearly to shreds. I haven't corrected Melissa's assumption, so every now and then she pulls me aside to give me these tidbits of encouragement, like I'm part of some step-program. I don't mind. If I told her the truth—the real reason I showed up at her church like that, the real people I was running from—she would send me right back without hesitation. I can't risk her knowing who I really am. I can't risk anyone learning the truth. Once they find out, they will never look at me the same.

Minnie gasps, catching my attention. At first, I think she's reacting to the slightly burned potato wedge in her hand, then I see the phone she's holding, and I realize she's just being a dramatic pre-teen.

"What's going on?" I ask, leaning over to see the glowing

5

screen.

Melissa sighs. "I told you no phones at the table, Minnie."

"No phones at the table during *dinner*," she corrects, batting her long eyelashes. "These are just the appetizers. Dinner hasn't been served yet."

"Just tell us what's got you gasping like that," I say.

She holds up the phone and repeats the bold headline. "New York City Boss found dead in his own home today."

My heart stops for a moment. We're in Norman, New Jersey—eight hours away from the City—but our town still gets news and updates about everything going on in the Big Apple. Reports from the City make headlines even in California sometimes. It's because New York is different. Lawless.

It all happened ten years ago when a cop was arrested for killing a civilian during a routine call. There were rumors the incident was racially motivated, triggering a countrywide protest to defund the police altogether. People marched and chanted for weeks, rallying in the streets and demanding justice. Officials faced immense pressure from the public.

Eventually, New York City gave in.

On March 19, 2021, exactly one year after the protests began, New York City defunded its police department. The decision forced the department to cut over half the police force, leaving one of the largest cities in the world virtually defenseless against crime. Without enough manpower to maintain law and order, the City fell into fiery chaos. From the ashes rose a new order.

Crime bosses took over, one borough at a time. Less than six months after the great defunding act, the mafia held the Big Apple in its hand.

Gangs had always existed in the City, but without the police, they were able to come out of hiding. They no longer had to worry about arrests, they no longer had to fear imprisonment. New York City was officially ruled by anarchy.

It's been this way for ten years now and I don't think it's going to change any time soon. People should have been afraid of what was happening when it'd first started, but they were fascinated instead. Life in New York sounded like something straight from an old gangster film. People getting killed in broad daylight, cops unable to do anything or solve any crimes. The media romanticized what was happening and the public became obsessed. Watching the local news suddenly felt like watching a violent reality TV show.

Ten years later and people are still obsessed. Minnie is proof of that as she holds up her phone and rattles off the names of known mafia bosses like she's naming her favorite celebrities.

"Maybe it was Jameson Willis, or one of his sons. It could even be a boss from the Moreno family, they're hardly in the news," she says, then lets out a dreamy sigh. "I hope it wasn't one of the Volkov bosses. They're my favorites."

"Minnie Hart, put your phone away!" Melissa orders sharply.

Her tone snaps me from my reflections, and I nod agreement. "You shouldn't be looking at New York news. It's never good."

Minnie frowns. "Can't I at least find out who died? This could end up pouring into Jersey."

"It won't come to Jersey," Melissa assures her.

She's right. As dark as New York City has become, the mafia's influence doesn't stretch beyond their borders. People might have sat back and watched the Apple rot, but they learned from the mistakes of the NYC officials. No other city in the country defunded their police departments after the mafia took control. In fact, cities nearest New York made an effort to fortify their borders and reinforce their own departments. That's how Arthur got to take the exam. Before the defunding happened, Norman held the police exam once every five years. Now, police recruitment happens twice a year. Being only eight hours from NYC puts this little town in a dangerous spot if the mafia ever tries to expand its reach but that won't happen. It's too risky for them and Norman is more than prepared to handle whatever riffraff flows out of New York. It's the reason I ran here when I escaped. It's a safe place to live.

Minnie sits back and blows air through her cheeks, still staring at her phone. "I still want to know which boss died."

I do too, but I keep my mouth shut as Melissa shifts in her chair like she's going to launch across the table and snatch Minnie's phone from her hands.

The young girl looks up in enough time to catch the look of fury on her mother's face. She cowers. "Sorry, Mama. I'll put it away."

"Did you find out who it was?" I ask slowly. When Melissa glances at me, I add, "Since you risked Melissa's wrath over it."

She laughs. "It was Giovanni De Luca. Boss of the Italian mafia."

The room tilts sideways, and I grip the edge of the table to steel myself.

Giovanni De Luca… It can't be.

My jaw begins to ache, and I suddenly realize I've been clenching it. As I relax my face, I glance up to see Melissa watching me closely. Her eyes are squinted, like she's peering right into my head and reading my thoughts. Good thing I have no idea what to think of this.

"Rose, are you—"

"I need to check the roasted chicken," I say, cutting off Melissa before she can finish her question.

I'm in the kitchen before anyone can stop me from leaving, reaching for the counter to stable myself as I'm racked by a wave of guilt and grief and joy all at once. Giovanni De Luca is dead. My nightmare is over.

Six months ago, I showed up on the doorstep of Trinity Baptist Church. I was taken in by this kind family and treated like their own. I told them my name was Rose Lucas, and that I was running away—trying to start over. That was only half-true.

My name is not Rose Lucas. It's Rosa De Luca. And Giovanni De Luca is more than the boss of the Italian mafia of New York. He is my father. Which makes me the princess of the De Lucas. Daughter of a mafia boss.

In New York, they called me the Flower of Manhattan. An Italian Rose. I was considered a mafia princess. But my life was nothing like the princess fairytales you read about in children's stories. My father wasn't a king ruling over a beautiful country with horses and knights to protect his precious daughter. He was a *kingpin*, ruling Manhattan with an iron fist.

I grew up in the mafia. I was raised on the other side of the law, even before the defunding. It wasn't until then that I realized just how screwed up my family really was. Before the mafia took over New York, we'd had to operate in secrecy, but with the police force largely out of the way, my family was set loose on the City. An animal released from its cage.

Violence, death, and war became everyday things. Right out in the open. I was only ten when the defunding happened. I didn't have a complete understanding of what was going on around me. But I learned very quickly. And I hated every second of it.

That's why I ran away. I managed to escape from the mafia—from my father—and ended up here in Norman. It hadn't been easy to get away, but it was even tougher to move on once I'd crossed the borders into Jersey. I had no money, no resources, and no name. There was no way I could walk around telling people my identity, that would have gotten me sent right back to where I'd come from.

So, when Melissa accepted me into her home, I told her my name was Rose Lucas. I let her believe I was running away from prostitution and drugs. I buried the truth about everything. Guilt flooded me every day—every time I heard the name Rose, instead of Rosa. Every time Melissa smiled at me and patted my cheek and told me everything would be okay.

I believed her when she told me that. I believed everything would eventually work itself out. And until now, I had only my hope and Melissa's faith to go on. But now my biggest enemy is finally dead.

I should feel safe. I should feel elated. But I don't.

I feel like I'm dying inside because Giovanni was a monster, but he was still my father. The fact that he was found in his own home sets my hands to trembling. I'm shaking so badly; I feel like I'm going to faint.

Found dead in his own home. The words repeat in the back of my head, and I lurch forward, gagging as tears flow down my cheeks. I'm sick with grief.

My father was found in his estate. In my *home*. The place I'd grown up in. Where I'd learned to walk, and played with my dolls, where I ran down the halls squealing in laughter as my older brother chased me. The place where I snuck out to meet my first boyfriend. And where I said goodbye to my brother before I walked out of his life for good.

Except now it doesn't feel like this is for good. It doesn't seem final. I don't feel safe. Even though one of the most powerful men in New York City is now dead, I have a hair-raising feeling that something is very wrong. That I am not safe at all.

How did my father die? Who could have gotten to him? Does it mean they're going after my brother, too? Or me?

No, I tell myself, swallowing my nerves and choking back a sob. *They all think I'm dead. They have no idea I'm here in Norman.*

"Rose—"

The sound of my name pulls me from my thoughts. I gasp as I look up and see Arthur standing in the kitchen entrance. Slowly, I work out his image as the tears blurring my vision drip down my cheeks and onto the floor. He's frowning, but not in anger. Somehow, Arthur looks more heartbroken than me. Like it was his father who just died on the news.

I suck in a breath and exhale a sob. It's all he needs to hear to cross the floor and take me into his arms.

I feel safe here. Holding onto Arthur as he strokes my hair. "Talk to me," he murmurs.

But I can't. I can't tell him I'm the daughter of a mafia boss who was just found dead, and the men responsible might be coming after me now. If I say that, he will know that I'm a liar. That I've never told him or his family anything real or true about me. The last six months of my life have been pure joy, but its joy built on the ashes of my burning morals.

I am willing to do whatever it takes to stay as far away from New York City as possible. Even lie to an innocent family. Lie to a man I think I might be falling in love with. Lie to a little girl who calls me her big sister. Lie to a woman who took me in for no other reason except that she's a good Christian woman who just wanted to treat others the way she would want to be treated.

I would rather die than return home. But my willingness to give up my own life doesn't make it okay to put the lives of others in danger.

So, when Arthur pulls away and holds my face in his, when he peers down into my eyes and asks me what's wrong, the tears that flow are no longer for my father. They're for myself. Because I know this family is no longer safe. Not as long as I'm here.

Once again, I have to pack up and leave with nothing but the clothes on my back. I can only hope Arthur and Melissa and Minnie are smart enough not to come after me.

Chapter Two

It's been over a week since I found out about my father's death. The news is still covering the entire event. Every. Single. Station. My brother, Gio Jr., has taken over the family estate and business. He's the new don of the Italian mafia and he's making moves that make no sense. I've read articles about him rearranging the business, writing up contracts with other companies we would never trade with. He even held a press conference, which was aired live, stating that he trusted the tiny police force of NYC to handle the situation.

I might be six months out the mafia, but I'm not stupid. Trusting the police is Junior's way of saying he's not investigating the crime. Which means he doesn't think it was a crime.

I don't want to entertain the deeper meaning behind his words—that my father might have been killed by someone in the family. That Junior is covering up for someone. Or he's too afraid to investigate.

My father might have been a monster, but he didn't deserve to die without his murder getting solved. That's just cruel. But I don't allow myself to dwell on any of the news. I ran away for a reason. It's better to put all this behind me— which is what I try to do as I squeeze Minnie's hand and walk out Trinity Baptist Church with her.

It's Sunday afternoon, which means we've got to get home and start prepping for Sunday dinner. The Harts always have a big meal together, just the three of them—four, including me. I didn't know much about cooking until Melissa took me in; since then, she's taught me how to make homemade buttermilk biscuits with honey, potato salad, macaroni and cheese—all kinds of foods I ate as a child.

I know, it's weird to think of an Italian Rose eating soul food, but that's what's so unique about my family. The mafia loves to make the most of every opportunity it's given. That includes marrying for the benefit of the business—not love.

New York City is divided into five boroughs, each of them is ruled by a different mafia. The Italians took Manhattan, leaving the De Lucas in charge. My grandfather, Gabriele De Luca, ruled our sector without issue for decades, but he ruled without ever expanding our territory, without ever taking any chances. When he passed away, my father saw an opportunity to make a bold move. He forged an alliance with a rival mafia—one that nearly doubled the territory under the De Luca's control.

This alliance was forged through marriage to my mother,

Laura Willis, the daughter of Jameson Willis, boss of the mafia ruling over the Bronx—also known as, the Willis Stronghold. She married my father almost thirty years ago, effectively uniting the Stronghold with the Italian mafia of Manhattan. Their union granted the business access to the Bronx and gifted them with two children of mixed race; my older brother Giovanni Jr. and myself—half Italian and half Black American.

So I grew up eating soul food and handmade pasta like it was normal. I also grew up hearing men getting tortured in my basement. Which wasn't normal at all. I just wish I would have realized that much sooner than I did.

Minnie is tugging my arm, forcing me to look down at her as we cross the parking lot of the church. "Are you excited for dinner? Arthur will be coming again." She smooths the wrinkles of her skirt with her free hand and smiles up at me, chubby cheeks dimpling.

I nod slowly. "Yes, I'm excited."

"Too bad you burned up the chicken last time."

I frown, thinking of the ruined roasted chicken from last week. That was the day I found out about my father. I don't blame myself for forgetting about the chicken, but Melissa and Minnie have no idea why I was suddenly so emotional. Basically, they think I got distracted and burned up the chicken for no real reason.

That's fine with me. I'd rather them believe I'm airheaded than learn I'm the Flower of Manhattan. Not even Arthur knows, though he almost coaxed it out of me with all his hugging and whispering and gentle touches that night. I

16

managed to hold out and convince him I was lightheaded and worried about gang violence pouring into Norman.

As a cop, he understood my worries and assured me I was safe. I wanted to believe him, but I know the truth. If someone is powerful enough to get to my father and leave Junior spooked enough not to investigate, then things in NYC are worse than I thought. That means I need to get away now.

But I haven't found the chance to leave. I'm still trying to find out where I should go. I can't just get on a bus and ride until my fare runs out. I don't even have the money to afford bus fare—unless I ask Melissa for it, but that request would come with its own set of questions I can't answer without lying. I don't want to lie anymore. I just want to get away.

I feel pathetic. Like a completely different person from the woman who'd boldly declared she was willing to do whatever it took to stay away from New York. Now I can't even get myself to lie for some measly bus fare. Maybe it's because I just got out of church.

Melissa is beaming with a smile when she gets into the car. "Are you ladies ready for dinner?"

It's early afternoon, but it'll take until evening for us to get everything cooked. I flash her a smile and nod, Minnie complains that we should just order a pizza.

"We had pizza last week," Melissa says, casting a sideways glance at me.

I suppress the groan that swells in my throat. We'd ended up ordering out after I ruined the roasted chicken.

When we get home, there's a package waiting on the porch.

I pick it up and immediately pass it to Melissa. This isn't my house, and no one outside the Harts knows I live here, so I never get mail or packages. But Melissa gasps behind me as I unlock the door and walk into the living room.

"What is it?" I ask, opening the blinds. When she doesn't respond, I turn and find her holding a bouquet of red roses. The smile she wore at church has doubled, stretching so wide I fear it may decapitate her.

I stare at the flowers. "You've got an admirer."

She shakes her head and holds them out to me. "They're for you."

My stomach clenches. "Me?" But no one knows I live here. No one should be sending me anything.

"They're from Arthur!" Melissa laughs like a proud mother and my lungs deflate.

It takes me a second to realize I haven't moved or breathed. Melissa is staring at me, her smile faltering. "Don't you want them?"

"Of course I do," I say, reaching for the flowers. "I'll go put them in a vase."

Melissa sings behind me, "I'll pick some baby's-breath from my garden to add to the bouquet!"

I don't hear whatever else she says. I'm too busy trying to ignore the erratic beating of my heart as I walk on watery legs to the kitchen. I should be excited Arthur sent me flowers. But I'm too overwhelmed by anxiety. For half a second, I thought my family had come for me. For an instant, I thought I'd been found. And the fear of that thought had almost made me lose my bowels right there in the living room.

I can't live another second under this sort of pressure. I need to get away as quickly as I can.

Minnie follows me into the kitchen. She leans against the counter as I search the cabinets for a vase. "How romantic," she sighs. "Arthur must really like you."

"A dozen roses is proof of that, right?" I say, exhaling nervously.

"Eleven roses," Minnie corrects.

I bump my head on the cabinet door as I stand upright too fast. "*Ouch*," I hiss.

Minnie glances at me, concern forming on her face, but before she can ask if I'm all right, I cut her off with a question. "How many roses?"

"Eleven," she repeats, staring at the hand I have pressed over the back of my head.

The pain in my head burns, but it's nothing like the clenching fear growing in my heart. Eleven roses. Not twelve. That's not a simple mistake on the florist's part—this was deliberate.

I grab the bouquet and turn away from Minnie, silently counting each red bulb, desperately hoping her math is off.

It's not.

There are eleven roses. One is gone. Because I'm that rose. The missing flower of the mafia. The Italian Rose.

It's a message only I would understand, and I've received it loud and clear. And it says so much more than just a poor number count. It says I've been found. That my family has known where I've been all along. That they're coming to get me soon.

There's noise in the living room, and for one horrible moment, I think the person who enters the kitchen is one of Junior's men come to drag me back home. But it's only Melissa with a bundle of baby's-breath in her hands.

She glances at me in confusion. "Everything all right?"

"Everything's fine," I tell her. Another lie.

Minnie purses her lips. "Rose hit her head on the cabinet."

"Let me take a look," Melissa says.

"I'm fine." I turn away and set the roses on the counter. I want to hurl them out the nearby window but that would be dramatic.

"It doesn't look bad." Melissa is behind me now, staring at the back of my head. She places her hands on my shoulders and turns me around so she can look at my face. Up close, she reminds me of my mother. Dark skin, age-lines running over her features, her brows wrinkled in concern. Melissa smells like the flowers she's just picked, and it takes everything in me not to wrap my arms around her and squeeze.

I love Melissa like I loved my mother. Sometimes I wish she was my mother. I've got light brown skin and dark curly hair, big, hazel eyes and full lips. I could pass as her daughter. I could pretend I grew up in a normal, loving family where we make Sunday dinner together and pick flowers from our gardens. But that would be too good to be true. It *is* too good to be true.

The truth is that I grew up attending funerals every other

20

week. And the only thing I was ever allowed to pick was the color ribbon I wore in my hair. My father decided every part of my life, even the sort of clothes I should wear as a proper mafia princess.

He was strict with me, as most mafia fathers are. Men in the business handle all the work while the women are kept safe behind the gates of our father's and husband's mansions. We are treated like prized dolls, dressed up and flaunted at balls and dinner parties, traded as wives for contracts and business. We even attend church—it's important for us to keep up an image, like we're sorry for the sins our fathers and brothers and husbands commit.

My familiarity with the church is probably what drew me so close to Melissa. She's the one who gave me the crucifix that dangles from my neck now. I subconsciously touch it as she tells me I don't look so well. The silver cross feels smooth and cool beneath my clammy fingers. My hand is shaking. I can feel it trembling against my chest as I clutch at my necklace.

Melissa is saying something else, but I barely hear it. She's probably praying for me. I hope she's praying for me. I might have come from the mafia, but I understand her convictions. I know that she means it when she pulls me into a hug and whispers, "God's got you. Don't worry so much."

I don't know how she has managed to see through the barrier I've built around myself the past week, but it crumbles at her words, and I don't try to fight it any longer. I squeeze her so tightly she lets out a little yelp, making me jerk away and laugh nervously.

"I'm sorry," I say.

"Want to talk about what's been bothering you?" she asks, patting my cheek.

I do. But I don't.

I can't.

Before I can answer, Minnie lets out a squeal. "Arthur is here!" she shouts, running out of the kitchen. Melissa and I laugh together, though mine has noticeably less mirth in it. I glance to the side, out the kitchen window, so I can watch Minnie run down the driveway to the car pulling in. It's a black car, a simple Camry Arthur bought before I came here. He loves that car, keeps it so clean I can see Minnie's reflection on the hood as she skips over to it. She's still in her yellow dress from church, it flows behind her as she runs.

I can't stop myself from smiling, despite how nervous and gloomy I feel. Because, for now, everything is all right. For now, I can enjoy a dinner with my makeshift family before everything between us changes. This will be our last supper.

I let out a sigh, my eyes still on Minnie. She makes it to the middle of the driveway—and then my heart squeezes.

The car doesn't stop. It hits Minnie full on—her small body jerks backward, her dress flies around her in a storm of yellow. As if time has stopped, I watch her head snap back; I can see her eyes are squeezed shut, her mouth is wide open— she's crying. She is crying for someone to help her. Then time catches up and she flops to the ground. I don't hear any sobbing and it isn't because I can't hear over my pounding heart. It's because Minnie isn't moving. She's unconscious. Or worse.

I'm shrieking as I run out the kitchen and down the driveway. The car is backing up and pulling away, tires screeching. I want to chase after it, I want to drag the driver out his seat and pummel him with my fists, but I know it's not possible. Melissa stops me mid-stride and we fall to our knees beside Minnie's limp body.

I can't look at her. I can't see past the tears burning in my eyes. I can't hear past the storm of blood rushing through my head now. I am dizzy and lightheaded and stricken with fear. First the flowers, now Minnie.

Minnie.

A twelve-year-old girl. One I consider a sister. Someone who is innocent in all this. She's just been hit by a car and there is no other explanation except that it's because of me.

Another message from my family. That they are willing to hurt the people I love.

Melissa is shaking my shoulder. "The police!" she shrieks. "Call the police! Call an ambulance!" She throws her body over Minnie's and lets out a horrific wail. It sends shivers down my spine, but I turn stiffly and run to the house.

I am numb. I am barely conscious as I go toward the kitchen where the landline sits on the counter by the fridge. This cannot be happening. I thought I was safe. I thought my family couldn't find me—couldn't reach me—this far out from the City.

I was wrong. I was so horribly wrong.

I need to leave. The thought works its way into my head again

23

as I take the phone and hold it up to shakily punch out the numbers, 9-1-1. I report what's happened in my calmest voice and then set the phone on the countertop.

I need to leave, or it will get worse.

I'm *going* to leave—right now.

I turn to run out the kitchen, but I don't make it more than two steps before someone grabs me from behind.

It isn't Melissa.

It isn't Minnie.

It isn't Arthur.

It's someone else. Someone who's been in the home, waiting. Watching for a moment when I'd be alone, and they could get what they came for.

I scream and throw my legs up, kicking at the air. But it's a futile effort. A strong hand clamps over my mouth. An equally strong arm wraps around my neck. I am silenced and choked until my lungs burn. Until my eyes water. And then, finally, everything turns black.

Chapter Three

When I woke up this morning, I did not know I'd have to deal with this crap. This was supposed to be an easy day, a relaxing day; instead, I'm being sent to take care of business because my men decided to pick up a Russian last night. A *Russian*. Of all the people to target, my grunts thought it would be smart to grab the *one* type of man they knew wouldn't break easily.

There are a lot of unbreakable men in this business. It's how you get ahead, how you stay on your game. In a world where secrets are worth more than gold, your grit is everything. And if there's one thing I've got to say about the Russians, it's that they know how to keep their mouths shut. Which is why I'm being called in. Because that's what I specialize in. Getting people to open their mouths. To tell me their secrets.

My driver opens my door and keeps a brisk pace behind me as I step out and walk into the warehouse my family keeps for this sort of work. I hate doing interrogations at the estate, it seems old-fashioned and unnecessary. I hear the Italians still do it in their homes. Torturing people in their basements like some sick scene out of a twisted Netflix show. That's why the Italians will never get ahead. They don't know how to adapt to the times. It makes everything worse that their don just died. I heard the news a few nights ago. Giovanni De Luca Sr. is dead. Found in his own home. Just six months after his wife died and his daughter ran off. It's a series of unfortunate events, but I'd be lying if I said I cared.

With the Italians scrambling, we now have a chance to start making moves. Serious moves. And as the underboss of the German American mafia, I'm not going to pass this chance up.

Before I can do anything, though, I've got to get this Russian to talk.

Douglass, my personal guard, is a step behind me as I stride through the halls of the warehouse. He brushes past me to get the door when I near the main corridor.

"Thank you, Douglass," I say with a nod.

He nods back, following me inside. "My pleasure, Mr. Jäger."

There are four people inside the small room when I enter, three of them are my men; two grunts who are here to stand guard, and my little brother, Wolfgang Jäger. The last man is the Russian. He's bloody and shirtless and has a collection of bruises and lacerations scattered over his chest and face. One of his eyes is swollen shut, the other is bloodshot and blinks at me weakly as I walk to the center of the room.

Fear unfolds over his face as he realizes who I am. It isn't every day you get to meet the Jäger underboss in person. He knows seeing me means his day just got a lot worse. I almost laugh but even I have to admit—nothing is funny.

Wolfgang let's out a howl. "Brother!" he says with a smile. His eyes are tired, but I can see the wicked joy dancing in his pupils. Wolf loves this sort of stuff. He gets off on the violence, enjoys the danger, thrives on the brutality of the mafia. Like a vampire drawn to blood, he feeds on the darkness. Embracing it. Desiring it. Like he can't get enough.

He claps me on the shoulder and leans in close to speak into my ear. "We went at him all night and he still hasn't said a word." He says this in German, so the others don't hear him asking for my help. It makes him look weak. But the fact that I'm here at all says a lot about the situation.

I glance at the other men in the room. They're tired too, too tired to care about Wolfgang's bruised ego. They just want to get their information and get home. I want the same thing, so I promise myself I'll make this quick as I remove my jacket and pass it to my little brother.

"Give me the room."

Wolf nods and turns to leave, though the grunts stay in case I need their help. Douglass is by the door, a dark shadow standing in the way, preventing any escape. One look at the Russian sitting in the chair and I know Douglass isn't needed.

My brother is many things. Violent. Gruesome. Cruel. He was built for this dark world we live in—some would say he's almost perfect for it.

Almost.

His weakness is his lack of patience.

The Russian isn't talking, just staring at me through his half-lidded eye. He is scarred and bruised, but he tries to hold his head high, shaggy white-blonde hair falling into his face in bloody clumps. I'll give him credit for his grit and all that, but I can tell he's close to breaking. If Wolf had held out for a few more hours, he would've started talking. But now I'm here. And he'll be singing like a bird in a few minutes.

"Do you know who I am?" I ask him.

He takes a slow breath, working his mouth like his jaw might be broken. Then he answers in a thick Russian accent, "You are Amory Jäger."

"That's right. Do you know what I'm here for?"

He spits a glob of blood onto the floor, right next to my leather shoe.

I stare at it a moment. Then, with a breath, I roll my shoulders back and walk to the corner of the room where a bloody mop leans against the wall. I grab it and snap it over my knee.

"Strip him."

The grunts peel from the wall and follow my command without a word. I watch as the man's one good eye triples in size as he is shed of his clothes.

"Bend him over his chair."

Wolf's men follow orders once again, shoving the Russian into a very uncomfortable position. They hold him in place when he starts to struggle. He's panting now, his fear filling the air, so thick it's almost palpable.

Slow, deliberate steps take me back to the front of the room, stopping right behind my victim. I tap the inside of his ankle. "Spread your legs."

He is naked and bent over a chair. No one blames him when the smell of urine penetrates the air. I watch him pee, stepping aside so it doesn't get on my shoes. Then I walk forward, dragging the broken stick along his flesh.

"I could do a lot to you in this position. With this stick." I squat in front of him, so we're eye level. "I'm sure you have a good imagination, so I don't think I have to go into details about that. But I do need you to understand I need information from you. Information that's useful to me. And I'm willing to do whatever it takes to get it."

He lets out a choked sob. "Th—They'll put a bullet in me if I talk."

"I'll put a stick in you if you don't." I hold it up to show him I'm serious.

He squeezes his eyes shut and starts muttering in Russian, undoubtedly praying, though I don't know why. If there is a God, He clearly hates this man.

I glance down at the Russian's left hand, there's a bullseye burned into his flesh. It's red and raw, probably given just this morning. That same mark is present on the backs of the left hand of every grunt in the room with me—Douglass included. It's the sigil of the Jäger family, the leaders of the German mafia. In my native tongue, the word *Jäger* means hunter. The bullseye is a fitting image.

We place that mark on the men we pick up, a sign that

they've been *hunted*. Wolfgang has a bullseye tattooed onto the back of his shaved head—because he's an idiot. But I appreciate his bold commitment to the family business. That bullseye lets everyone know the Jägers got to them. That we got them to share all their little secrets. That way, if they do manage to escape from us, they'll never be taken back into their mafia ranks.

One thing this organization doesn't tolerate is snitches. The mark is important, it's something you can't hide unless you chop your hand off. So the men who bear it undoubtedly belong to us.

As cruel as it is to kidnap and brand people, the Jägers can be merciful. We allow the Hunted men to join our ranks as grunts. It's the lowest position within the mafia, but it's better than a bullet to the back of the head.

Douglass is proof of our mercy. We picked him up when he was just sixteen—at the time, we didn't know he was a distant relative of an underboss in the Willis Stronghold. We were just picking up new recruits—snatching men off the streets like children kidnapped in the night. Once we got Douglass in an interrogation room, he sang every song he knew. His information was good. So good, I took him under my wing. He's spent the last six years working his way up the ranks to become my personal guard.

My father, the boss of the German mafia, doesn't approve of Douglass's position. He thinks I should surround myself with good German men. But he doesn't know that it's the foreign grunts I trust more than anyone. Because the grunts have to work for everything they get. They have to earn my trust. They have to prove their loyalty. People like Wolfgang, people born into the organization, don't have to earn anything. We trust each other because we're related. Because it's convenient. But that's not good enough for me. Because relationships built on convenience never last.

My gaze lingers on Douglass a moment. He's come a long way from the sixteen-year-old kid we picked up six years ago. He's over six feet tall, built like a linebacker, with dark brown skin and a clean-shaven head. He looks like he could break me in two. Not that I'm much smaller than him. I'm not as packed with muscle, but I'm nearly as tall, and I've got typical German features. Brown hair, so dark it's almost black, smooth pale skin, and sharp grey eyes. I'm the opposite of Douglass, but I wouldn't have anyone else guarding my back. Not even another German.

"It doesn't have to end here," I tell the Russian.

He stares at me like I've lost my mind.

"You've been Hunted. You know that means you can never return home. But you can join us. You'll be a grunt. But you'll be alive."

He doesn't speak, as if he's thinking this over.

"But you only get to join us if you start talking," I say. "So you might as well tell me something I can use against the Volkovs now." I tap his nose with the broken tip of the stick. "Or I can resume my other plans."

We stare at each other for a long moment—longer than I'm comfortable with. For a second, I think I'm going to have to use this stick, but when the air smells sour with urine for the second time, I know I've got him.

I push to my feet and drop the stick to the floor. "He's ready to talk."

Douglass opens the door for me as I turn to leave. "Good job, Mr. Jäger."

"Thank you, Douglass." I stop in the hall, just outside the door. "He'll probably be singing for the rest of the morning. Set up a dinner this evening. I want to celebrate whatever we learn."

"I'll have beer delivered from the distillery," he says, pulling out his phone.

"No. Tonight, we drink Vodka."

Douglass smiles. "We'll toast to the Russians."

Chapter Four

Wolf is right behind me as I walk back to my car, his guard opens the warehouse door to let us out. Once we're outside, he turns to me with a grin. "Thank you, brother," he says in German—something he does only when he's serious.

I slide into my car and make room for him to join me. "You're welcome."

He's still grinning when he settles against the leather seats which makes me sigh as I scroll the messages on my phone. "What else do I have to clean up?" I ask, because I just *know* Wolfgang has somehow managed to screw something else up in the short time I was in that interrogation room. He's twenty-six—five years younger than me—but he acts like he's twelve most of the time. That's why I only trust him with the dirty jobs. Hunting men, interrogating, even taking out some of our enemies. You can't really screw up an assassination unless you let the guy live, but Wolf has a disturbing enjoyment of killing so he hardly ever messes that stuff up.

Everything else, though…

He lets out a chuckle I've heard him give me a thousand times. I love my little brother, but I'm *this* close to telling Douglass to turn the car around so I can go get that stick I left and beat him with it.

"What is it, Wolfgang?" I grunt, ignoring a call from my father. My phone buzzes only once before I punch the reject button.

"You should have answered that," he says, peering down at the phone.

I shift my body so he can't see my screen anymore. "Why?"

"Because Vater called a family meeting while you were inside with the Russian."

"*Vater*," I say the word slowly. It isn't often I speak German—I was raised to appeal to our American clients—but our father has always insisted we use our native tongue with him.

I hate saying that word. It makes me feel less like an underboss and more like a son. A child.

Vater… The man has never been anything like a father to me.

"I've got business with the Morenos this morning," I tell Wolf when I realize he's still staring at the side of my face.

"*Spaniards*," he hisses the word, and it sounds like venom on his snake-like tongue. I'm not surprised. The Jägers have hated the Morenos for generations, but I've been trying to ease the tension lately.

The mafia has had control over New York City for a decade now. But we've been ruling separately. The Italians own Manhattan, the Willis Stronghold is set up in the Bronx, the Russians hold Staten Island, the Spanish mafia owns Queens, and the Jägers control Brooklyn. In a way, having a borough for each gang helps keep the peace. We don't cross into each other's territory unless we're scouting for recruits or trying to do business. But having such strict and clear borders has also made it too easy to start a war.

Before the defunding, the entire mafia was forced to work underground. Forced to work together. To cooperate for the sake of the overall industry. But now that we don't have to worry about the police, we have time to fuss over our bridges and borders and territory lines. Travel is strict—sometimes it's not even possible to cross into the other boroughs without having a full security escort, and even then, some low-ranking grunts might get stupid and fire at us just to take a shot at taking down an underboss.

I've been trying to smooth things out with the Morenos lately because I hate being patted down and nearly strip searched every time I want to cross into Queens. They have the best nightclubs, so I'm there more often than I should be. That might not be the best motivation for wanting peace, but hey, we've got to start somewhere.

It also doesn't hurt that the Morenos have tight control over the flow of cocaine into the city. With their connections, we could triple our cash flow. It's a good investment.

"You were planning to meet with Spaniards?" Wolfgang's

question pulls me from my thoughts.

"Yes," I say, glancing out the window. "Just a five-minute meeting right here in the car. Nothing more."

He curses in German. "You would have a Spaniard in your car. On these *seats*."

I had a Spaniard in my bed last night, but that isn't the type of meeting Wolf needs to know about.

I sigh and look over at him. "It'll help the business."

"Well, now you have other business to deal with."

I look at my phone again as it buzzes in my hand. Another call from Vater. This time I answer. "Uwe." I use his first name to let him know I'm not in any better mood than he is. I ignored his first call, so I know he's ticked and ready to explode.

He breathes into the phone for five full seconds before he says, "Amory. I called a family meeting."

"I was busy. And I'll be busy until this evening. So if it's not an emergency—"

"It is."

"Well, Wolf is right here with me." I switch the phone to speaker so my brother can hear. "Let's do this now."

Another few seconds of angry, heavy breathing. I imagine my father at his grand cherrywood desk, all six feet of him towering over it, hands splayed on the surface as he glares down at the phone. His dark hair, grey at the roots, slightly disheveled from running his meaty hands through it. His three-piece suit unbuttoned and wrinkled because he's likely been throwing things in a fit of rage since I ignored his first call. He has a very short temper. It's bad for his blood pressure, but I'm not going to warn him about it. Hopefully, I can piss him off enough to send him into cardiac arrest. Then I won't have to deal with his crap anymore.

"De Luca is looking for you," Uwe says. "I want to know why."

"I won't know until he finds me."

Wolfgang shifts uncomfortably. I glance up at him, but Uwe is speaking again, and my attention is immediately pulled away.

"I want you to meet with him when he contacts you."

I frown. I'm never going to meet with the Morenos at this point. But my father is right. I should meet with De Luca. With Gio Sr. dead, it's more than strange that Junior wants to see me right now. There was once a time when Junior and I saw each other daily—we were friends growing up, and then I turned fifteen and was officially inducted into the German American mafia. I had to cut all ties with anyone Uwe didn't approve of. The De Lucas weren't our allies. So our friendship faded.

A year later, Junior was named as his father's successor, so we were able to see each other on occasion—whenever I shadowed Vater at business meetings or attended dinners and trade-offs involving the Italians. But that was all business.

Whenever I saw Junior, he was by his father's side, just as I was by mine. I'd had all my hair cut off and was dressed in a suit—with a rainbow of bruises decorating my face. Vater is old-fashioned. He initiated me into the mafia the same way we took in our Hunted grunts. I was snatched out of bed one night and beaten to a pulp until I sobbed like a girl and begged my father's men to stop.

They didn't. Not until Uwe told them to.

I've still got scars from my induction night. One on my chest and a few on my back that still throb sometimes. Like they're fresh. A constant reminder of who I am. Of how I got here. Of how I don't ever want to go back to what I used to be. A nameless grunt, naked and crying on the floor of one of my own warehouses. Just like that tortured Russian.

I unlock my phone and send a message to my assistant to cancel my meeting with the Morenos. Then I sigh. "Alright, Uwe. I'll meet him later. Anything else?"

He lets me know there's nothing else by hanging up without another word.

"That was interesting," Wolfgang says.

"That shouldn't have been a family meeting," I mutter, leaning forward to tap the partition separating me from my driver. Douglass glances back long enough for me to tell him to take me to Junior's estate.

We might not be close anymore, but not much about Junior has changed. If he truly wanted to contact me, he could have called my phone. But he knew I probably wouldn't have picked up because there's nothing I need from the Italians right now. Manhattan is useless to me with the De Lucas scrambling. Junior knows this. So instead of wasting his time making calls he knows I'll ignore, he went out of his way to ask around town and let everyone know he was looking for me. Now that Uwe knows, I have no choice but to go see what he wants.

I grind my teeth until my jaw aches. It's not until we're outside Junior's apartment building that I notice Wolf is watching me closely. That's when it dawns on me. His nervous looks. His uncharacteristic anxiety.

"Is there something I should know about what's waiting for me inside Junior's home?" I say darkly.

He gives me that stupid chuckle again. "Brother—"

"What am I cleaning up now?" I snap.

He looks away, slinking back into the leather seats like a little boy who's just been disciplined by his father. He needs more discipline. But he's too old and I'm not his daddy. So instead of yelling at him more, I shoulder my door open before Douglass has even put the car in park. I'm halfway to the front doors when two Italian guards step forward, guns aimed.

I hold my hands up so they can search me. They take the gun I have holstered at my hip, and the small knife up my sleeve. Then they let me in.

Giovanni Jr. is the leader of the Italian mafia here in NYC, appropriately nicknamed, the Garden of Manhattan. He lives in a penthouse overlooking the borough, and if I cared about his riches and luxury, I'd make on about the breathtaking views and the floor-to-ceiling windows and the artwork flown in from Italy to decorate his walls. But all I care about is getting this done and over with. Whatever this is.

Junior is sitting on a snow-white sofa when his guard escorts me into his living room. His hands are folded in his lap, his legs are crossed, his white suit is crisp and clean. He smiles at me, flashing perfectly white teeth that stand out against his olive-toned skin. "Amory."

The sound of my given name makes me pause. Not everyone gets to call me that, especially not with a smile on their face. But Junior is still something like a distant friend to me. If not at least an acquaintance.

"What do you want, Junior?" I say almost angrily.

His smile widens. "I want your hand in marriage."

I'm glad his guards took my gun because I'm *this* close to shooting him dead. Before I can tell him this, he rises from the couch and holds his hands up defensively. "I have an offer for you."

"Obviously one involving marriage."

He nods.

No wonder he didn't bother calling me. If I had known he interrupted my business plans with the Morenos for this, I would have hired a hitman to kill him just for ticking me off.

I am not a man made for marriage.

I'm the German underboss of Brooklyn. I'm Amory Jäger, the Hunter of New York. I don't do relationships. I don't want to get married. I woke up next to a beautiful Spanish woman this morning and I intend to sleep beside another tonight—if I ever manage to get away from my father, brother, and childhood friend, that is.

Junior knows all this about me. He knows how I feel about marriage. Even if he didn't, we're mafia men. Marriage isn't something we take seriously or lightly. I know, that sounds like I'm contradicting myself, but let me explain.

In this dark world, we don't marry for love. We marry for business. For contracts. For deals that benefit our organization. Our marriages are taken seriously on paper, but that's about it. All that's required is a consummation and an heir. After that, I'm free to live as I please. Enjoy as many women as I want—like I'm still single. So long as I keep my mistresses away from important functions and dinners, I won't be scolded for my behavior.

Faithfulness isn't expected from men in this business. Our women are different. They're loyalty *is* expected—*demanded.* Because we take care of them. We are the ones out here doing the dirty work. Making deals, doing drug exchanges, serving time in prison when there was one. In exchange for our money and protection, our wives remain loyal. It isn't fair, but it's the mafia. Nothing about who we are and what we do is fair.

But the fairness in marriage isn't what's most important here. As an underboss, getting married means more for me than anyone else. My position is important. It's high-ranking. I am second in command of the entire German American mafia. I hold a lot of power in this city. That means I can't take marriage lightly. It means holding out as long as I can, waiting for the most beneficial arrangement possible—which I know for a fact isn't with the broken De Lucas. The Garden of Manhattan is rotting. I'd be an idiot to marry into their gang right now.

On top of that, Junior has no one to offer me for marriage. He has one little sister—she's over ten years younger than me and isn't even in the city anymore. Rosa is her name. I knew her when she was a kid. We never spent much time together since I'm so much older than her, but I met her a few times. Right before the defunding, we spent an entire day together. She was just ten years old at the time, I was twenty-one, so it was more like babysitting. Junior had asked me to do it when one of their guards was taken in by the Russians. They couldn't trust anyone on their payroll and Rosa needed a guard, so he asked me to watch over her until he vetted his men again.

It was an easy day of work. I took her to the park, stopped for burgers at a greasy joint, bought her a vanilla ice cream cone, and then walked the strip with her—window-shopping. She fell in love with an overpriced, rose-shaped hairpin from Tiffany's, which I ended up purchasing for her. And then Junior called and said they had the problem solved. I took her back home and that was it. I haven't seen her since.

And I don't expect to see her again because last thing I heard; she ran away from home. Escaped the mafia to start over in Jersey.

I narrow my eyes at Junior. Because I suddenly know where this is going.

Gio Sr. is dead. The De Lucas are slipping, losing control over Manhattan. So to reinforce their ranks, they want to form an alliance with the Jägers. They don't have anything to offer us—no drugs, weapons, or even men to add to our ranks. So Junior wants to forge a pact through marriage. Which means … he must have found his sister.

"Junior," I say as calmly as I can. He's still smiling at me, like no matter what I say, he knows I'll end up agreeing to this insanity. "I'm not having any part of this."

Slowly, he glances down at the coffee table between us. For the first time, I look down and notice the pictures scattered over the crystal surface. They're pictures of a Russian woman. A dead Russian woman.

My blood goes cold as I stare at the images.

I know that woman. I used to see her every day. I used to believe she would be part of my family for the rest of my life. Until this happened...

I can't peel my eyes from the photos. Can't get myself to look away from her swollen face, her bruised skin, her bloody body. You can't even tell how beautiful she used to be. Can't even tell that she was once a happy, smiling woman who believed in silly things like love and laughter and joy.

I'm staring for so long; I don't notice when Wolfgang enters the room. It's his sharp intake of breath that pulls me from my trance. I pivot and find him standing just behind me, his gaze locked on the images, too.

His eyes flicker up to me and then quickly drop to the floor.

And suddenly I understand. I know why he's been acting so funny. And I know why I can't refuse Junior's offer now.

Because those pictures aren't just sick images Giovanni dug up for jokes. They are crime scene photos—the woman's death was ruled as a random attack. Something that happened during a mugging. But I know the truth. Wolfgang knows the truth. Junior knows the truth—and he is willing to use it against me. Blackmail me into this marriage or send the Russians after me with everything they've got.

If he was smart, Junior would have taken the photos to the Russians and worked out a deal with them to help get the Italians back on their feet. But he's come to me instead. Because a deal with the Russians would have been dangerous. They could have worked with him. Or they could have killed him just for holding on to the truth for this long. For letting them think the princess of the Russian mafia was killed in a random mugging.

Junior makes a noise—something like a laugh—and I force my eyes from my stupid brother back to him. "I thought your sister was gone," is all I can say.

He sighs. Runs a hand through his thick hair. "She was. But we got her back yesterday."

"You're selling me damaged goods, June. The Jägers won't benefit from this at all."

He smirks. "You get to take your secret to the grave and avoid a war with the Russians. That's your benefit."

My hands ball into fists. "And how do I explain that to my father? To the rest of the German mafia?"

"Vater doesn't have to know," Wolf says behind me.

I whirl and shove him so hard he trips three steps backwards. "Shut up!" I holler.

I am outraged. I want to shove him to the floor and beat him until he looks like the woman in the photos. Until he feels everything she felt, and then some. Because this is all his fault. If he wasn't such a screwup. If he wasn't so irresponsible. If he wasn't so uncontrollable when he's in his drinks.

44

I am sick of cleaning up after him.

Coming in to finish an interrogation is one thing. But being blackmailed into a terrible marriage is another thing entirely. This will impact the entire organization. The rest of the German mafia will feel the effects of this arrangement. It will tie us to the Italian gangs for life. That's not something to take lightly. But Wolfgang doesn't understand that. And he never will. Because he's my little brother. He's my spoiled, stupid little brother. Not the underboss. Not even a guard like Douglass. He's just Wolfgang. Uwe's second-born. He has no responsibility. No discipline. And now I'm paying for that.

I turn back to Junior, who's still smirking at me. Like he's won.

He *has* won.

"She's damaged goods," I say again.

"She's not all that bad," Junior insists. "She 'found God' when she was away." He smiles and shrugs at this like it's funny. "I had eyes on her the entire time. She kept her identity a secret. Stayed holed up with a nice little church family. Even knows how to cook now."

I shake my head, too angry to speak.

"Even so, I had my doctor check her out. She's still a virgin. If that's something that interests you."

Mafia women are held to a high standard. Our girls are raised for the purpose of being given in marriage for deals just like this. It's old-fashioned to demand them to be chaste, but when you're signing deals of this caliber and the payment is flesh—it'd better be worth it.

That means we expect our wives to be virgins when we marry them. Or the deal is off.

"Come take a look at her." Junior jerks his head toward the hallway.

I follow him, and in an angry daze, I mutter, "I don't care if she's broken."

Believe it or not. I'm not interested in Rosa's virtue. I might be mafia, but I don't care about who she's been lying with. I care about who she's been talking to. She's a mafia princess. She has a lot of knowledge. Deep knowledge that could hurt more than just the Italians. She could ruin all of New York by talking to the wrong people outside the city. That's why no one ever leaves. That's why we don't *let* anyone leave. Because our secrets are everything. They protect our way of life. They ensure our business—our legacies—will live on.

There was a time when Rosa De Luca was known as the Italian Rose. The Flower of Manhattan. But when she ran away, she ruined herself and her family. Her mother was killed in her great escape. Her father died six months later. And the Italian businesses suffered losses the entire time she was gone.

Her virtue might be intact. Her newfound faith might be something her brother is proud of. But Rosa is ruined. She showed her true colors. That she isn't loyal to the mafia. That she cannot be trusted.

In a world like ours, trust—*grit*—is everything.

Rosa De Luca is not the Flower of Manhattan anymore. She's a withered rose. And she's going to be my wife.

46

Chapter Five

I am an idiot. To think that I was ever safe. That I had ever truly gotten away. The only person I was fooling was myself. Reality was the only thing I'd escaped. No one ever leaves the mafia. No one ever gets away. Not for long, at least.

I remember when I finally returned to consciousness. I'd glanced around in fear, only to immediately calm at the familiarity of my surroundings. I was back inside my home. In my own bedroom.

Slowly, I'd blinked away the dried tears on my face as I sat up in my bed, hands brushing the plush throw blanket I used to love.

"You're up," said a voice across my room.

It was then that I noticed the figure sitting in my chair beside my desk. Giovanni Jr., my older brother. He is the opposite of me in many ways. Taking after our father as much as I take after our mother. His hair is chocolate brown, smoothed into gentle waves compared to my mop of dark coils. His skin is deep olive while mine is the color of brown sugar. His eyes are a gentle green that sparkles when he smiles, mine are hazel and always seem to be filled with fear or tears— or both. Junior is the spitting image of our father, and as he stepped into the dim evening light cast in by the window of my bedroom, my heart broke a little, knowing that this was as close as I would ever get to seeing my father again.

He's dead. Just like my mother. Just like I will be soon. And it's all my fault. I'm an orphan because I tried to escape. I got innocent people killed because I tried to get away. And it was all for nothing because here I am again. Right back where I started.

Maybe this is what I deserve.

I didn't try to argue with that thought as it worked its way into my head, whispering into my mind, blaming me for everything.

Gio didn't smile as he stared down at me. "Welcome home," he'd said, his voice low and blunt and not at all welcoming.

I swallowed.

"It's been a long six months."

"How did you find me?" I managed to squeak out.

The corner of his mouth turned up, almost offering me a smile. "Rosa, we never lost you."

Horror hammered into my gut. He had known all along. He'd let me get away and dragged me back when it was convenient for him.

I shivered at the thought, wondering what the deal was all of a sudden. He didn't bother retrieving me for our father's funeral. So what did he need now?

He must have read the expression on my face because his eyes focused on me as he said, "I have plans for you. You will behave and get them done, Rosa. I let you have your fun in Jersey, but it's time to come back to reality. Back to the business."

To the *mafia*. I wanted to correct him, but I bit my tongue and dropped my gaze to his leather shoes instead. Italian leather, something our family had imported from the businesses we ran in our home country overseas. My father had always worn the finest leather and the finest suits. I wasn't surprised to see Junior following his lead. He is the new don of the Italian mafia. He's the Godfather now.

"What do you want from me?" I'd asked, praying to God he couldn't hear the trembling in my voice.

Junior had every right to have me whipped for what I'd done. For the impact it'd had on the family business. And no one would stop him as don. But instead, he was standing in my room, ready to make plans. To include me in the discussion. If I wanted to survive, I had to behave. If I ever wanted to escape again, I had to cooperate—just for now.

"I want to make sure you don't slip away and make another mess," he told me. "I want to fix everything you screwed up."

"I didn't kill our father," I said defensively. My hands clutched at the covers bundled around me as I tried to keep my voice from rising. "That happened while I was away. The businesses failed because our clients didn't want to deal with *you*." Junior might be don and he might be wearing the same expensive clothes as our father, but everyone knows he isn't our father. He's a terrible businessman. Which is why Papa was so hesitant to name him as his heir. I wouldn't have been surprised if our father had named one of our cousins as his successor instead.

Gio knows this. That's why he took two steps forward, so fast I gasped and crawled backwards, my butt hitting the headboard. His face was etched in rage, a muscle spasmed in his jaw as he ground his teeth together.

"Our businesses started slipping the moment you ran, Rosa. The Italian Rose escaped New York with all her secrets. Every organization in the city started cutting ties, scrambling to distance themselves from the potential snitches of the mafia." His hands curled into fists as he spoke, a slow demonstration of the anger boiling inside. "Our mother died the day you got away. And so did our alliance with the Willis Stronghold. They retracted our claim to any Bronx territory and took a fourth of our men with them." He stopped to heave a sigh, his nostrils flaring. "Father couldn't handle it."

No.

I slapped my hand over my mouth before he said the words, hoping to somehow stop the sob I felt clawing its way up my throat.

"He took his life, Rosa."

I broke. Burying my face in my blankets and letting out a strangled cry. I had tried to convince myself that Papa's death was an inside job. That June had been too afraid to start an investigation because he feared the killer would come after him. I had even entertained the dark idea that maybe Junior had done the job himself, but I'd known better.

Gio's revelation had broken the dam inside me, releasing a wave of pinned up guilt to crash through me, but his next words turned that wave into an uncontrollable flood. "He killed himself because of you."

I choked on the tears I was already drowning in, drenching my blankets and sobbing like a child. I felt like a child in that moment. Like a lost little girl—a little *orphan* girl now, because of my own actions.

Warmth bloomed on the back of my head, and I shifted to see Gio standing beside my bed, leaning down to pet me on the head. He's ten years older than me and has always treated me like a child. Even now, despite the fact that I'm twenty years old and this is all my fault. But his gentleness only lasted a moment as his eyes locked with mine and I watched the coldness creep back in, frosting over the warmth that'd flickered through them for that fleeting moment.

"We have a chance to fix this," he told me, cramming the hand he'd just used to comfort me deep into his pocket. Like he didn't trust himself not to reach out and touch me again. Like it was wrong to offer kindness to me.

"I can't fix this," I said, sniffling. I had no power. I was the lost princess now. The withered rose of Manhattan. Junior was the one with our father's ring on his finger. He might not be the same businessman as Papa, but the truth was, if anyone could turn our organization around, it was him. He'd told me he had plans for me, so I assumed something was already in place.

I assumed right.

The next moment, he smiled wolfishly and took a step back. The ashen moonlight curled in from the open window and cast a tower of shadows over the room. Half my brother's face was covered in darkness as he grinned and said, "I'm going to make a deal with the Jägers."

"The Jägers."

He nodded. "You will marry Amory Jäger."

My heart stopped. I'd always expected to be married young, had even expected my parents to pick out my husband for me, but I hadn't ever expected to be given to someone outside the business. My father had married outside the family, choosing a Black American bride from the Stronghold instead of an Italian Rose from the Garden. Our connections back home in Italy had been livid, but when profits from the trade deals happening in the Bronx started rolling in, my father's progressive marriage was hailed as the most successful business arrangement our organization had ever established.

I grew up hearing about the hardships my mother endured during the first years of her marriage to my father—how she was mistreated by the old-fashioned members of the strict De Luca household. By the time I was born, their relationship was openly accepted by almost the entire family, but all the stories I'd heard had led me to believe that I would be given to an Italian man to marry. Not passed off to the German mafia.

I stared at my brother, trying to see if there was a hint of a joke or insanity in his eyes. There was nothing but that blank coldness stirring in his wintergreen orbs.

He took a breath. "Amory Jäger is the underboss of the German mafia in New York. This is the best possible arrangement you could hope for."

I sank deeper into my blankets, as if I could crawl under them and hide from all this. "I don't want to get married."

The words tore a barking laugh from my brother. "You think I care what you want, Rosa?" He leaned forward, jerking his hands from his pockets to place them on my mattress for support. "You ruined this organization, now you're going to fix it. You will do this, sister. If I have to drag you down the aisle myself. Now…" his eyes glanced away for a moment, and I saw a flicker of the brother I'd known six months ago. The way he hesitated, unsure of himself for just a second. Then he regained his composure and lifted his chin. "You haven't ruined yourself, have you?"

I felt the blood rushing through my face before the blush appeared, spattered over my cheeks and nose until my entire face was flushed red. It wasn't an entirely outlandish question. I did have something of a relationship with Arthur during my time away, but I didn't escape the mafia to sow my wild oats across Jersey. I left so I could live a decent life. A Christian life. And I had found that with Melissa and Minnie and Trinity Baptist Church.

Arthur never would have touched me, even if I'd asked him to. Which I hadn't, of course. But Gio doesn't know that for certain. Despite having my exact location, I guess he didn't watch me 24/7, or else he would have realized I'd only had the chance to see Arthur a few times a week and it was usually with his mother and sister around.

Still, the question made me feel like a child and I couldn't keep myself from blushing and squirming in my bed. "June," I said quietly.

He grunted in anger and met my gaze, his face hard and void of emotion. "You're the little sister of a don, the only daughter of a former don. Your virtue is important. You know that. Now answer the question, Rosa."

I shook my head. "No one's touched me." Anger bubbled through my chest. "But not because I'm the sister of a *don*. I kept my virtue intact because it's what God wanted for me. To save myself for marriage—"

He laughed, silencing me in an instant. "Yes, I know you found God while you were away. You don't have to explain the Bible to me."

I hadn't found God while I was away. I'd always known God. Mafia life wasn't strict just for fun. It was strict because it was built on hundreds of years of tradition—traditions established on a very old, very Christian foundation. I grew up reading the Bible as much as I read the notes on the other mafia members and their connections to our businesses around the world. I was taught to be good and chaste because God wanted me to be, as much as my father did.

I even went to Catholic school, sitting beside the daughters of other dons and underbosses and high-ranking members of the mafias of New York. The only difference between my faith in Jersey versus here in Manhattan was that I was allowed to fully embrace it in Norman.

I was raised to be chaste, but also expected to turn a blind eye to my father's drug ring. I was raised to be quiet and demure, but also taught not to utter a word when my father raised a hand against my mother. I was raised going to confessions with the priest at St. Joseph's Cathedral, but I was also told to pretend I never noticed the rose tattooed onto his right hand—the symbol of the De Luca family.

Every member of the Italian mafia wore that mark somewhere on their body. A red rose. The number of petals represented the rank of the person who bore the tattoo, each thorn on the stem was a life taken by their own hand.

Father Serrano has nine thorns on his rose. Sometimes I would count them as I stared at his aged knuckles while I confessed my sins.

The faith is a joke here in the mafia. Something kept in place out of tradition. Used as a tool to keep the girls in their place and tell the boys it's okay to kill and steal and destroy lives, as long as they confess it later on.

I learned differently in Jersey. I learned the truth.

Pastor Marcia told me it wasn't enough just to confess. That repenting wasn't only telling God what you did wrong, it was turning away from those sinful things and habits. Even if you messed up and committed those same sins again in the future, the repentant heart—the desire to change—was what God was looking for.

But no one in this business wanted to do better. No one truly wanted to change. They just wanted to be able to sleep at night. And if Father Serrano couldn't give them that false sense of peace, then they'd find it at the bottom of a bottle instead. Whatever worked best.

I hadn't expected Gio to understand my faith if I ever saw him again. But I hadn't expected him to laugh at me for it, either. I'd glanced up at him as he howled, shoulders bopping in amusement. My hand subconsciously went to the crucifix around my neck, clutching the jewelry Melissa had given to me.

Dread hit me like a truck—like the vehicle that'd hit Minnie. "You put a *child* in the hospital to get me back," I whispered. "A child I loved."

"I had to let you know I was serious." Gio wiped a tear from his eye. "She's fine, Rosa. Just a broken leg."

"How do I know that?"

"You don't. You'll just have to trust me."

"Trust you," I repeated drolly. "The man who had me choked out and transported back to New York."

His eyes hardened as they focused on me. "My man didn't choke you out until *after* you placed the call for an ambulance. That should tell you something."

It did. But I didn't want to acknowledge that because it would mean part of my brother was still kind. Still the man I used to know. I wasn't sure how to cope with that—how to handle his subtle kindness combined with his open brutality.

"If you behave," he went on, "I'll let you call your little Christian family later. Maybe you can pray for them."

Maybe they can pray for me, I thought.

Gio turned to the door. "I'll have my doctor examine you just to make sure you're telling the truth. After that, I want you to get cleaned up and rest. You'll be busy planning a wedding soon. Enjoy this day off."

He left me alone to wait nervously for Dr. Rizzo to come in and conduct her examination. She checked for injuries as much as she checked for my ... uh ... virtue. But the whole thing was painfully awkward, nonetheless. I couldn't get into my shower fast enough once she was gone.

After that, I got dressed and remained locked in my own bedroom until Gio had a meal delivered. I picked at it like a bird and then drifted off to sleep. It was the same routine this morning. Gio sent breakfast, I got washed up and dressed, and then I sat around waiting.

Now, I can hear steps approaching my bedroom door. I assume it's a servant come to grab the breakfast I didn't eat, but when the door swings open, I glance up and find my brother. He's wearing a perfect white suit with a dark green tie that matches his eyes, but it's the man behind him that catches my attention.

A tall creature who strides in and stops in the middle of the room like he owns the place. His grey eyes are like a storm, swirling with emotions that put me on edge. There is nothing but anger and resentment on his face. Like he hates this entire ordeal. Like he hates me. He isn't a huge man, but I feel so small in his presence. Like he takes up more space than he should. I can't get away from his searing gaze. It pins me in place, lazy eyes blinking beneath the shadows of his dark bangs. A few strands of his hair have fallen into his face, he doesn't bother to wipe them away. He just stares at me, eyelashes fluttering as if they could fan away the stray hairs. I get a wild, inexplicable desire to reach out and brush the strands away. To run my hand along his square jaw and feel the coolness of his pale skin beneath my fingers.

I control myself.

Because I realize who he is when he opens his mouth and says my name with a subtle German accent. "Rosa."

It's him. It's Amory Jäger.

I blink at him, recognition washing over me. I haven't seen this man in ten years. I'm sure there were times we attended the same functions and events as members of the head families of our respective organizations. But I don't think I've been face to face with him like this since I was a child.

He's different. Not that reserved twenty-something-year-old I remember who struggled to hide his smiles and never let me catch him laughing at all the silly things we discussed that day.

That simple day … a decade ago.

It had been the best day of my life. I'd told him that. Had even confessed that I didn't want it to end. That I wished my father would hire him as my personal guard. And he'd ruffled my curly hair and told me he would make a terrible guard because he'd just stuff me full of ice cream. I hadn't seen anything wrong with that at the time, so I was devastated when he dropped me off and told me goodbye. I remember crying

58

crocodile tears, clutching his shirt and hoping that if I just held on, he wouldn't walk away. But he had. He'd left me there on my front steps.

And now he's standing in my bedroom while I discreetly try to cover my bare legs with my blankets. I'm still in my pajamas—since Gio hadn't let me out or sent me any visitors, I'd showered and thrown my oversized sleep shirt back on. Now I severely regret that decision.

Amory doesn't notice my attire. His eyes are locked on mine, the anger slowly drifting away. But it isn't replaced with a gentle joy that curves his tightlipped expression into a smile. The anger fades and his eyes are left empty. Blank. Almost bored, as he regards me the way you'd look at a stale box of cereal, trying to decide if you're just hungry enough to eat it.

It's been ten long years and it shows. He's in his thirties now. An underboss in the German mafia. His success is evident in his expensive suit and shoes and the watch worth the price of a house that decorates his wrist. But with his success undoubtedly came hardships.

I can see the lines around his mouth, earned from years of frowning and grimacing and glaring. I can see the hints of grey hairs at the edges of his face, right above his left ear—exactly three strands that stand out starkly against his otherwise dark head. But, more than anything, I can see how tired he is. How years of gruesome work turned the reserved young man I knew a decade ago into this detached—distant—man before me.

The fact that I'm expected to marry him sends a shiver down my spine.

Chapter Six

There are eight people sitting at the table, including myself, Wolfgang, and our father. The others are generals within the business, people who have spent their lives carving out a name and a living through the German mafia. One of my uncles is present, along with my father's best friend, two distant cousins, and a man named Hans; the only one of us who was born and raised in Germany—in Bremen, to be specific. The boss of Bremen sent Hans over to us when the defunding happened. We're not the best of friends, but he gets things done. And he's had a serious influence over my father in terms of keeping the business rooted in German culture and tradition. Which is why Vater is livid as he sits at the head of the table and spews curses at me over his breakfast.

"Marry an *Italian*?" Uwe curses again, this time in German. "An Italian *mixed-breed*?"

I clench my jaw at the insult. It's common knowledge the

De Luca head family is of mixed heritage, but it was never something I saw as a problem. Maybe I'm too modern—too *woke*—but I saw the benefits of the marriage as much as Gio Sr. did. Their arrangement was completely untraditional for a mafia head family, but the alliance between the De Lucas and the Stronghold is exactly what turned the Italians into the powerhouse of Manhattan.

At least until Rosa ran away and ruined everything. Which is why I'm being forced into a new alliance with the De Lucas—tainting my own 'precious' German blood. According to my father, at least.

"How could you even consider this?" Vater shovels a forkful of his potato omelet into his mouth, the crisp edges of the potatoes crunch loudly under his teeth.

It takes me a moment to realize he's actually expecting an answer. I reply in German, "It will help the business."

It won't. At all. And Vater knows this, which is why he jerks forward to spew more foul language at me. He ends up choking on his food instead and stutters through a fit of coughs. After a second, my uncle Oberon passes him a glass of water and speaks in a much gentler tone. "You are smart enough to see how terrible this arrangement will be," he says to me.

Hans chuckles, it's a deep rumble I swear I can feel through the hardwood floors. "Maybe the baby Hunter has been blinded by the beauty of the Italian Rose." He leans forward, his tie coming dangerously close to dipping into his semolina pudding. "Have you smelled her petals, Jäger? Have you tasted her thorns?"

I grip the fork by my plate, and everyone shifts, resting a hand on the hip where their gun is holstered—everyone but Vater, who simply holds up a hand and clears his throat. "Careful, Hans. The Rose of Manhattan might be withered, but she is Amory's fiancé now. Whether we like it or not."

"I don't like this any more than you do," I say as calmly as I can. "But you will respect Rosa as my woman."

Hans tilts his chin up, it's a big, round chin covered in a carpet of dark hair. His beard is as thick as the ugly sideburns decorating the edges of his face, like black bars desperately trying to cage his monstrous visage. The rest of his head is bald and gleaming, but it doesn't outshine the ring in his nose. It glints off the morning sunlight washing in from the wide windows that line the grand breakfast room. I try to focus on that ring instead of the smirk tugging at his chapped lips. If I look at him directly, I know I'll lose the tiny remnants of patience I walked in here with and kill him where he sits.

"My apologies, underboss," Hans says with no hint of sincerity. "But if you don't like this any more than we do, why did you agree to it?"

I can't say, *because I don't have a choice*. I can't tell them it's because I'm trying to avoid a war with the Russians that will get myself and Wolfgang killed. I can't say it's because I owe Giovanni Jr. a favor I could never truly repay.

No one besides Wolfgang knows I had help covering everything up. No one besides Wolfgang, Junior, and me is even aware there was anything to cover up. Like the Russians, they believe it was all a random mugging. As proud as I am to see how great of a job we did at keeping everything a secret, I can't help but wish we hadn't right now. Because no one in this room will ever understand why I have no choice but to marry Rosa. And I will never be able to explain, not without Vater losing all faith in me. He might even disown Wolf for this.

All I can offer Hans is the same pathetic reason I've been saying since I got home yesterday and first told Uwe the news. "Because it will help the business."

"That's not good enough." Vater shakes his head.

I glance at Wolfgang, who's been disturbingly quiet this entire time. He's sitting between one of our cousins, Morgen, and our father's best friend, Klaus Brandt. For a moment, I wish we were twins so I could telepathically tell him how much I hate him right now, instead I settle on scowling. With the way he's avoiding my gaze, I suspect the scowling is enough, but I can't glare at him too long or else the others will realize this whole thing has something to do with him. Something to do with the dead Russian woman we all pretended to forget about four years ago.

I never forgot. Couldn't forget if I wanted to—I *did* want to. Because she didn't deserve to die. And Wolfgang didn't deserve to live. But here we are.

Here I am.

There he is. Sitting with his hands in his lap like he's got nothing to do with this. Life will go on for him like none of this ever happened once I say, 'I do.' The same way it went on four years ago. Once again, I'll be the only one affected by my brother's mistakes.

I sigh. "Rosa De Luca is sister to the current Italian don and granddaughter to the current boss of the Willis Stronghold. Marrying her will create a three-way alliance between the Bronx, Manhattan, and Brooklyn. We may not benefit as much from Manhattan right now, but I can turn that around in a year. By then, I'll have an heir from Rosa and our ties with the Stronghold will be solidified. It's a solid plan."

"A *long* plan," my cousin Conrad grumbles.

"But a solid one," I assure him.

"What if you don't get an heir in a year?" Vater asks, casting a very conspicuous glance at Conrad. My grumpy cousin has been married for three years now and hasn't produced a son or a daughter yet. No one at this table wants children, but one of the points of marriage in this business is to produce a child. That seals the alliance in blood—a blood that's stronger than the virginal consummation of the wedding night. Because a child is flesh and bone, a living heir who cannot be questioned the way a woman's virtue could.

I smile at my father, finding genuine humor in his concern. "I won't have a problem producing a child."

He nods at this, seemingly satisfied with my response. "If you don't get one out of her, we could annul the marriage."

It's a rare thing to do, but not unheard of—at least not for someone of my status in the mafia. Being an underboss makes the birth of an heir that much more important. If Rosa doesn't give me one within a year, I could blame it all on her and demand an annulment so I could find a more fitting wife. One that could give me the son I need. Preferably a German one, if my father has a say.

I don't like the sound of it. It's a slippery plan that could go wrong in so many ways. The mafia holds marriage sacred—if only because of all the business deals riding on the union. So it isn't easy to get out of them. I don't even know any men in the organization who've gotten a divorce.

First, I would have to prove that I actually tried to have a child with my wife—tried enough times to legitimately call her barren. Knowing how spiteful and old-fashioned Uwe is, he would do things the German way and have us ... ahem ... *perform* in front of his chosen witnesses as proof.

Once that humiliation is over, I'd still have to wait for Rosa to take a pregnancy test—hope I didn't get her pregnant that time—and then file for an annulment.

And after that, we would have to convince the priest who marries us to release us from the vows we'll take before man and God. That part wouldn't be too hard, our priest has been working with us since I was a child. He christened me and even blessed me for my fifteenth birthday. Right before my father's men snatched me out of bed and started my brutal initiation into the gang. He's a great priest, if you can't already tell.

I don't like the annulment idea, but it's all I've got to work with if I ever want to get away from Rosa De Luca. At the very least, I don't mind keeping the suggestion in my back pocket, so I nod agreement to my father and stand to leave.

He looks at me with a question in his eyes. "Where are you going?"

"I have to present myself to Rosa's grandfather. He's a mafia boss, just like you. He'll be expecting me to pay my proper respects."

Uwe laughs, and I spot a bit of spinach stuck in his teeth. "Enjoy the Bronx."

Believe it or not, I'm actually looking forward to my trip to the Bronx. Dealing with the Stronghold will be much less of a headache than breakfast with my own family. Probably because I'm going to the Bronx to deliver gifts.

It's a longstanding tradition within the German mafia to give gifts to the family of the bride as a way to say thank you for allowing me to marry your daughter. Obviously, the Stronghold isn't German, but Jameson Willis is the Godfather of the Stronghold. He'll be expecting something from me, especially since I'm lower rank than him as an underboss. It won't hurt to start things off on the right foot.

Normally, I would ask my fiancé what she thinks her grandfather will expect, but Rosa and I haven't spoken since we saw each other yesterday. And even then, we hardly exchanged more than a few words. We spent the first minute after I walked into her bedroom just staring at each other. It'd been ten long years since I'd seen her. She was only a kid then—with a gap between her two front teeth and a childish joy I almost couldn't understand.

Now, she's a woman. With perfect teeth and a perfect body

and absolutely no joy. That much I could tell just from looking at her as she'd sat on her bed trying—and failing—to cover herself with her blanket. Her expression was just as shocked as mine, but behind those almond-shaped, hazel eyes, I could see the anger and sadness and fear swirling uncontrollably.

Anger, because her brother is forcing her into a marriage she wants no part of. Sadness, because she's lost the freedom she fought so hard to get. And fear, because she's marrying me.

After staring blankly at each other, Junior cleared his throat and snatched both of us from our thoughts and memories. That's when he started laying down dates for the wedding and asking if we could do this as quickly as possible. His eagerness reminded me that I wasn't there to stare at a beautiful woman, I was there to check out my new bride—like I was inspecting a nice steak I intended to enjoy for dinner.

I don't even remember if I felt sick of *myself*. But I did feel sick. And irritated. And as angry as Rosa—because she wasn't the only one being forced into this arrangement. But it was easier to just grin and bear it than fight and start a war with a rival gang. So after I left Gio's estate, I broke the news to my father and then made arrangements to meet with Jameson Willis today.

I've got Jameson's gift tucked into my lap as I ride out to the Bronx. Wolfgang has joined me for this venture, following me around like a lost child ever since yesterday morning. Normally, his shadow wouldn't bother me—I wouldn't even notice him, to be honest—but right now, his mere presence makes me want to strangle him and then tell Douglass to pull over so we could dump his body somewhere.

He has caused me so much trouble.

When I glance up, his wide, round eyes are glued to me. I can tell he wants to say something, but he's too afraid. Instead of speaking, he offers me a tightlipped smile and then turns to stare out the window.

I do the same.

Besides, I'm positive I'll enjoy the view outside my window far more than any conversation with him right now. That's not just because Wolfgang has backed me into a corner with this marriage, it's because the Bronx looks nice.

Ten years ago, this borough was called the Concrete Jungle. But once the defunding happened, Jameson Willis rose to power and changed everything about the Bronx. It is no longer the stomping grounds of petty criminals and smalltime gangsters. United as one force—one *Stronghold*—the gangs of the Bronx became the mafia we know today.

Clusters of projects and ghettos were torn down and replaced with skyscrapers, villas, and luxury hotels. Jameson Willis did for the Bronx what every mayor of New York has been promising since before he was born. He did it illegally, of course, but this sector of the city praises him for it, nonetheless. They call him King James, and I can't say the title isn't fitting. Because the Bronx isn't a stone jungle anymore, it's a flourishing kingdom.

I don't stop myself from looking up, tilting my head all the way back, as I step from my car. We're at the front gates of the Willis estate. It's a mansion that dwarfs every other building in sight, with marble pillars holding it up and a fountain spurting crystal blue water in the circle of the driveway.

Wolfgang is beside me, whistling. "What a place."

"Are they expecting you, sir?" Douglass asks.

I glance over at him and then turn to face him fully. Douglass is originally from the Stronghold, a fact I am immediately reminded of when I see his dark brown skin and familiar visage. Then my gaze drops to the bullseye burned onto his left hand.

"They are expecting me," I say, staring at the mark. "But just me. You don't have to come inside."

He bristles, straightening a little. "I'm not ashamed of my mark. I'm German now, sir."

I pat his shoulder and look him in the eye. "You are German. But Jameson might see it as an insult if I flaunt your loyalty in front of him."

Understanding weighs on him, making his shoulders sag for just a moment. Then he glances around—at the guards standing beside the marble pillars and walking the pristine lawn a few meters to our left. He notices the way they eye us, the way they eye *him*, and he takes a sharp breath.

To me, Douglass is a loyal brother. An invaluable Hunter who cannot be replaced. He is as good as the German brothers I eat with every night. But to the Stronghold men with assault rifles in their hands, he is a traitor. Someone who should be shot for drinking German beer and driving around a German underboss.

I shouldn't have let him drive me here.

But it's too late now.

Douglass nods and then turns to reach for the driver door. "I'll pull around once you're ready, sir."

"This won't take long."

Wolfgang and I are patted down, our weapons confiscated, and the package I have for Jameson is examined. Once we're finally let inside, a lovely looking woman in a sleek black dress guides us through the mansion to a room with grand double doors. She opens them slowly to reveal Jameson Willis and a crowd of people I assume are his family or his underlings.

There are at least ten people present, all seated at an oval-shaped table. There's only one empty chair at the far end, which I take without hesitation, forcing Wolfgang to stand beside me like my lapdog. I smirk.

"Something funny?" King James says. He's looking at me through dark brown eyes, almost hidden below his heavy eyebrows. Jameson Willis is old enough to be my grandfather—the oldest don in all five boroughs. He is dressed like an old pimp, instead of a businessman, but I think the look suits him. He's big and stocky, seems to take up more space than humanly possible. There's a solid block of gold on the pinky finger of his right hand—his boss ring. It's big and gaudy and shines as bright as the gold chain around his neck, but it's nothing compared to the twinkling rock on the hand of the woman seated beside him.

I glance at her for a second, trying not to let my eyes linger. She is Monique Willis, Rosa's grandmother. The woman is an exact replica of her late daughter, it's almost startling how much alike they looked. Smooth skin and perfect full lips, eyes that seem to smile even when her mouth doesn't. If it weren't for the hints of grey peppering her shoulder-length curls, I would swear she hasn't aged since the nineties.

"Is something funny?" King James repeats. There is a thread of anger woven into his voice that makes me answer quickly, "No. I'm just overwhelmed to be in the presence of royalty."

He stares at me a second, then lets out a low, reverberating laugh that spreads through the rest of the table. I look at each person, Jameson's two living children—twin brothers, Trenton and Tyrese Willis. Trenton's wife, Diamond, is also present, as well as their two daughters, Adella and Nona Willis. There are four others at the table, but I don't recognize any of them. I haven't had many dealings with the Stronghold before. This is my first time inside the king's palace.

Something uncurls within my chest as I watch the table full of people laugh at my remark. Something foreign and unfamiliar.

Anxiety.

I don't know where it comes from. I don't know why it's even there. But it is and I quickly swallow it down before it can prick through my pores in a nervous sweat. I cannot let them see me like this.

"You're trying very hard to make a good impression, little Hunter," King James says.

I take a deep breath. "I'm hoping my gift will impress you more than my words."

Jameson nods at the package in my hand, so I unwrap it and lay it on the table as if on display. A dozen diamonds, each one no less than five full carats. I also decided to throw in three rubies the size of eggs. I heard Monique likes them.

My resources are right because Monique leans forward in her chair, a greedy look in her eye. But Jameson only frowns.

"You came in here with pretty rocks?"

"These pretty rocks are worth millions," I tell him. "They're the best my business has to offer."

I'm actually telling the truth—well, part of the truth. These aren't the best the Jäger jewelers have to offer, but they are excellent diamonds. It's what we're known for in this industry. The Morenos have their cocaine, the Russians enjoy selling flesh, but the Jägers sell pretty rocks. We mine them overseas—illegally, of course—but they're still the best this city has to offer. Jameson knows this, he's just being greedy. But I've got enough resources to feed his appetite.

"I have more to offer my future grandfather-in-law," I tell him.

"I don't think I'll be interested." He waves a hand, but Monique waves hers, too, as if to dismiss his silliness. She rolls her eyes at her husband and then plants those burning orbs on me. "I love the jewels."

For a moment, I don't know what to say. It isn't common for mafia women to openly disagree with their husbands. Then again, it isn't common for women to join the men at the business table like this, either. That's one of the unique things about the Stronghold—their women are actively involved in their gang affairs. That's probably why the Stronghold is so … *strong*. And also why Rosa was bold enough to even *try* to run away from her family. She was raised by a strong woman who wasn't afraid to speak her mind to her husband, despite his position as the don of the Italian mafia.

For a second, a small part of me feels an inexplicable sense of excitement at the thought of Rosa crossing her arms and trying her best to stand her ground against me once we're married. She might be the daughter of a Willis, but she's still a flower. And flowers are easy to break.

"Thank you, Mrs. Willis," I say, inclining my head. "But I hope you'll still accept my second gift."

"What is it?" Jameson asks.

"I'm expecting a new shipment of raw diamonds next week. You can have first pick and do whatever you want with them."

King James leans forward, resting his chin on folded hands. "How many diamonds will I get?"

"Three. Each worth five carats."

He smiles. This time, it isn't a smirk that leads to cackling laughter. It's a grin so large it reveals a gold tooth on the left side of his mouth. He's pleased. Because he knows I'm not talking about jewelry at all.

If I can finish up my delayed business with the Morenos, I'll be able to get my hands on a full shipment of cocaine. I'm offering Jameson first pick of the raw supply—three truckloads, worth 50 million each. That's 150 million dollars-worth of drugs. Throw in the pretty rocks still on display on the table between us, and you're looking at a wedding gift worth one quarter-*billion* dollars.

Rosa is not worth all the money I'm spending, but I knew I would have to shed a large sum for this. The Stronghold doesn't trust the De Lucas anymore. They blame Rosa for her mother's death and all but cut ties with their Italian allies after everything went down. Accepting my gifts will mean accepting the marriage between myself and Rosa. It will mean accepting this new three-way alliance and accepting Rosa as his granddaughter again. She will be treated as a Willis, entitled to his protection and a portion of his assets once he dies. Assets that will go to me, as her husband.

Jameson may not like the idea of being tied to the girl he blames for killing his daughter, but he can't turn down an opportunity to strike a pact with the Jägers. The De Lucas might be tumbling downhill, but he knows for a fact that *we* aren't. Plus, the cocaine won't hurt. And neither will the diamonds. Especially not the diamonds.

Because drugs are a trillion-dollar industry, but only as long as there are addicts to sell them to. NYC has no shortage of fiends looking for their next hit, but not everyone wants cocaine. In a lawless city like this, there is always a new drug available. Things shipped in from overseas—experiments from distant drug lords trying to test their new product. Synthetic drugs trying to make a quick buck. Cocaine is valuable, but it won't last forever.

Diamonds, *jewelry*, on the other hand… People will always want something that sparkles. That's why the Jägers specialize in selling pretty rocks. It's also beneficial that our customers aren't a bunch of addicts. We can deal with clients from the good side of the law. We've sold jewels to hedge fund managers, celebrities, and NFL stars. Just last month we cut a diamond for an engagement ring ordered by the quarterback of the NY Jets.

The diamond industry is a legitimate business venture. The Jäger family has a dozen different stores outside the City—one of them is personally owned by me, four are located overseas, and all twelve are completely legal. That means we have something to fall back on if everything in NYC goes up in flames. I could start over as an honest jeweler. I don't see myself working nine to five, selling rings to blushing brides, but it beats slinging dope on street corners.

Jameson sees the value in this. He knows no matter how bad the De Lucas are doing; it will be beneficial to form an alliance with the Jägers. I can see the understanding unfolding in his eyes as he nods and stands. The rest of his entourage stands, too, which I take as my signal to rise.

King James walks around the table, meeting me at my chair with an extended hand. "I accept your gifts."

I let go of a breath I didn't know I was holding. "Thank you, Mr. Willis."

Chapter Seven

Junior is being nice today. It puts me on high alert, but I've been locked in my bedroom for the last four days—I'm too deprived to let the anxiety linger. The only person I've seen is the servant who brings me food. She doesn't speak to me, likely because of Gio's orders, so my time in this penthouse has been quiet and lonely. Until today.

Today, Giovanni has decided to let me out of my room. The door is left unlocked—which I only realize after noticing the woman who brings in my breakfast doesn't have to use her key before coming in. As soon as she leaves, I throw my covers back and run to the door. Sure enough, it's unlocked.

After cleaning myself up in my bathroom, I run back and check the door again—still unlocked. So I change and tiptoe into the hall.

Now, I'm walking barefoot through my brother's home. There are no servants milling about, dusting bookshelves or vacuuming the expensive rugs. There aren't any guests lounging in the living room. The library is empty. The gym is dark and cold. The pool is lit up, its filters working to clean the chlorine-blue water—but it's empty.

I am all alone.

In Norman, I was never alone. There was always someone to speak to, or laugh with, or even sing songs with. Melissa took me around to the shelters she ran at least a few days a week. I was familiar with the women she worked with, and I had friends from the congregation of Trinity Baptist Church. Most of them were ladies, since it was a women's ministry. But Pastor Marcia always brought her husband around, and their three sons. Plus, there was Arthur and even a few other cops from the police department.

It was one of the loveliest places in all of Jersey. And I'd been ripped away from it. Violently. Mercilessly. Still, I was treated better than Minnie who was hit by a car driven by one of Gio's men. And I was treated better than Melissa who had to witness her own daughter's senseless accident.

I haven't spoken to my Norman family since being dragged back to New York, so as I turn the corner into the kitchen, I make a mental note to ask Gio about the call he promised me. I'm about to find a drink from the fridge when I hear voices coming from the lounge area beyond the sunroom.

They don't belong to my brother or his guards—all the voices are female, which sends me across the kitchen, leaning against the door with my ear pressed to the wood.

I hear laughing. *Giggling.*

Before I change my mind, I push the door open and gasp.

My best friend and two of my cousins are seated comfortably on the sofa and chair, a glass of orange juice in their hands, croissants and mini fruit tarts held delicately between fingers. They all glance up as I enter; smiles erupt onto their faces.

"Rosa!" they say in unison.

I rush over to them, taking my cousin Nona into my arms. She's from my mother's side of the family, but I've always been close with her and her older sister. When she sets me free, I give Adella a hug and then sit on the sofa, right beside my best friend.

Olivia Romano. She is tan and tall and elegant, with dark brown hair kept short in a pixie cut. Her eyes twinkle as she smiles at me, and I remember the girl I grew up with. Olivia is the daughter of Niccolò Romano, the man Gio named as his underboss. He was best friends with my father, which is why I'm best friends with her. Growing up, she was at my estate almost every day—enough to know Nona and Adella by name.

I can't keep myself from grinning as she pulls me into a hug, but my smile fades when she pulls away, and I catch the glimmer of the diamond ring on her finger. She hadn't been engaged when I left.

"That's new," I say, staring at the giant jewel.

She blushes and holds it up so I can get a better look. "It's from Marco."

I blink, hoping it isn't the Marco I'm thinking of. "Marco *Segreto?*"

Slowly, she lowers her hand, and her voice comes out softly, barely more than a solemn whisper. "Yes. Marco Segreto."

Even Adella and Nona wrinkle their noses. Marco is a general within our mafia. He controls all the business that flows through Harlem and owns three hotels near Central Park. He's a successful mafioso, by and large. Any high-ranking member of the Manhattan Garden would be pleased to offer him their daughter. I'm sure my own father would have entertained the idea of a marriage between us ... if Marco was thirty years younger.

He's near his sixties, as old as my father was before he took his life. But he's never been married, so he's technically still an acceptable match for Olivia. Women of our stature aren't raised to be the *second* wife of anyone in the mafia. Not even a general. Not even a *don*.

Still ... being passed off to someone nearly the same age as her father is almost an insult. I can only imagine the arrangement is some sort of punishment, and I don't have to wonder what for.

It's because of me.

The realization makes me stiffen. As an attempt to keep her safe, I never told Olive anything about my plans. If my father suspected she'd helped me, he would have punished her and Niccolò, too, for failing to control her. Olivia had nothing to do with my great escape, but she's still my best friend. It isn't farfetched to imagine my father at least had his suspicions about her assisting me somehow.

Unable to prove her association, he likely ordered Niccolò to marry her off. Preferably to someone undesirable and with a firm commitment to the Italian mafia. Marco Segreto was the perfect choice. He's old enough to embarrass the Romanos for their suspected aid in my escape and experienced enough to be wholly dedicated to the Garden. He won't let Olivia get out of line the way my father had allowed me to.

I shiver as I stare at her engagement ring, guilt flooding through me. *How many lives have I ruined?* I wonder, but when Olive glances up at me, I see no judgment in her eyes. Knowing her, she was probably happy for me when she learned of my escape. She grew up with me, as close to me as Adella and Nona—my own kin. She knows the hardships of being the daughter of a high-ranking mafioso. She knows the struggles we face—understands how they could have pushed me to the point of fleeing.

She probably wanted to flee, too. But I'd been the only one brave enough to try. And I'd failed. And ruined things for her in the process.

"When's the wedding?" I manage to ask.

She smiles dolefully. "It was supposed to be two weeks from now. But it's been postponed." She doesn't have to explain why. It's because of my wedding. Yet another arrangement being forced onto a mafia princess.

"Speaking of weddings," Nona cuts in. "We were invited over to help you out today, Rosa."

I tilt my head to the side. Confused. "Help me out?"

Adella turns and snaps her fingers; on cue, a line of staff

members enters the lounge with large boxes and garment bags in their arms. "I'm guessing Gio hasn't told you yet, but we're your bridesmaids," Adella explains, carefully avoiding diving into further details. Everyone knows I ran away, but they've probably been instructed not to say anything about it. I'm glad.

"We wouldn't be doing our job right if we didn't help you pick out your gown," Nona adds.

I stare open-mouthed as the staffers unbox and unveil the gowns brought in for me to try on today. This is why Gio let me out of my room. He wasn't being nice; he was trying to get started on the wedding plans.

Oh well, I sigh. I could be angry about it and order the staff members to pack up and leave. But that would only make Gio angry and cause him to make things worse for me—or worse for Minnie and Melissa and Arthur. *I won't enjoy this*, I think, nodding as a hefty woman with glasses holds up a gown for me to examine. *But I'll do it with a smile anyway.*

My cousins are stuffing themselves with sweets while Olivia prattles on about her own wedding plans. She doesn't look happy about her *groom*, but she is happy about the wedding.

"Sometimes it's the festivities that tug your lips into a smile," she says, eyeing her ring again. "Not the reason behind them."

I nod my agreement as two women button my gown and then step away for me to turn around and show my bridesmaids my dress. It's a strapless gown that's sleek and formfitting, but way too long. I can't help that I'm short, but even with alterations I don't think this dress will be right for me.

My ladies agree with rigid smiles and stiff nods.

I take a deep breath. "This isn't the one."

"No," Adella shakes her head without shame. She's the oldest here and the only one of us who's married. I'm not surprised since she's almost Gio's age. Nona is closer to my age at twenty-three and Olivia is only ten months older than me. The two of them frown and offer me apologies as I tiptoe behind the changing screen for the next dress.

I try on five more with no success.

A short, backless dress that barely comes to my knees. It's meant to be unique, but it will likely get me shunned by everyone in attendance if I dared expose so much skin as a new bride. Next is a puffy dress so large it looks like a monstrous prom dress. A traditional Italian style dress that'd been flown in from Tuscany comes next. It's totally black and gorgeous but given the fact that I don't actually want to get married, it feels more like a funeral dress than a wedding gown. Another formfitting dress that I think I like until I put it on and realize it's entirely made of lace and will reveal my underwear underneath. That dress makes Adella yell at the staff.

"This is a wedding for the Flower of Manhattan—not the Harlot of Harlem!"

Embarrassed, the seamstress and her assistants rush me behind the changing screen again and I'm forced into a vintage style dress inspired by the 1950s. It's off-shoulder with a fluffy tulle skirt but it makes me look younger than my twenty years and since Amory is already eleven years older than me, I decide against it.

With a huff, Nona throws in the towel and tells the staff that we're ready for lunch. I accept a glass of sparkling water from Olivia and relax onto the couch as tables are set up and trays brought in. We're served Italian wedding soup—which I don't eat—a garden salad, and grilled chicken breasts. Adella complains the food is too light, but Olivia only laughs.

"Some of us are trying to get our bride bodies. This food is perfect."

"I forgot you're not allowed to be fat on your wedding day," Adella says sarcastically.

I shrug one shoulder. "I'm not very hungry anyway."

"Too excited to eat?" Olivia asks.

I frown at her, genuinely shocked by her question. "Why on earth would I be excited? I hate every part of this."

The small smile on her face shrinks even more and she silently scoops a spoonful of soup into her mouth.

"I'm sorry," I mutter.

"Things could be worse," she says. "You may not like Amory, but at least he's young and handsome. And he isn't like his brother."

His brother? I don't get to dwell on the question before Nona jumps in. "Or you could still be single like me, with no arrangements or wedding date in sight." She sighs and pushes her salad away.

I suddenly feel like I've ruined lunch.

"It's hard for me to feel grateful. I know that sounds

inappreciative, but don't you at least see where I'm coming from?"

"No," Adella says boldly. "You are a mafia princess, little cousin. You were raised with the understanding that you would not pick your husband, and with the expectation to marry him without complaint. That duty remains, no matter the reason behind this arrangement."

I fiddle with the stem of my glass. "I suppose you're right. I just thought I could confide in my own cousins and friend."

"We're here for you." Olivia reaches for my hand. "We understand what you're facing better than anyone."

"Just don't act like you're the first woman to ever face it," Adella says, staring at the ring on her own finger.

"Or the last," Nona adds.

I nod slowly. *No one is going to pity me through this. Not even my closest companions.* And why should they? I'm the very reason Olivia is engaged right now. And even though Nona's husband will be picked out for her just like ours was, she still wants to get married. She looks forward to trying on dresses with her bridesmaids and arranging her own wedding. I probably seem like a spoiled brat to her right now.

But I won't let anything blind me to the fact that I'm being forced into an arrangement that will lock me in the mafia. My bridesmaids will never understand the real reasons I don't want to be tied to Amory. They will never understand that my faith is far more important than the mafia or any handsome man who might be willing to accept me as his bride. And they certainly won't understand how both Amory and this entire city stands in the way of the freedom I'd had in Norman. Freedom to love and worship God openly.

Lord, I silently pray, *if there was ever a time to get me out, it's now.*

I don't get a response to that, but I'm not exactly expecting one. I know God hears me. I know He'll get me out of this marriage and out of the city again. Back into the arms of the Christian man who's truly meant for me.

My heart leaps at the thought of Arthur. I have to see him again. I have to find a way. Before I say, 'I do.'

I find the strength to try on a few more dresses. The last dress captures everyone's attention. It's a boho style gown; off-shoulder with a sweetheart neckline and a straight skirt. There's a split up the right side that goes up to my thigh, exposing my entire leg. It teeters the line between modest and racy. I absolutely love it.

So do my girls. They're grinning ear to ear when I step from behind the changing screen. Adella even gives me a very womanly nod of approval, lifting her glass of lemon water in salute.

"I think we have a winner," she says. The other ladies show their approval by raising their glasses, too.

I can't help but smile. I may not know my groom. I may not even want to get married. But at least I'm going to look beautiful doing it.

___.X.___

I am left alone after the seamstress takes my measurements and

85

my girls are finally ushered out. For a moment, I entertain the thought of trying to leave with them, but I know there are guards posted at every exit in the building. I wouldn't make it to the elevator before getting stopped. Besides, it's late afternoon now and I'm exhausted—too exhausted to attempt another escape, but not exhausted enough to go back to my room. I'm afraid of being locked inside again, so I walk through Gio's penthouse until I find the living room.

This place is too big and too quiet. Nothing like Melissa's little home or the estate we lived in as children. Gio had all my things brought over to his place before he kidnapped me, but I've been here enough times to recognize the artwork on the walls and the expensive cream-colored sofa with the Italian imported throw pillows. There is a statue in the far corner of the room, it's half-finished and looks to be a hundred years old. Beside it is a bookcase that stretches to the ceilings, casting a bit of shade as a reprieve from the lazy sun pouring in through the grand windows lining the living room walls.

As I stand at the edge of the room, I can see all of Manhattan. One sweeping glance gifts me a view of the borough I once called home. Skyscrapers and high risers, business suites stacked to the clouds. I can see Central Park and the Met and the edges of Harlem as the clouds move away from the sun.

This was once my home. This was where I was raised. And somehow it feels foreign to me, despite only being gone for six months.

"How was it?" Junior is by my side, staring straight ahead.

I jump back in surprise and blink at him. He's dressed casually in a button-down shirt tucked into grey slacks and shining leather loafers.

I clutch my chest, trying to calm my frightened heart. "What are you doing here?"

"I live here."

"Not in the living room."

He's still staring out the window as he asks again, "How was the dress fitting?"

"It was fine," I snap. "What do you want with me?"

"I want you to cooperate."

"I haven't been fighting you." I've been locked up for days. I haven't had the opportunity to fight. I even picked out a stupid gown like he wanted.

He sighs and finally drags his eyes from the view of the city down to me. I'm an inch shy of five feet tall, he's at least six feet so it's an effort for him to crane his neck and look me in the eye. I carefully push up on the balls of my bare feet so I'm a tiny bit taller. "I appreciate your cooperation. I'll need more of it this evening."

"What's happening this evening?"

"I've arranged a date between you and Amory."

I take a step back, but before I can protest, his hand whips out and grabs me roughly by the arm. "He's going to be your husband in two weeks. You need to get used to spending time with him now."

"*Two* weeks?"

He sighs dramatically. "Rosa—"

"I haven't even coped with the fact that my father is dead, and I've been kidnapped. I can't get married in two weeks— especially not to a man I barely know."

"You do know Amory. We were friends as kids, you practically grew up around him."

I blink at him, because even he knows he's stretching the truth here. "You and Amory were friends until you were inducted into the Italian mafia."

He shrugs. "So what?"

"So, you were *fifteen* at the time. Which means I was only five—too young to remember any part of your great relationship with Amory Jäger."

But I wasn't too young to remember the fateful day we spent together ten years ago. If there was any evidence to prove my brother had once gotten along with the German underboss, it was my day with Amory. The fact that Gio didn't trust anyone else to watch over me except a forgotten friend from the past speaks volumes to how close they once were.

Now Amory is coming back into both our lives. Permanently. But I don't have time to wonder how my brother feels about being reunited with his childhood buddy. I have to somehow wrap my head around the fact that I'll be marrying that man.

Yes, Amory Jäger is a handsome, rich, powerful man. Yes, he was once close friends with my older brother. Yes, I can't ignore the fact that it was exciting to see him again after all these years. But I don't want to marry him.

I want nothing to do with this dark world of crime and

violence. I just want to get back to Norman. I want to make Sunday dinner with my family. I want to go to church again.

I feel myself growing weaker every day. Slipping further away from God. There's a King James Bible in my bedside drawer, I read it every morning and night. I pray to the Lord every day, begging Him to save me from this place.

I don't get an answer.

But I cannot stay here. I won't stay here. And marrying Amory Jäger will only complicate things. It'll be much tougher to run away as Mrs. Jäger, the Huntress of New York, than as Rosa De Luca, the Withered Rose.

June pulls me back to him and grips my other arm with his free hand. "It doesn't matter if you knew Amory growing up or if you just met him yesterday. I need you to cooperate. We have one chance to fix everything you ruined. Do not screw this up."

I twist free of his grasp. "Amory already agreed to the marriage. I don't think one bad date could mess things up that badly."

"It isn't just a date," he tells me, stuffing his hands deep into his pockets.

I squint at him. "Then what is it?"

"You'll be meeting his family—"

I groan and roll my eyes.

"Amory's father is the boss of the German mafia. You will be expected to pay your respects to him as his future daughter-in-law."

That's why Gio has let me leave the room and walk the

halls of his luxurious home. He's trying to butter me up. Trying to lower my guard.

It doesn't work. I don't want to go to the Jäger estate. I don't want to meet the German mafia. If my behavior or my attitude can at least give my brother a headache, then I might actually try to screw this up on purpose.

Giovanni is watching me closely, like he knows what I'm silently planning. He frowns. "Rosa, please do this for the sake of the De Luca name." He drops his gaze to the floor. "For Father."

That isn't fair.

Throwing Papa into this to make me feel guilty—to make me want to curl up and die. As if I needed a reminder that all of this is my fault in the first place.

My resolve withers at Junior's words. But only part of it. If I'm going to do this, I need to know it'll be worth it in some way, other than making Gio's life as a mafia boss easier.

"I'll be on my best behavior, June," I tell my brother.

He flashes me a cautious smile. "You will?"

"If you let me call my folks in Norman."

The smile vanishes.

"You promised I could call them when I first woke up."

He's frowning now, deep lines forming around his downturned lips. "It's too risky, Rosa."

"You promised."

"I know, but—"

"What could one Christian woman and her injured daughter do to the mafias of New York?" I place a hand on his

90

sleeve, it's rolled up to his elbow. "One call. Ten minutes."

His eyes slowly close as he shakes his head, but he digs into his pocket and retrieves a cellphone anyway. "Five minutes," he says sternly. "And put it on loudspeaker."

I nod, dialing Melissa's number before he can change his mind. It rings only once before her worried voice comes over the other line.

"Hello?"

I gasp, tears instantly filling my eyes. "It's me, Mel!"

"Oh, Lord! You're alive! We thought you were dead!"

"I know." I swipe at the tears running down my cheeks and take a shaky breath. Gio is standing right beside me, his face hard and his eyes narrowed as he stares at the phone. He says nothing. He makes no move to step away and give me privacy. He doesn't even acknowledge my own presence. His sole focus is the phone in my hands and the woman's voice sobbing on the other end.

"I don't have much time," I say quickly. "I just called to let you know I'm all right, and to check on Minnie."

The phone goes quiet a moment. "Rose, what's going on?"

"Is Minnie all right?" I ask, ignoring her question.

Mel pauses again, wasting precious time. "Her leg is broken. But she's got a cast on it and plenty of pain pills. She likes all the attention from Arthur."

His name sends pain arrowing through my heart. I clutch at my chest as images of him pop into my head. His strong arms pulling me into his embrace. His deep voice murmuring comforting words into my hair as I cried into his chest. Words that had been encouraging and uplifting. Words that had reminded me that I'm a Child of God and because of that, everything would be okay.

Why couldn't I marry a man like that?

"How is Arthur?" I ask shakily.

Melissa's tone brightens. I imagine a smile on her plump face as she says, "He's worried about you. We've all been worried. We thought—" she pauses, "We thought you'd been killed."

"No, I'm alive, Mel. I'm all right, I promise."

"Is it him?" she asks slowly. "Did you go back to him, Rose? Or did he come get you?"

By *'him'* she means the pimp she thinks I ran away from six months ago. My heart sinks into my gut. Because her voice doesn't sound accusatory or judgmental at all. It sounds full of emotion and concern. She doesn't blame me for what happened to Minnie. She just wants to know how she can help me get out of this horrible situation.

More tears flood my eyes. Because there is nothing she can do. If Gio even suspects Melissa will try to enter New York, he'll send his men to do a lot more than break Minnie's leg.

I have to convince her everything is fine, or she won't give up. She might even send Arthur out here to help if she thought he could truly make a difference. He is a cop, after all. A fact that used to bring me comfort and security, but now it only opens a pit of dread in my chest.

Melissa snooping around is one thing, but a police officer from outside the city asking questions is another thing entirely.

Arthur could actually do something to stop them. He could get other departments involved and begin dismantling the city from the outside in. If he was determined enough. If he had the resources. If he cared enough to get me back.

Does he? I wonder, then I shake my head. Because it doesn't matter how Arthur feels. I refuse to let him put his life in danger by even entertaining the thought of rescuing me.

"Listen, Melissa," I say, trying to make my voice sound strong and stern. To my side, Gio holds up two fingers to let me know I'm almost out of time. I nod at him. "I am safe, okay? What happened ... It was my fault. But I'm going to fix it. You won't ever be in danger again. I promise."

"Okay," she says slowly. Then the line goes silent for too long, but when I open my mouth to say more, Melissa cuts me off. "Arthur just walked in. He wants to speak to you."

No, if I hear his voice, it will break me. But he's talking before I can hang up. "Rosie?"

I choke on a sob. "Arthur..."

He sighs slowly. "How can I fix this, Rosie?"

"There's nothing to fix," I say, eyeing my brother. He holds up one finger now, his face stony as he stares at the phone.

"Where are you? Back in New York?"

"Arthur, don't ask questions."

"Minnie and Mama filled out police reports on what happened. I'm not letting this go."

"I'm telling you to let it go," I say, harsher than I want to.

"They hit my sister, Rose. And they took you."

"Please," I whisper softly. "If I have ever meant anything

to you—anything at all—you will let this go. For Minnie's sake. For Melissa's sake."

He breathes into the phone. "You did mean something to me, Rose. I just realized it too late."

I squeeze my eyes shut and cry into my free hand. When Junior steps closer to retrieve the phone, I yank away. "I've got to go. Tell Melissa I love her. Tell Minnie I'm sorry. And…" I pause. "I love you guys."

"We love you, too, Rosie."

Junior takes the phone and hangs up. It is disturbingly silent for the next few moments as he watches me wipe at my leaking eyes.

I feel warmth on the top of my head, and I know it's his hand, petting me like a child. Like I'm still ten years old to him.

"Are you happy?" I say, glancing up.

His face is anything but.

He takes a slow breath and shakes his head. "But I am proud. I know that was hard to do."

"Do not patronize me," I hiss.

He retracts his hand and nods at me, the brief gentleness in his eyes ebbing away. The coldness returns as he puts his phone back into his pocket and says, "You have an hour to get ready. Meet me back here to leave for your date."

Chapter Eight

My future bride looks pretty in pink. She's wearing a white blouse tucked into a blush-pink chiffon skirt that brushes just past her knees. Very chaste. Very girly.

Apparently, I'm turned on by girly things because I feel my chest tighten at the sight of her as I step from my car and approach the front doors of Junior's penthouse. She's waiting with her hands clasped in front of her, clutching her little purse for dear life.

"I don't bite," I tell her, offering a smile.

She frowns up at me, like she's never heard a joke before. "Why would you bite me?"

I ... don't know what to say to that. So I thrust the rose I have in my free hand at her. It was Wolfgang's idea. *Because she's the* Rose *of Manhattan*, he'd said when I told him Rosa would be joining the family for dinner tonight. It's not until I'm watching her glare at the red flower that I realize Wolfgang is an idiot.

Or I'm an idiot. I shouldn't take dating advice from a man who enjoys a different woman every night.

Then again, my love life isn't any better. I'm not as wild as my little brother, but I've had my fair share of ladies and I've never had to *date* them before. I'd pick them up at bars and clubs or have them brought in and pay them when they leave. Or not. They didn't always want money, some of them just wanted me.

The point is, I don't know what I'm doing right now, but it's obvious I'm not doing this right.

Rosa hesitantly takes the rose and winces, drops it to the ground.

"What's wrong?" I ask quickly.

She holds her finger. "The thorns, they pricked me."

I curse in German and stoop to pick up the flower. "I'm sorry."

"You didn't clip the thorns?"

"I didn't know I had to."

She stares down at me. From this angle, she looks immensely disappointed. Like I've ruined the entire night before it's even begun. I could get angry and tell her it's just a stupid flower and she's being a big baby about it. But I'm too distracted by the way her lips pucker as her gaze shifts to focus on her injury. She brings her hand to her mouth and sucks on the very tip of her finger.

I almost groan. And then I think, *what am I doing?* When did I become such a ... a *pervert?*

I cough violently, trying to clear my thoughts. Rosa jumps

in surprise, glaring as she watches me rise with the flower in my hand. I toss it on the ground a few feet away. "I'll get you a bandage when we get to my estate. How's that?"

She nods, her finger still in her mouth. It takes an embarrassing amount of effort not to stare at her lips. Since things are already awkward and can't get any worse, I grab her hand and yank it from her mouth.

"Stop doing that."

"Hey!" She frowns, clutching her hand.

"You shouldn't stick your fingers in your mouth. It isn't sanitary."

"Can we just go now?" she complains.

I turn and head back to my car without waiting for her, then I remember this is supposed to be a date, so I turn back, but I don't realize she's following right behind me, so I end up bumping into her.

She gasps as I step on *both* her small feet and then she's stumbling back. There's a moment of stillness, where everything slows down. Rosa's tipping backwards, a look of fear on her face before she topples over completely. I sigh. Then the stillness passes, and time catches up, along with gravity, but I'm quicker than I look. I reach out and grab Rosa by the wrist, pulling her into my chest. My other hand goes around her waist, stabling her.

"You're okay," I tell her.

Her eyes are wild with panic. It takes an extra moment for her to realize I've caught her and she's in my arms, not flat on the concrete. When she comes to her senses, the panic is replaced by embarrassment. I watch as a gentle blush works its way over her cheeks. We're close, close enough for me to smell her perfume. She smells like a rose. I don't know if she wore that fragrance on purpose or not, but it makes my chest tighten again and I have to look away from her large, hazel eyes or else I might kiss her.

I feel like a teenager on his first date. Not a grown man out with his fiancé. I don't even want to marry Rosa. This arrangement will hurt my organization more than help it. But that doesn't mean I have to ignore the fact that Rosa is absolutely beautiful. That she fits perfectly in my arms. That her innocence feels familiar to me. Like she's still the girl I knew ten years ago. The girl I'd been charged with guarding and protecting for a single day. Now I'll be protecting her for life. And it won't be anything like it was before.

Rosa's all grown up. But I still feel protective of her, like my job as her personal guard never ended. Inexplicably, I want to keep her safe. Preserve the precious innocence that has somehow survived her mafia childhood. The kindness and concern I'd extended to her years ago is still there, echoes of my past capturing my heart.

I blink at her, not realizing that she's brought her hand to my chest, gently pushing me away. I let her go.

"Thank you," she says, taking a step back and staring down at the ground.

That's when it hits me.

I'm attracted to Rosa. Honestly, genuinely, legitimately attracted to her. But she isn't drawn to me. She probably wants

98

to scramble back to Jersey first chance she gets. I didn't expect her to walk down the aisle with a smile on her face, but I also didn't expect to be taken by her. Not like this, not so suddenly.

This marriage is supposed to be business. Business I'm not going to enjoy.

I mean, I plan to enjoy our wedding night and all the other nights we'll share. But looking at Rosa, at how she can't even meet my gaze, I don't think she wants to share anything with me. Not even this car ride. For some reason, that makes the tightening in my chest turn into a dull ache.

I sigh and open the car door for her. This is going to be a long night.

Our car ride passes mostly in silence, but when I can't take it anymore, I glance over at Rosa and say slowly, *"Gutten Tag."*

She blinks. "What does that mean?"

"It's a common greeting in German. Simple enough for you to learn, right?"

She understands now and nods, repeating the words in a very bad German accent. "Gutten Tag."

I lean over, cup her chin, and gently press my fingers against her cheeks so her lips pucker for me. *"Gutten Tag,"* I emphasize.

She blushes and says it again. This time, her accent is slightly better. *"Gutten Tag."*

"Good girl." I let her go and fix my jacket, buttoning it as my home comes into view. It's the same mansion my grandfather lived in when he was the *Jägermeister*, large and grand and gated off. An estate built of brick and sitting back far enough for us to have an expansive lawn and half a dozen guards milling about. They don't pay us any mind as Douglass opens my door and lets me out, then Rosa. She pauses as she sees him for the first time, her eyes dropping to the bullseye on his left hand.

They stare at each other a moment, then Douglass glances away and nods at me. "I'll pull around if you need me." He says this in German, which takes me by surprise. Douglass started learning the language when he was first hunted, but he rarely uses it. Now, I suppose, he's just showing off in front of Rosa. A granddaughter to his former Boss. They probably knew each other as kids. Douglass is the nephew of a Stronghold general, after all.

If they had any connection, neither of them shows it. Douglass gets back into the car and Rosa simply turns to me, a very forced smile on her lips. "Ready?" I say, offering her my arm, her hands are trembling as she takes it. I feel like I'm the only thing keeping her on her feet right now. I don't want to make things worse for her, but I have to let her know before we enter my home, so she isn't taken by surprise. "My family is here. Everyone. My little brother, my parents, my uncle, and cousins. A few generals from the organization. They're all here to meet you. So they'll be asking questions and trying to greet you. Don't let anything they say get to you—but if someone steps out of line, let me know."

She looks up at me. "All of the German mafia is inside your

house right now? To meet me?"

I laugh. "I'm the underboss. Besides my father, there is no one more powerful than me in our organization. They have to come out and meet my future wife or it will be seen as a sign of disrespect." I walk to the front doors and nod at the guards. "But not everyone is here. The lower ranked men aren't important enough to enter my home."

She nods, swallowing hard as the double doors swing open. I lead her through the open foyer and into the lounge area where most of my guests are waiting with drinks in their hands. Wolfgang sees us first and thrusts his glass into the air.

"Brother!" he exclaims.

The rest of the guests turn and do the same, raising a toast to my awaited arrival.

"Welcome!" Wolfgang pushes his way over to us and takes Rosa's hand. "What a beauty. You're a lucky man, Amory." He says this in German, but I glare at him, and he quickly looks away. I made it clear to everyone here tonight that we'd be using English only. It's tough enough for my fiancé—being forced to marry me and all that—I don't want to make this any more insufferable by talking around her like she isn't there. But before I can remind my brother of his manners, Rosa squeezes his hand and says softly, *"Gutten Tag."*

Wolf's eyes widen and nearly pop from their sockets. His jaw hangs open for a moment, then he gasps up at me, a teasing smirk spreading over his lips. "She speaks German like an Italian. I love it."

I do too, but I don't say this because Rosa's staring up at

me now, blinking. Waiting for some sort of gesture of approval.

I smile down at her and nod at my brother. "Wolfgang speaks four languages. You can use Italian with him tonight if you want."

He gives her a vulpine smile I've seen him use on women before. *"Buona sera."* His voice is husky and low and makes Rosa grip my arm even tighter, but she hides her discomfort well. Instead of shying away like I expect her to, she leans forward and starts speaking Italian with him like they're best friends.

They fire off a conversation right in front of me, like I'm not even there. I could be angry, but instead I take this moment to step away and grab myself a drink.

"How is she doing so far?" my father sidles up to me. I'm two inches taller, but not nearly as beefy. He looks like a walking pile of meatballs. His sharp eyes narrow as I take a long sip of my drink.

"She's getting along with Wolf."

"All women get along with Wolf."

I almost laugh, but the truth in his words sap all the humor from the conversation, especially when I remember the woman my brother is currently charming is my own fiancé. I glance over at them; Wolf is showing Rosa the bullseye tattooed onto the back of his head. He keeps it shaved to show off his mark. Rosa seems confused but impressed as she nods and smiles. I can't make out every word, but I can tell from here they're still speaking Italian. I'd better go over and stop them before Vater starts to feel insulted.

As I move to walk away, he grabs my arm. "Did you show her the gift yet?"

I shake my head. It didn't seem like something I should do as soon as I saw her tonight. Vater isn't upset about it, though, he actually smiles as he says, "Good. Present it before dinner."

"In front of everyone?"

"She will be the wife of an underboss in two weeks. She needs to get used to being surrounded by nosey Germans."

He's right. "Do you want to meet her now?"

Vater shakes his head, eyeing Rosa closely. "I want to watch her meet Christina first."

I peer through the crowd to see my mother walking up to my fiancé and panic hits me like a lightning bolt. I love my mother—dearly—but I know she can be more trouble than my father when she wants to be. Which is exactly why Uwe keeps her locked away in the estate most of the time. She gets off on giving everyone a headache.

"I should go." I pull away from Vater and dip into the mass of guests, nodding to my cousins and Uncle Oberon, ignoring Hans who doesn't even bother smiling, just stares at me through his unblinking black eyes. When I make it to Rosa, she's shaking hands with Christina, a gentle smile on her full lips. A slender woman is by my mother's side, long-legged with wide hips and bleached blonde hair. It's Petra Preuß, my cousin from my mother's side.

It's actually a good thing Petra's here, Rosa will need a female friend once she joins the family. I can't think of a better woman for the job. She's been raised in the mafia, just like Rosa, and she's high-ranking, being my own cousin and having just gotten engaged to Eike Brandt, the son of my father's best friend—Klaus Brandt. Normally, Petra is a good girl, except when she's spent too much time with Christina and has had too much to drink. Like tonight.

Somehow … *somehow*, at only six in the evening, both my mother and my cousin are swaying in their six-inch stilettos. Christina is licking her wet lips and eyeing my fiancé closely as she shyly explains how we spent time together ten years ago. It's a cute story. And I'm sure it would be much appreciated on, like, girls' night over a bottle of pink champagne, but right now my mother looks like she's going to spill her drink and vomit on Rosa. I have to end this conversation before something happens and my chances at making it through this dinner without a migraine are permanently ruined.

"*Mutti*," I say softly, reaching for her arm. She smiles, though her eyes are glossy and unfocused. She's drunk because of Vater. Because this is the first time he's let her out her quarters in over a month. He doesn't even allow Wolf and I to see her when she misbehaves, treating her like a prisoner, locked up in her own house. It's better than when he used to take the belt to her, like she was a child who needed discipline. Some nights, I'd hear the strap whacking for hours. Hear Christina shrieking until she passed out. I'm grateful I never inherited my father's cruelty. I do what I have to to keep the Jäger name alive. I'm in the mafia, I don't pretend this is a bright and happy day job. But I don't forget my humanity, either.

Wolf does. He's inherited all the bad parts of our father, especially his brutality. Which is why he's still single—no one wants to give their daughters to him, despite being the son of the Jägermeister. His reputation is that bad. It's what got me here in the first place, marrying a woman who'd rather run for the hills than say, 'I do.'

Christina leans into me, muttering in German, "She's pretty. Get her out of here."

The warning sends a chill down my spine, but I shake it off and offer a fake smile to Rosa. "My mother isn't feeling well."

"She feels fine," Petra says, pointing her glass at me. I don't think she realizes its empty. "Leave her alone, Amory. We just want to meet your pretty, foreign wife."

"She isn't my wife yet. And you've met her. Now take Christina upstairs, please." I move my mother a step away, but she fights me, slamming a pathetically weak hand against my chest as she curses in German. "Don't take me back there! I won't go!"

Rosa's eyes are the size of oranges, watching in increasing fear as my mother acts out. This is getting bad. If Christina keeps going like this, Vater will have her locked away for another month. Maybe even take the strap to her again if he's in the mood. Right now, he's only laughing. Standing in the crowd with Hans by his side, chuckling at this entire ordeal.

I hate him for this. I hate that he's done this to my own mother, a woman who used to be beautiful and sober and loving. I hate that he's sitting back and enjoying the embarrassment unfolding before him—before our entire family. Before Rosa. The woman who's expected to join this madhouse in two weeks.

We were supposed to make a good impression. We were supposed to welcome her to our home. Not send her running back to Jersey. If Wolf weren't beside her, gripping her arm to keep her from darting to the front doors, I think Rosa would be halfway to Norman by now. I would be, at least.

"Mutti," I say softly, pulling my mother into a hug. "Calm down. No one is locking you away. I just want you to lie down for a moment."

She struggles to twist away, but I hold her firmly, whispering into her white, feathery hair. "It's all right. Petra will take care of you. And I'll come get you for dessert."

She leans away and blinks up at me. "Promise, Amory?" she asks in English. "Promise you won't let him lock me away."

I kiss her forehead. "I promise."

For a moment, it seems like I've finally calmed everything down. Petra takes Mother under her arm and begins to guide her away, but she jerks back and whirls around, holding up her hand for my fiancé to see her wedding ring. "Diamonds are just pretty shackles in this life." She croaks out a drunken laugh. "They're only nice until you say, 'I do.'" Then she starts sobbing so loudly people begin to stir.

I take a step forward, but I'm shoved to the side by a large arm. When I regain my footing, I realize Hans has pushed his way through the crowd. Petra's eyes widen in fear as she sees him coming, but there is nothing she can do. He grabs my mother roughly by the arm and drags her toward the stairs in the back of the room without a word.

Christina shrieks the entire time. Pleading in German for him to let her go, crying for Vater to hold him off. I glance back at my father. He isn't smiling anymore. But he doesn't order his lapdog to let her go. So we all wait in silence until Hans ascends both flights of stairs, Christina shouting for help the entire time. It isn't until the heavy door at the top of the staircase closes behind them that Mother's screaming finally stops. Her voice echoes through the lounge for a few extra moments. Her final cries for mercy. The sound of it is haunting. An unwanted reminder of my harsh childhood in this nightmarish manor.

When the door shuts, the crowd heaves a collective sigh, but our nerves are still unsettled. Petra disappears in the mass, likely afraid that Hans will come for her next. I don't have time to dwell on her or him or even my mother. Rosa is still beside me, her eyes huge and filled with raw panic. I can't think of a single thing to say that would make this situation better, so I reach into my pocket for the gift I've prepared and drop to one knee.

This is as good a time as any to ask my involuntary bride to marry me. As if she actually has a choice. This is all for show anyway. Something to entertain my guests with. It'll be the only time they get to see me on my knees, so I hope they enjoy it.

They do.

Wolfgang lets out a howl and I hear Uncle Oberon calling for a toast. All at once, the mood is immediately lightened as frowns are replaced by smiles and headshakes turn into nods of approval. The joy is strangled, but it's there.

Somehow, it still hasn't reached Rosa.

She stares down at the ring in my hand and then lifts her gaping eyes to my face. Drops them back to the ring. And starts to shake her head.

I don't expect her to be excited about all this. I don't even expect her to smile. But I am absolutely stunned when she turns and bolts away.

I am left alone on one knee with a ring in my hand. In front of every important member of the German American mafia. The room is dead quiet as I rise to my feet.

Because I don't know what else to do, I laugh, pocketing the ring. "Italians," I say. "Always running."

Chuckles ripple through the crowd as Wolfgang steps forward. "Go get her. You're a *Jäger*, brother. Enjoy the hunt."

I smirk and turn toward the doors. "I'll be back before the first course."

Chapter Nine

Rosa ran toward the back doors. They won't take her to the lot where my car is parked. They'll take her to the patio outside. That's where I find her, leaning against a stone fixture, her hand clamped over her mouth. When she glances up and sees me, she visibly stiffens. Good.

She knows what she's done is wrong. She knows she should be punished for it. But I'm not my father. And I refuse to scare her even more than she already is. But I *am* angry, and I *am* going to address the situation. Because she needs to learn her place before we walk down that aisle. Or else my family won't be chuckling the next time she embarrasses me like that. They'll be sending Hans after her, to drag her back so I can teach her a lesson. In front of everyone.

"I'm sorry," she gasps, wiping at her tears. "I panicked."

"You can't do that, Rosa," I tell her as calmly as I can. "I know what happened with my mother was startling—"

"She was dragged away in front of a room full of people!" she shouts. "And no one tried to stop it or help her."

"Rosa…" I take a step forward, but she takes a step back.

"No," she says firmly. "Is that what's waiting for me once I marry you?" Her eyes glisten with angry tears. "Once I'm *shackled* to you?"

A muscle in my jaw ticks as I clench my teeth. I'm on my last ounce of patience. "Stop acting like this is new to you," I snap. "Your brother didn't drag home some innocent Christian girl off the streets of Jersey. He brought home the Flower of Manhattan. You were born into the mafia, Rosa, just like me."

She straightens her back, lifts her chin. "So I'm supposed to be okay with what I just saw in there? I should be *happy* about being forced into this marriage? Should *I* get down on one knee and beg *you* to marry me instead?"

I release a shaky sigh, trying with all my might not to lose it out here. "You need to learn your place," I warn her. "Before I have to teach it to you."

She crosses her arms. "Your mother was right. That ring is a shackle."

"You knew that before she ever said it."

My words are like a slap to her. She actually reels back like she's been hit, but she regains her composure quickly. I respect her for that.

"You knew good and well there would be a day when all this unfolded. You might not have expected your mystery groom to be me," I pat my chest, "but you knew you'd be marrying someone you didn't pick yourself. You knew you would never truly be free in this world. Not as a woman. Not as the daughter of a don and especially not as the wife of an underboss. So quit fighting this, Rosa. Because it's happening. Whether you like it or not."

She glances away, her arms crossed and her lips pouting like a petulant little girl. "I had freedom in Norman," she says. "I had a family who treated me with love and respect. And I had a man who would have loved me as Christ loved the church. A man God would be proud of me for marrying." She uncrosses her arms and balls her hands into little fists by her side. "So I will never stop fighting you, Amory. Because I know what God truly wants for me."

I cannot believe this. I cannot believe of all the women in New York City, I have been saddled with the one mafia princess who takes her faith seriously. I stare at her like she's crazy—she *is* crazy—and I don't know if it makes me want to drag her back inside or pull her into my arms.

How has she managed to hold on to her faith in a world like this? How could she believe God exists—and that He *loves* her? If that were true, she wouldn't be here. With me.

But Rosa believes it anyway, and even though I don't hold those same beliefs, I still admire her for them. Though, I'll never tell her that. Because it's easy to look at the world around us and deny the existence of an ever-loving God. But it takes unspeakable strength to look at all this madness and still believe there is Someone who can make it all better.

Rosa De Luca is truly a flower. Somehow growing in the darkness of the mafia, given life by the Light of Christ.

But as much as I admire her for this, I have to stop her from shouting all this insanity out here on the patio. She's still talking about God and her mystery man from Jersey, which washes away my admiration and replaces it with anger.

"Arthur is twice the man you will ever be," she's hissing. "Because he's a man of *God*. He isn't afraid of you—or anyone from the mafia."

I have never wanted to hit a woman before now. But instead of silencing my dear fiancé with my fists, I use a far more effective weapon. I take a large step forward and hush her with a kiss. She's so surprised she actually gasps in shock, her lips parting just enough to give me entry. I deepen the exchange, sliding my tongue over hers, enjoying the way she tenses in surprise and then melts into pleasure. I back her into the wall, running my hand from her small waist, along the curve of her back, to her neck … and then I grab a fistful of her curly hair.

She yelps as I tug, pulling her head back to look me in the eye. "Now that I have your attention," I say darkly. "Let me make this clear to you."

She struggles, her hands flying up to my fist tangled in her hair, but I tighten my grip. "*Stop it*," I snap.

"You're hurting me."

"I don't care."

She lets out a whimper that doesn't faze me.

"Listen to me, Rosa, because I'm only going to say this once." I glare at her, making sure she can see the seriousness in my eyes. I don't want there to be any doubts from this day forward. "You belong to *me*. Not Arthur. You are *my* fiancé. Not Arthur's. You will be marrying *me*. Sleeping with *me*. And giving *me* children. Not Arthur. *Never* Arthur. Understand?"

I loosen my grip on her hair just enough for her to nod, which she does with tears in her eyes.

"If you ever speak of another man that way, and I find out about it, I will find him and kill him. And I will let him know it's your fault he is dying. And I'll make sure you watch me do it. Understand?"

She nods again.

"You're a woman of faith. That's fine. But I am not a Christian man, and this will not be a Christian marriage. You will learn your place as a *mafia* wife, Rosa. It would be wise to learn it quickly."

She nods once more, though this time I wasn't expecting her to. It's fine. I like that she's cooperating now. I like this version of her far more than the one who left me on one knee in front of my entire family. It's never been my intention to frighten or harm the woman I marry. I prefer a wife who walks down the aisle, not one I have to drag down. But if Rosa insists on being a brat, she will be treated like a brat.

I release my hold on her and she sags against the wall, sliding down to the ground with a sob. I look away. Still angry. Still unbothered by her tears.

"I am not like your brother," I tell her, reaching into my pocket. The diamond ring I was supposed to give her earlier twinkles in the moonlight as I take it out and drop it in her lap. "If you cooperate, I won't treat you the way he has. But I will not allow you to ruin this family the way you did your own."

She stares at the ring, wiping at her red-rimmed eyes.

"Put it on," I order. "We have to get back inside."

She obeys, sliding the ring onto the appropriate finger, but she mutters something as she does so, and I lean down to hear better. "Come again?"

"You *are* like my brother," she repeats.

I blink.

"There aren't any bruises on my face. But that doesn't mean Gio hasn't punished me for what I've done." She lifts her head to look at me directly; for the first time, her eyes are filled with anger instead of fear. "Someone else took my punishment for me. A twelve-year-old girl named Minnie Hart. A girl I love. A girl I call my little sister. One of Junior's men hit her with his car the day I was dragged back to New York." She stops to let out a bitter laugh. "Her own mother took me in. It's her older brother who's stolen my heart. And Gio is holding them all hostage. If I mess this up for him, he will take his anger out on them."

I gulp, suddenly feeling dizzy as she finishes, "You're exactly like my brother, Amy. There is no difference."

Amy. The nickname I've only heard a handful of times. A name only Rosa has ever called me—back when she was just a kid who looked at me with stars in her eyes. She called me Amy because it was easier to say than my full name. It was girly, but not any more than Amory—by American standards, at least. I didn't mind the nickname. In fact, I sort of liked it. It was like a secret between the two of us. Like, to her, I wasn't Amory

114

Jäger, the mafioso. I was just Amy. A twenty-something kid who could make her laugh until she squealed and smile until her cheeks hurt.

I am not that man anymore.

It hurts. Staring down at her as she cries … it hurts now. Because she's right. There is no difference between myself and Gio, or my father, or my brother. I'd boasted a big game, declaring I would never hit a woman, that I was only as cruel as I needed to be.

But look at me now.

I threatened to kill Arthur because she loves him—as if she cheated on me, somehow. And I … I grabbed her by the hair. I hurt her.

I lower to my knees in front of Rosa. I don't know what to say. There is nothing I *can* say. She sees this. I can tell as she looks at me, that she knows I'm sorry.

A delicate hand extends, and she brushes my jawline with the gentleness I should have used before. I shiver beneath her touch. "I'm sorry. I hurt you. And I shouldn't have."

"I embarrassed you," she says, as if that makes this all okay.

I find the strength to look her in the eye. "Rosa, I won't ever hurt you again. I promise."

She nods.

"I was angry. And I was…" my voice trails off, hesitation seeping in. "I was jealous."

"Jealous?"

That you have someone else. Someone you could look at the same way you used to look at me. Someone who could protect you better than I ever could. Because I've become the monster now.

"It doesn't matter," I say with a sigh. I push to my feet, the chill breeze of the night sending whispers of cold crawling over me, pulling me back to reality. Back to the fact that I am not Amy anymore, I am Amory Jäger—the next Jägermeister— exactly who I need to be. I think I might be falling for Rosa, but I can't let those emotions take over. She has no feelings for me. She's in love with another man. And I don't think her precious God would approve of me.

But deeper than that … loving Rosa could make me weak. Turn me into a man on my knees before his woman, instead of the man who puts her in her place. In this dark world, I can't afford to be the man on his knees. I can't afford to be the man who puts her in her place, either. I need to be the man who makes sure she never gets out of line to begin with. Because the Jägers will have both our heads before they suffer the shame of what she brought to the De Lucas.

The quicker Rosa learns her place, the safer we will be.

I roll my shoulders as I offer her my hand and help her to her feet. When she's upright again, I hold her there, stopping her from pulling away. She looks up at me, confused. "What is it?"

"I promise I won't hurt you again—"

"I know."

"But you've got to promise me something, too."

She regards me with a look I can't place. Something between caution and curiosity. "Okay," she says slowly.

116

"Promise me you won't fight this anymore. I know neither of us asked for this arrangement, but that doesn't mean we have to go into it kicking and screaming. We can try to make the most of this."

Hazel eyes glimmer against her brown skin as she blinks in thought. I can't believe she even needs to think about this, but I know where her hesitation is coming from. I know *who* she's hesitating over. Arthur Hart. Apparently, the Christian Prince Charming.

I resist a very strong urge to roll my eyes as I tell her, "I'm not asking you to love me. I'm just asking you to try. To get along with me."

She presses her lips together, still unsure. Still thinking about stupid Arthur, even though I've gotten on my knees for her tonight. Twice. Even though I've apologized and promised never to hurt her again. Even though I've kissed her—and I know she felt something in that kiss. It's still not enough to push that man out of her mind.

"Rosa, work with me. Even if you don't want to." I pause, unsure how much of my heart I should let her see. "Even if you don't want *me*."

Rosa stares at me, realization slowly working over her, leaving its evidence blushing against her cheeks.

She knows I want her.

"Okay," she mutters, looking away. "I promise I won't fight anymore."

The amount of relief her words bring me is almost embarrassing. I shouldn't be this worked up, but I'm stressed *all* the way out. I can't take this—this whole marriage thing. On top of everything else I'm responsible for. I want to lie down on the patio and sleep for the night, but I've still got a dinner party to attend, and I'm meeting with the Morenos once more before morning.

I glance at Rosa who still can't look me in the eye. At least this part is taken care of. At least I won't have to worry about her shaming me again like earlier or trying to run away. Once the wedding is over, things will get easier. She will forget about Arthur—I'll make sure of that. We'll be sharing a lot more than a kiss. More than enough to guarantee she'll never think of him again.

Until then, we've still got this dinner party.

I squeeze her hand. "We should go inside."

She nods and smiles, so I turn to lead the way because it's my house, but not before stealing a quick kiss from her lips because she's my woman. She blushes, but I ignore the flutter in my chest, reminding myself that the ring on her finger belongs to me, but the love in her heart belongs to another man.

I want to kill him. I don't care what I promised.

Chapter Ten

"If he wanted you to promise to try then it's probably because he wants this to work." Olivia is sitting at my desk with her feet up, painting her toenails while I fight my unruly curls into a thick braid. Adella and Nona are both lying in my bed, smirking as they watch me struggle.

My bridesmaids came to visit for another dress fitting and to pick out their own dresses. Yesterday, we picked out the floral arrangements together; that was when Nona noticed my giant diamond ring and the questions about my engagement started. I avoided answering for as long as possible, but when the girls arrived this morning, they broke through my defenses. Now that the seamstresses have left and we're alone for the next hour—until I've got to leave for whatever Gio has scheduled for me today—they won't leave me alone.

I knew it would only be a matter of time before my friends managed to get information out of me. I love both of my cousins like they're my sisters, and I can't keep a secret from Olivia unless my life depends on it. Which is why the only secret I've ever kept from her is the one where my life was hanging by a thread. Ironically, that's the secret that got me here, braiding up my hair in preparation for another date with Amory. My new fiancé.

I turn to look at Olivia, glancing down as she wiggles her toes. "I think he wants things to work out, but not because he loves me."

"Then why?" she asks, stroking on a blush pink paint.

"Because he's tired," I say. "He seems very stressed."

"He's the underboss of the German mafia." Nona rolls onto her side and hugs one of my plush pillows. "Of course he's stressed. Adding a fussy wife to the mix is the last thing he wants."

I want to argue that I have every right to be fussy about this, but I already know how my bridesmaids feel about the situation, so I keep my mouth shut and start on my braid again.

"Besides," Olivia says, fanning her toes so the paint will dry quicker, "Amory isn't a bad pick. You should be happy he wants this to work."

"He's handsome," Nona gushes, squeezing my pillow tighter.

Adella rolls her eyes. "He's important. That's what matters most." She points her finger at me. "A man like Amory—the next Jägermeister—he's got power in Brooklyn. Which means you'll have power as his wife."

I shake my head. The Hunters of Brooklyn aren't like the

Stronghold. They're traditional, just like every other mafia in New York. The women are pretty, silent dolls, while the men are the muscle—doing all the dirty work, handling all the business. In a way, I'm grateful for it because it means I'll never have to get my hands dirty. I won't have to do anything that would go against my faith. But that doesn't mean I want to spend my life as Amory's housewife, at his beck and call, giving him my body for his pleasure, giving him sons to turn into gangsters and daughters to marry off just the way I've been.

I want to live a normal life, like the one I had in Norman. With Melissa and Minnie. And Arthur…

I force thoughts of Arthur from my head as quickly as they come. Amory might have shown me a piece of his heart when he'd all but confessed that he's attracted to me—that he wants me—but he'd also made himself more than clear on the issue of Arthur Hart.

He said he would kill him. And any other man I thought I might admire.

I've already done enough damage to the Hart family; I couldn't live with myself if I knew I got Arthur tortured and killed just for mentioning him to my fiancé again.

I sigh, realizing the girls are staring at me, expecting some sort of response.

Adella says, "Something else on your mind?"

"I don't think I'll have as much power in the Jäger family as you might think." An image of Christina being dragged away by that giant German monster pops into my head. I don't push the thought away. I want to keep it there in my mind for as long as possible, to remind myself of who the Jägers really are. Of what I'm getting myself into.

Olivia and Nona are naïve. They've got stars in their eyes, blinded by Amory's good looks and stature. But they weren't there. They didn't see Christina's fear, hear her panicked shrieks and cries for help. They didn't look her in the eye as she warned me—*diamonds are just pretty shackles.*

I glance down at my engagement ring. A silver band with an oval cut diamond—7ct. I can feel its weight on my finger, a constant reminder of the man who gave it to me. Of the wealth and power he holds. I should be happy with the bachelor I've scored—with his prosperity and prestige, but all I see is more resources at his disposal to track me down.

Amory will be an even bigger problem than Junior.

Adella is in front of me now, snapping her fingers. "Focus, Rosa."

I blink up at her. "Sorry. Did you say something?"

She presses her lips together and swats my hands away from my hair. "Let me handle this."

I laugh. Adella's always been better at braiding than I have. She scoops a little product onto her fingers and works it through my curls before separating them into sections.

"When I was at Amory's estate, his mother had some sort of episode."

Olivia glances up from her toes. "What do you mean?"

"She got really drunk and caused a scene. When she wouldn't settle down, Amory's father had one of his guards drag her away. She was screaming the entire time—begging for

122

her husband to show mercy.'"

The room falls silent, even Adella stops braiding my hair for a moment. The look on Olivia's face is raw fear; she's likely thinking of her fiancé. Wondering how he will treat her after she says, 'I do.'

"Amory isn't like his father," Nona tries to reassure the room.

"You don't know what he's like," I mumble, wincing as Adella pulls my hair a little too tightly. She apologizes and loosens her grip, but I'm no longer paying attention. All I can think of is the way Amory grabbed my hair when we were out on his patio. How angry and violent he had seemed. And how, moments before that, he'd pulled me into his embrace and kissed me like I'd never been kissed before.

For just a moment, he was Amy again. The older man I'd had a secret crush on ten years ago. The guy I thought of whenever I imagined myself as a woman, hanging on the arm of a strong, handsome gentleman. I had expected to marry an Italian within my own mafia, but I'd secretly dreamed of Amory as I'd grown older. Wondering what my life would have been like if he'd stayed when I'd asked him to. If my father had hired him as my personal guard and he'd never left my side.

For thirty seconds, Amory Jäger was that man again. My Amy. The guy I'd fallen for before I'd even known what love truly was. And then, in an instant, he became a different person. The Jägermeister he strives to be. A shadow of his father.

Instead of dragging me around in front of his entire family, he spared me the public shame and grabbed a fistful of my hair to privately put me in my place. To remind me that I belong to him.

But he apologized, I remind myself. He admitted his behavior was wrong—and he'd promised never to do it again. Except his promise came in exchange for a vow of my own. He didn't pledge to never hurt me because it's wrong to grab a woman's hair, he promised not to hurt me because I promised to behave. To act properly, as a good mafia wife should. I can only imagine his promise would go out the window if I ever broke my end of the bargain.

Adella taps my shoulder and turns my chair so I can see the mirror of my vanity. She's given me a braided crown and twisted the rest of my curls into an elegant bun. I'm afraid it looks too formal, but I decide to wear a simple yellow dress and low heels to offset the look. I don't want to dress up for this date. I don't mind upholding my promise to Amory—at least for the sake of keeping Arthur and the others alive—but that doesn't mean I have to impress him. Or even care about how he might feel about me.

The thing is … I think he might actually have feelings for me. If not because of that kiss, then because of what he'd said afterward. How dejected he'd looked when he confessed to knowing that I don't want to marry him. But if he had feelings for me, he would have asked me on another date.

I haven't gotten so much as a phone call from Amory since he dropped me off back home after dinner at his house. I'm not even sure this date was his idea. Gio is the one who told me about it. Had me scrubbed clean and set out a collection of clothes for me to choose from just for today. I'm sure he's more excited about this than I am. When I told him I didn't want to go, he made a face and said, *This is an opportunity, Rosa. You have to find happiness wherever you can in this life.*

I don't know what to expect today. If I'll be able to find happiness with Amory. I suppose most of that depends on him. Will I get the Amy who kissed me and seemed hurt by rejection? Or will I get the future Jägermeister who threatened to kill Arthur and have me watch?

I shudder as I step into my shoes and turn around for my girls to get a look at my outfit. They beam with joy and walk with me to the elevator. It's activated by a passcode that I don't know. Only Gio and a few of his guards have it, so I can't leave on my own. When I get back from the outings Junior allows me to go on, a guard is always waiting to punch in the code and walk me straight to my bedroom. They even shut the door behind me, like I'm not allowed to be in any other part of the penthouse unless my brother is home.

A black car is waiting for me when I walk out the front doors. My girls turn and kiss me goodbye before they climb into their respective vehicles and drive off. That's when my driver steps out and my eyes widen in shock. It's Douglass, Amory's driver.

He doesn't speak—or even look me in the eye—as he helps me into the empty backseats and then settles in the front. I don't bother asking him where Amory's at or where I'm going, I know he likely won't tell me. I do want to ask him a hundred other questions, though.

Douglass is from the Stronghold, he's a few years older than me, but not old enough that I don't remember him from before he was Hunted. He's a distant cousin, someone who used to be a lanky kid with long legs and skinny arms. Now, he's a beast of a man with a trimmed beard and a gun strapped to his hip.

I always knew Douglass would grow up and work in the mafia, it's the life he was born into. But I didn't know he would be working for the *German* mafia when he got older. I remember when he was first taken; my mother was called away to a family meeting in the Bronx that lasted three days. There were rumors of war going around, even plans to storm Brooklyn and demand Douglass's return. But grandpa had ultimately decided against it.

Douglass was a mid-level soldier in the Stronghold. Important enough for us to be insulted by his kidnapping, but not worth the struggle of getting him back. And once we realized he'd started singing to the Germans, his fate was sealed.

He wears his bullseye like a badge of honor. Speaking German, drinking beer, not even trying to hide his traitorous loyalty. I'm disappointed in him, but I try not to judge. He's probably disappointed in me for running away to Norman. We all have our reasons. Besides, having drama with Douglass will only cause problems. It'll be much easier for us to just put our differences aside and get along. In fact, Douglass could even be my ally if I play my cards right.

The ride is long enough that I find myself nodding off in the backseat, but just as I think sleep is inevitable, the car pulls to a stop and my door is opened from the outside. I almost fall out the car, but a strong arm grabs my elbow and lifts me upright. I glance up to find Douglass smiling awkwardly at me.

"Be careful, Ms. De Luca." He quickly releases me and takes two big steps back. Guards and grunts aren't allowed to touch mafia women, especially not one of my status. He could lose his hand for grabbing me, even though he'd helped me. If Gio or Amory were here, he would have been punished for that little gesture, and he knows this. I can tell from the way he's watching me that he's wondering if I'll snitch.

I smile at him. "Thanks for helping me."

He nods, one nervous jerk of the head like he's headbutting the air. "You're welcome, Ma'am."

I glance past him, squinting at the afternoon sun. "Where is Amory?"

Douglass gives a long, contemplative look. "Up ahead," he finally says. "Just walk along the sideway to the end of the street. He should be waiting."

I nod and turn to leave, but I hear his voice behind me. "Mr. Jäger is waiting, Ms. De Luca."

You just said that, I think, but I turn and wave with a smile to let him know I heard him. Douglass gets back into the car and waits for me to begin walking before he starts the engine again.

I'm suddenly happy I decided to wear the low heels. I have no idea why Douglass couldn't take me to wherever Amory is waiting, but it is what it is. I walk down the street, passing cafes and arcades and boutiques jampacked together, before I meet the entrance of a small parking lot. That's when my heart stops.

There's another black car waiting right at the lot's opening. A Camry with its engine running and a man leaning against the hood. The man is one I never thought I'd see again. His dark brown skin smooth in the sunlight, his handsome face smiling, his broad shoulders bunched in anxiety. I realize, with a breath, that he's waiting for me, and I immediately take a step toward him.

"Arthur…" I whisper.

Chapter Eleven

Arthur runs over and wraps his strong arms around me, lifting me from the ground. "I found you," he breathes.

"How? What are you doing here?"

He grabs my hand and pulls me toward the car. "We don't have much time."

I let him help me into the passenger seat and wait for him to slide into the driver's seat before I turn to him and speak again. "I don't understand."

"Strap up," he says, clicking his seatbelt into place.

"I need answers."

He glances into the rearview mirror, puts the car in reverse, and backs out to merge onto the main road before he replies, "You have allies in New York."

Douglass. It must have been him. I think of his last words to me, wondering if he was trying to tell me something. *Mr. Jäger is waiting…* but it was Arthur who found me. *Is* Amory still at the end of the street? Waiting for a date who'll never show up. Or was this part of Douglass's plan all along? To help his distant cousin get out of New York.

I glance up at Arthur, overwhelmed with emotion. I'm leaving. I'm getting out of New York. Out of the mafia. Out of an ungodly marriage.

The thought of marriage makes me blush. Maybe now I can marry Arthur. He's a man of God. He believes in Christ the Messiah. He risked his life and came all the way to New York to get me back. That must be love.

I reach for his hand; he's gripping the steering wheel like his life depends on it, but he softens at my touch. His fingers interlock with mine as he lifts my hand to his mouth and kisses it. I feel butterflies zing through my stomach. That gentle touch does more to me than the feel of Amory's lips pressed against my own, his tongue invading my mouth without notice or permission. It was a passionate kiss, but it wasn't intimate. It wasn't pure. Not like the way Arthur kisses my hand, a sweet gesture that both calms and excites me at the same time.

"You came for me," I whisper.

He nods. "Did you really think I wouldn't?"

"I…" I think of Minnie … and Gio and Amory and all the threats they issued. "This is dangerous," I say, looking out the window. Buildings and cars zip by, my last look at New York. I will never return after this. I'll never get to tell Olivia goodbye, never get to hear Adella's sound advice, or Nona's complaining.

I don't care.

Arthur squeezes my hand. "I know this is dangerous. But you've got friends here, Rosa. We're okay."

Slowly … I peel my eyes from the window and look up at him. This is the first time he's said my name. It isn't the name he's known me by.

"Rosa," I repeat.

He glances down at me, still smiling. "Yeah. That's your name."

"How do you know that?"

"You've got friends," he says, kissing my hand again. "They told me the truth."

It's a perfectly good explanation, but it does nothing to stop the sheer panic that skitters through me. I can't focus on the panic, though, because I'm immediately assaulted with the realization that Arthur has learned the truth.

"So you know…" I can't hold his gaze anymore. "You know who I really am."

He lets out a heavy sigh. "Rosa De Luca."

I wish he didn't know my real name. I wish I was Rose Lucas. The girl he'd met me as. The girl he'd fallen for.

"I don't care about your past, Rosa." Arthur lets go of my hand to steer better. He switches lanes and then looks over at me; his smile is still there. I can't help but smile back, and not just because of his grin; I'm smiling because of his words.

Arthur doesn't care about my past. He doesn't care that I'm mafia—*former* mafia now. To him I'm not the withered rose at all, I'm a blossoming flower. I've been forgiven for my sins, for my lies and deceit and the problems I've brought the Harts.

I've been made new. A fresh new flower in rich soil, fertilized by the loving kindness of a good Christian man and my Savior Christ Jesus.

"I can't believe this," I whisper, willing myself not to cry. "You're too perfect, Arthur."

He grins at me, and it melts my heart. "I'm not perfect, Rosa. But I try my hardest. I just want you to be happy. And you weren't happy in New York. I knew it as soon as I heard your voice on the phone."

"You have no idea how hard it was to make that call," I confess. "I thought I'd faint afterward."

"You're better now," he says confidently. "You're safe."

"And I'm happy." I reach for his hand again.

He takes it, kisses it. "I can't imagine what you went through in that wretched city. I can't imagine how hard it must have been for you."

"It was difficult. But I did have some people who made it bearable."

"Friends," he says.

I nod, thinking of Olivia and Adella and Nona, and maybe even Douglass. All the people who probably played a part in this. "I don't know if I could have survived without all of them. They gave me strength, despite being part of the world I wanted to escape."

Arthur squeezes my hand. "You have to find happiness wherever you can in this life."

I look at him.

First my real name. Now this.

"Where did you get that from?" I ask.

He glances over at me, still holding my hand. "What do you mean?"

"That saying. Where did you hear it from?"

He laughs. Shrugs. "It's just a saying, you know? Something I've always lived by."

"That's funny." I can't breathe. "My brother has always lived by that saying, too."

Arthur kisses my hand again, but it's not like the first time he did it. There are no butterflies, no zings of joy and whispers of affection. I am not blushing. I'm staring open-mouthed at Arthur's profile as he avoids eye contact.

"How do you know Giovanni?" I ask quietly. "What aren't you telling me?"

He drops my hand. "I'm so sorry. He wanted to test your loyalty."

I shake my head, praying this is all some sick joke.

"Why didn't you just keep walking?" Arthur asks. "Why didn't you ignore me and go on your stupid date like you were supposed to?"

"What's going on?" I whisper.

"That's the question I should have asked you months ago. When I first found out who you really are."

A shiver spider-walks down my spine.

"How long have you known?"

He chuckles. It's low and dark.

"I found out exactly one month after you showed up at the church."

"And you never said anything."

"Neither did you."

"I couldn't. I kept everything a secret to keep you safe—but you," I shake my head, "you're just a liar."

His gaze lands on me like a tongue of fire. I've never seen so much anger, so much rage, on Arthur's face before. I actually lean away from him, sinking further into my seat, as if I could escape out the locked door.

"Don't you dare call me that," he says. "I thought I was taking in an innocent woman who needed help. Someone who was truly a victim." He laughs again. "But I was housing a demon."

"How did you find out?" Because my 'friends in New York' is obviously a lie. Arthur's known my identity for months—*five* full months before I was dragged back home.

"Gio told me."

"My brother?"

He nods, squeezing the steering wheel. "If you think the mafia's power doesn't extend beyond the borders of the City then you're a fool, Rosa. They've got their hands in everything. They've got this entire country by the balls."

His language makes me frown. It's a sort of vulgarity I've never heard from him before. It makes me wonder just how much he's been keeping from me.

"I don't understand," I admit.

"Of course you don't. You were too busy housed up in a billion-dollar mansion to notice the world crumbling beyond your gates."

"Don't judge me," I say hotly.

"You were a pampered mafia princess—"

"I didn't ask to be born into the mafia!" I'm nearly screaming now. "I never asked for any of this! That's why I ran away. But I ran right into the hands of the enemy. All along. I never knew..." my voice trails off as I choke on a bitter sob.

"Never knew that I work for your brother," Arthur finishes. The car is silent as I try to digest his words. Arthur has been working for Giovanni since before I met him. He's known my identity all along. He could have sent me back at any given time. But he waited for Gio's call.

The same thing happened to my mother during my first escape. Everyone blames me for her death, saying I got her killed when I'd tried to run away. But no one knows the great escape was all her plan. She'd made all the arrangements, kept all the secrets, handled all the deals she'd needed to make for it all to be possible. And then, when it was time, she woke me one night and passed me a duffel bag.

We got into a car and drove away from our home without looking back. The plan was to have my mother's personal driver drop us off at a train station so we could ride out of the state. But he betrayed us, and my mother didn't realize until it was too late. Still, she was a stubborn woman, solely focused on getting her daughter out of New York. Out of the mafia. So she did whatever she could in that situation to get me out.

My mother grabbed the steering wheel and drove us off the road. We jumped the safety railing at 90mph and rolled three times before I passed out. When I came to, the driver was gone—thrown through the front window and into the grass— but my mother was still there. Pinned to her seat by the bent metal of the car door. Her eyes were still open, seeing nothing, yet somehow, still staring right at me. As if she'd spent her last moments watching over me, making sure no one came to drag me back home. Not while she was there.

With nothing left to do, I climbed from the wrecked vehicle and limped my way to the nearest building. It turned out to be Trinity Baptist Church in Norman, New Jersey.

The irony of this situation doesn't escape me. I have been betrayed exactly the same way my mother was. My driver lied to me. My rescuer deceived me. But I'm not like my mother. I don't have the guts to grab the steering wheel and crash the car. I don't have the faith to believe I'll survive a second accident.

So I sit in my seat and let tears pour down my face as I acknowledge my bitter defeat. I think of Melissa and how disappointed she would be in Arthur right now. And I think of Minnie, who suffered all that pain for no reason whatsoever.

"Did you have anything to do with what happened to Minnie?" I ask, wiping a tear from my cheek.

His grip on the steering wheel tightens. "That wasn't supposed to happen. No one was supposed to get hurt."

"Then why?"

"Because I waited too long." He glances at me. "That's what's so messed up about all this. I actually like you, Rosa. I think I might love you."

"I love *you*," I say desperately. "We can just keep driving,

Arthur. We can forget about all this and run away."

He shakes his head. "If you loved me, you would have told me the truth back in Norman. You would have let me help you."

"I lied to keep you safe!"

"And yet …" he looks over at me, his eyes full of resentment and rage, "Minnie still ended up in the hospital."

My desperation churns inside me, boiling into an anger that rivals his. "She was hit by a car owned by your boss."

Arthur swerves, gripping the wheel so tightly I fear he might yank it off its gears. "Do you know why your brother is my boss?" He starts to yell. "Because guys like me can't get ahead with the mafia wielding so much power. Norman has more than tripled its police force, but the funding hasn't kept up. Cops are making less now than they did before the defunding." He jabs a thumb at his chest. "I have bills to pay. I have a mother and a sister to look after. So when I got an opportunity to earn a little extra cash, I took it."

"You swore an oath as a cop—"

"Don't lecture me, Rosa. I've been lecturing myself since I started working for your brother."

"Then why continue to do it?"

He sighs, his anger calming somewhat. "Because I don't have a choice now. Minnie was hospitalized because I didn't deliver you when Giovanni first asked." He shakes his head. "I waited *two* extra days and they rammed my sister with a car just to prove a point. They won't let me escape now. I'm in too deep."

137

"What exactly have you been doing for Gio?"

He taps a thumb on the steering wheel, I imagine if we were sitting on a sofa instead of in a car, he would probably bounce his knee instead. "I gave him lists of all the names of the women who joined my mother's shelters every month."

I frown, trying to figure out what on earth Gio would want with that.

Arthur explains, "My mother takes in a considerable number of women running from the City. She trusts me with her files, so I have complete access to the system. I'd go in at the end of every month and make copies of all the new entries. Then I'd stuff everything in a folder and drop it off in a mailbox. It was always a different one, Gio was careful. A few days later, I'd get an envelope of cash in my own mailbox. And that was that." He glances at me. "I didn't even meet Gio face to face until I delivered the list with your name on it. Your fake name."

Now it makes sense.

"He met me and told me to keep an eye on you. Said I should stay close to you and see if I could get any information out of you. But you never said a word about your past. You stuck with that runaway prostitute story like it was the truth."

"It was the truth I needed you to believe."

"If only." He starts tapping his thumb again. "Your brother is a horrible man, Rosa. I didn't have a choice except to do what he said."

"You could have gone to the FBI. You could have tried."

"You could have kept running straight through Norman to

138

some other place. Take your cursed baggage with you."

His words hurt. Ten minutes ago, I was his blossoming flower. Now I'm cursed. A rose with thorns.

"I know better than anyone how terrible Gio can be."

He clenches his jaw. "Did you know Gio sells the list I give him? Passes it off to other people in the mafia—the Russians, I think."

I close my eyes. The Volkovs make their money by selling women the same way the Morenos sell cocaine. They're human traffickers. And Arthur has been providing them with victims.

"How many women from Melissa's shelter have you sent to New York?"

He shakes his head. "I don't know. Some of them just pack up and go. Leaving nothing but a handwritten note behind, or simply disappear as if they'd never been there. But I know the truth. I know its Gio's men, or the Russians, taking them away."

"Why don't you do something?"

He hadn't been cornered until he'd met me. But there had been plenty of time for Arthur to do the right thing before then.

I scoff. "Or is the money that good? How much does Gio pay you for the lists? A thousand per name?"

"I'm not the only one making money off the lists," Arthur says quietly. "How do you think my mother gets her funding for all the shelters she runs?"

I stare at him, my eyes wide open and unblinking. He can't be serious. "Mel would never take dirty money."

"She doesn't know where the donations come from."

I almost laugh. Of course she doesn't. "Because you control the books." He'd said it himself; he's got full access to her files and systems. He can cash and deposit checks all day long without Melissa ever knowing. He's *been* doing that without her ever knowing. Washing dirty money through the ministry, accepting donations from the De Luca Foundation, not to mention whoever else buys the lists off him.

No wonder he's stuck under Gio's thumb. If Arthur doesn't do what he's told, Minnie could be killed, and Melissa could lose all her funding. Her ministry would crumble overnight, and then all the women who sincerely need her shelter would be put back onto the streets—or swept up by my brother.

This is worse than I thought. But right now, the only person I blame is Arthur. The man who stole my heart and lied to me for almost six months.

"You're a dirty cop," I say venomously. "You're the reason the mafia has so much control outside of New York."

Arthur lets go of an obnoxious laugh. "You think I'm the only one they've got on their dime?"

I swallow hard. Even if Arthur weren't a traitor, where would I be able to go if I ever got away again? The mafia is everywhere.

"I thought you were a Christian."

I half expect Arthur to laugh again, to remind me of my foolish naivety for ever trusting him. But when I look over at him, I see the hurt twisting the features of his face.

"I was a Christian," he says almost in a whisper. "But God wasn't there when I couldn't find a job to pay my own bills. And He wasn't there when we nearly lost the house. It was the mafia and their dirty money that put food on my table."

"And the mafia who hurt Minnie," I say.

"Well, where was God when my sister got hit!?" he yells.

I glare at him. "Where were you?"

Arthur doesn't answer, just whips the car onto the nearest exit and finishes the drive in silence. I try to think of ways I can get out of this, ways I can try to convince him not to hand me over to Gio, but before any plans can solidify in my head, I feel the car slowing down.

We've pulled up to Gio's apartment. I can see him standing on the front steps of the building, his hands in his pockets, an amused look on his face, and beside him is the date I stood up. Amory is fuming in anger, his temper barely contained as he glares at me through the window of the car. I try not to look at him as Arthur opens his door and comes around to let me out.

"For what it's worth," he says to me, "I do wish things could be different. I wish you really were just Rose Lucas. Then maybe one day I could have made you Rose Hart."

His wishes mean nothing to me. Not even an hour ago, I was willing to entrust my life to Arthur so we could run away together. I was willing to leave everything behind because I thought it meant I could be with the man God wanted me to be with. But Arthur is a liar. He doesn't even believe in God anymore.

I have no idea where that leaves me. What that means for

my own faith. I thought this escape was God's doing. I thought the Lord was getting me out of New York and back into the arms of a man of God. But I'm back home an hour later, and I'm about to be passed into the gripping arms of my outraged fiancé.

God, I pray silently, *are You there?*

I don't see His Hand in this. I don't understand what the plan is. I don't know what He wants me to do. But I'm not going to be like Arthur. I refuse to give up trusting in Him just because I can't see the bigger picture.

Arthur steps aside and waves me on. "Goodbye, Rosa."

I don't reply. I just clutch my purse and start toward the stairs, my head held high, my chin tilted up. I won't cower. Not now.

Gio is laughing as I climb the front steps of our home. "Welcome back, sister. Did you enjoy your ride?"

"You're a cruel man, Gio," is all I manage to say.

"Get inside so we can deal with you."

I do as I'm told, turning away without another word. I can feel Amory glaring at me, his burning grey eyes a storm of rage and betrayal. He steps to the side as I pass into the house, his only words to me a hiss against my cheek. "You promised."

Chapter Twelve

Rosa is a liar. That realization sends anger jolting through me, pouring from my mouth as I sneer at her, "You promised." I hate the way I sound when I say that. Hate how much of a punk they make me feel like. I'm not angry because she tried to get away again, I'm angry because I care.

She promised she wouldn't fight me anymore. She promised she would try to make this work. I told this to Gio when he approached me, saying he wanted to test Rosa's loyalty before the wedding. We have a week before its time to strut down the aisle, so I was reluctant. I reminded Gio of how our first date didn't turn out to be a disaster, and I even told him she'd promised me she would behave. But he'd insisted. And I'd doubted. And now here we are.

I have been made a fool of.

I trusted Rosa. Believed every word she'd said outside on my patio. I'd been fooled by the innocent look in her eye, how wide and round they were, blinking away the wetness of tears pooling with her emotions. She had looked so beautiful in the moonlight; lips puffy from our kiss, hair disheveled, cheeks red with blush and shame and heat. Heat I'd brought out of her. Because I know she felt something in that kiss. I know she thought about it after it was over.

She had melted into me. Had turned to putty in my arms, gasping into my mouth, surrendering herself to me. I could have taken her right there on the patio if I'd wanted. That's how willing she had been.

So then, why?

I grind my teeth together as she walks past me, chin up like she's got something to be proud of. It takes everything in me not to grab her by the hair and drag her away. But I'm not like my father. I'm not like my brother. She might have broken her end of our deal, but I've got more reasons than just a weak promise to honor my word.

I will not turn into Wolfgang.

Every time my anger flares up and I feel myself wanting to be violent like him or Uwe, I think of the girl who isn't here anymore. The one who lost her life to my brother's temper. And I am immediately calmed. Immediately reminded of what that uncontrollable anger could lead to.

So instead of yanking Rosa away to beat her half to death, I turn to her brother. "Give me some time with her."

Gio eyes me a moment, his silly grin growing stupider as it stretches across his face. "What will you do to her?"

"Teach her a lesson."

144

He shrugs one shoulder. "Have her home by dinner."

Rosa has turned back around to face us now, her wide eyes darting back and forth between us. She takes a step back as I reach for her, but I'm faster—and angrier—I've got her wrist locked in my grasp before she can even think to run.

"Let's go," I grunt, marching down the steps. The idiot who wants to die is waiting by his car. As much as I'd like to grant his wish, I choose to ignore him and storm to my car where Douglass waits.

Arthur is his name. He works for Giovanni. I didn't know that, and now that I do, it makes me want to put a bullet in him even more. The only thing that stops me is the way I catch Rosa looking at him as I shove by. Her face is torn up. Pinched with betrayal and sorrow. It's enough to make my throat feel sore as I swallow the strange lump of emotion welling within me. But I don't let it show.

She trusted him. She truly trusted him. Because she loved him.

But that love is gone now that the truth is out in the open. I don't have to entertain thoughts of killing him anymore because he has broken Rosa. Whatever love and admiration she had for him before is gone now, replaced by a deep seeded grief that might last the rest of her life.

She is too delicate for this world. Too gentle for the treachery and deception of the mafia. It's a wonder how she's managed to make it to age twenty without getting her heart broken a number of times with how she wears it on her sleeve. But I remember her father. Gio Sr. He was a kind man, as far as dons go. He sheltered her, kept her shielded from the worst of this dark world. And her mother helped, feeding her scriptures and Bible stories throughout her childhood. Convincing her there was a God in the clouds who loved her and wanted her to experience nothing but rainbows and sunshine. But this world is a barren land, void of all things good and light.

Rosa doesn't belong here.

But she *is* here. And now she's my problem. Her fairytales have fooled her for long enough. They would have gotten her killed if I was any other sort of man. They just might get her killed if she doesn't smarten up. That's why I'm going to teach her a lesson.

She gets into the car without a problem, though she's pouty during the ride. She refuses to even look at me, which just pisses me off because she's making me feel like I've done something wrong. *I'm* the one who's been insulted here. *I'm* the one who's been betrayed.

"You promised," I sneer again, glaring at her across the backseat of my car.

I am livid over this girl. Pissed off because she didn't just break her promise to behave—she tried to run away again.

"You tried to leave me," I mutter.

Now, she looks at me. Lips parted, throat bobbing as she swallows, like she wants to say something but doesn't have the words.

I don't either. Because I've already said enough, and I refuse to utter the rest.

146

Am I really that bad? Would marrying me be such a nightmare?

Douglass pulls over once we reach our destination. I fly out the door and go around to Rosa's side. She just sits there when I open her door, staring up at me with her arms folded.

"Let's go," I grunt.

She blinks. "Where are we?"

"Get out the car, Rosa."

"I just want to know—"

I slam my hand on the roof of the car. "You can either get out on your own or I can drag you out, but you are getting *out* of this car!"

She's standing beside me a second later. I can't see past the blaring red rage flashing in my vision as I grab her hand and yank her toward the bustling building looming over us. Thankfully, Douglass knows enough about me to just pull away and wait for a call or text. I can't think right now. If I let any other thoughts into my head except my goal, I might end up doing something I regret. Like focusing on how absolutely irritated I am that this woman would leave me.

That she really doesn't want me.

It isn't even that I want her so badly. It's that I've never been rejected before. So hard. So cruelly. She would rather risk her life and live on the run than be with me. I'm the enemy here. The monster in her perfect love story.

She hasn't seen a monster yet.

"Where are we going?" she squeaks out. The panic in her voice is almost enough to pull me to a halt. But I ignore her pleading tone and keep up my pace as we rush inside—I do loosen my grip on her hand, though I don't think she deserves even that bit of kindness.

I feel her relax beside me as the double doors open to reveal a busy lobby. Phones ring, people rush by wheeling carts and pushing patients in chairs.

"We're in a hospital," she says.

I glance over my shoulder. "There's something I want to show you."

Rosa keeps my pace as we make it to the elevator and ride up to the ninth floor. I let go of her hand once I'm convinced she won't run off again. When the elevator doors open, she waits for me to take the lead and I guide us to the end of the hall. There's a room with a guard outside the door. I nod at him, and he steps aside to let us enter.

Rosa gasps once we're inside. I don't blame her. There's a person in the bed, barely recognizable as a woman. Her face is swollen, eyes purple and bulging, lips fat and parted to reveal shattered teeth. Her hair is missing on one side of her head. Her hand is broken. Three ribs are cracked. Her hip is dislocated.

Mercifully, she doesn't feel any pain. She's unconscious, lost in a coma and kept alive by the beeping machinery around her. I don't know this woman personally, but I do know who did this to her.

"What..." Rosa whispers, taking a step back. I'm standing right behind her, so she ends up stepping on my foot and tripping into my chest. I grip her elbow to stable her, holding her in place. In her fear, she turns and clutches a handful of my shirt, craning her neck to blink up at me. "What happened to her?"

I cram my hands into my pockets. "My brother did."

"W—Wolfgang?"

I nod.

"I don't understand."

Neither do I. I don't understand how he can be fun and loving and dumb when he's sober, and then turn into a woman-beating demon when he's drunk.

"Wolf gets violent when he drinks," I say. "Especially toward women."

She frowns, daring another glance at the nameless lady in the bed. "Who is she?"

"I honestly don't know. I found her passed out in his bedroom a few nights ago. Could be a prostitute. Could be a girl he's been dating that I didn't know about. She's been in a coma since I brought her to the hospital. We won't be able to find out her identity until she wakes up."

"He did this for no reason?"

I nod again, hating the look in her eye. The question blooming in her head that she won't dare ask aloud.

Is this what I'll do to her?

I sigh. "I'm not a monster, Rosa. I could be. But I'm not. And I don't want to be."

She nods slowly.

"You could have been sold off to any man in the mafia. But you got me. Things could be a lot worse."

She knows I'm right. She could have gotten paired with

Wolfgang and then she'd be this woman lying here. She could have been this woman weeks ago when Gio first brought her back home. There are plenty of men in the mafia who'd argue her brother's a fool for not punishing her attempt to escape. But they don't know she *was* punished. They have no idea an innocent twelve-year-old girl is the one in a hospital instead.

"I wasn't trying to escape from you," Rosa says softly. I let out a little gasp, stepping closer to her, towering over her as she continues. Her hand still clutches my shirt, gripping the white material, my tie bunched to the side. Her other hand fiddles with the crucifix around her neck. I stare at it as she speaks. "I was running away from the marriage. From being stuck in the mafia."

So, it wasn't just me.

I gaze at her in silence, letting the quiet linger until she gets uncomfortable. That's when she shifts—not knowing what else to do—and bites her lip in thought.

There it is.

I watch the little action. Her lower lip slowly going into her mouth, swelling from the pressure of her bite, her teeth leaving marks I'd like to kiss away. Then she's done biting, her lip is set free so she can pucker them and glance up at me.

"You aren't the only one being forced into this marriage," I tell her.

She tilts her head to the side.

"This woman isn't my brother's first victim. He's been this way for a while now, but the worst of it happened four years ago. When he hit his fiancé and didn't stop until she was dead."

Rosa's eyes triple in size. "He killed his own fiancé?"

"Yes," I say quietly.

Sofia Volkov. The oldest daughter of Mikhail Volkov, the boss of the Russian mafia. She was a beautiful woman—smooth pale skin, white-blonde hair, a full smile with deep dimples, and a laugh that could bring you to your knees with joy.

I'd been jealous of Wolf when the deal was struck. Our father had been against marrying anyone who wasn't German, but even he saw the value in working with the Russians at the time. The paperwork was drawn up, contracts signed, and they were betrothed.

Six months later, Sofia was dead in a hotel room.

I never got the real story out of Wolf. He'd called me up one night and said he needed help. I never knew just how much help until he opened the door to his room, and I saw all the blood. When I asked him what'd happened, he just said she'd made him angry. That he'd caught her flirting with one of his security guards and when she'd denied it, he'd gotten mad. Mad enough to kill her with his bare hands.

That was the first time I'd ever felt thankful of my position as the eldest in the family. Wolfgang would run the German mafia into the grave if he ever became Jägermeister. He can't control his anger. I can barely keep mine contained. But even I have the self-control not to take my rage out on my own woman. Especially not a woman like Sofia.

She was kind. She was good. She was everything Wolfgang isn't. And he'd killed her.

But I don't tell all this to Rosa. She doesn't need to know the gritty details; it'll make her want to run away even more.

"I helped Wolf cover up the murder. We cleaned up the room and took her body to a dark alley. Made it look like a random mugging gone horribly wrong. I even gave Wolf a black eye to make it look believable."

That was a lie.

I actually beat him within an inch of his life for what he did. He looked worse than the woman in the hospital bed behind us when I was finished with him. But, again, Rosa doesn't need to know that.

She looks horrified, even with this modified version of the story.

"You helped him get away with killing someone."

I've done worse. *I've* killed people. I'm a mafia underboss, you don't get to where I'm at without taking a life or two—or twenty. I suffer every day for it. The pain in my back, in the scars left by my father's own men. The suffering in my nightmares every night. The times I've been hospitalized— deals gone wrong, shots fired, just missing my heart or lung or major artery. I take it all in stride. This is the mafia. Pretending its anything else will only get me killed.

"He's my brother," I tell Rosa. "But I wasn't the only one who helped."

She squints.

"Junior helped me. Since it happened in Manhattan, I needed him to get the cops on his payroll to hand over the evidence and reports they'd filed. He promised me he'd have it all destroyed. It wasn't until you showed up that I realized he'd lied."

She sucks in a breath. "He's blackmailing you."

"He never got rid of the evidence of what happened to Wolf's fiancé. And he's threatening to expose Wolf and me if I don't marry you."

She nods, finally understanding that she isn't the only one being thrown into something they'd rather not be a part of. She's just the only one fighting against it.

Rosa lets go of my shirt and steps closer to the bed. I half expect her to break down into tears, but she bows her head and starts muttering to herself.

She's praying.

The sight makes me burn with an emotion I can't place.

I almost admire her for it. For the hidden strength she has inside. Because it takes more than a little hope to believe in a loving God when faced with the gruesome image before us. There is a woman lying in a bed with her face swollen and her bones broken for no reason except that my brother is a madman. And Rosa's first instinct is to pray for her. She doesn't even know this girl. But she wants God to heal her, to protect her, to keep her safe from Wolfgang once she leaves the hospital.

I envy Rosa. I envy her faith. And part of me wishes I could share it with her. To feel a sense of comfort in the midst of pointless death and violence. I wonder how she sleeps at night. If her whispered prayers do anything to keep the darkness at bay. The scars on my back throb, reminding me of my own darkness. Of my own nightmares that haunt me.

I watch Rosa for a few seconds more, straining to pick up what she's saying. It's her faith that's driven her mad. Pushed her to the point of truly believing she could ever get away from New York. She reminds me of Sofia, obsessed with childish dreams of hope and faith and true love.

I don't follow Rosa's beliefs, but I can protect them. Like I should have protected Sofia. Like I should have guarded her and given her a place to feel safe in her beliefs. In her hopes. In her dreams. But I didn't. I failed Sofia. I couldn't protect her from the monster that is my own brother. But I can protect Rosa from the monster of myself.

I can carve out a life for her where she doesn't have to trade in her morals or compromise her faith. I have the power to do that. I *want* to do that. Because every time I look at her, I see the little girl I knew ten years ago, and my heart breaks a little. She's not a little girl anymore. She doesn't have stars in her eyes, blinding her to the world she lives in. She's a woman now, and she's woken up from that fairytale to realize she's living in a nightmare. But I don't have to be the monster in her dreams. I can be the hero of this nightmare. I can turn it back into a fairytale, in some small way.

I can protect Rosa the way I should have protected Sofia. I can be her shield. I can stand in the way of all the darkness of this mafia life. I can take all her sins; I can carry her cross. I'll let her cast her cares upon me because I care. That's what it means to be a husband. To be a protector and provider.

I can do all that if she would just let me.

Rosa stops her praying and turns back to face me. She plays with her engagement ring as she says, "I'm scared."

"You don't have to be. Not with me."

"I thought you were going to hurt me when we left my home."

"I'm not like my brother."

"But you helped him cover up his fiancé's murder. And so did Gio…" she glances away. "Everyone has secrets."

I know she's thinking of Arthur. Of how many lies he's told her over the last six months. As much as it hurts to see her torn up like this, I don't let any sort of emotion surface. Rosa wouldn't be so hurt if she hadn't tried to leave again. She'd be happily blind to the truth if she would have just kept her promise and given us a fair chance.

"I will never treat you the way Wolfgang treats his women," I say. "I will never lie to you the way Arthur did. But I won't let you go, Rosa. I'm not going to chase you around New York every time you want to get away. You will be my wife. And you will stay with me. No more escaping."

She sniffles, letting go of the tears I knew were coming. She's finally been defeated, broken, crushed. And like a withered rose, she crumples into my arms as she heaves a sob. I let her cry into my chest, my arms going around her waist, pulling her close.

"I'm not going to be a cruel husband," I say. "If you stick around long enough, you might realize I'm not so bad."

But I know she isn't convinced. I know all she's thinking of right now is the woman in the hospital bed, me covering up

Sofia's murder, and Arthur's betrayal. Every man in Rosa's life has disappointed her so far. Why would I be any different?

I don't know how to answer that.

Chapter Thirteen

I no longer expect my days to go as planned. Arthur's betrayal is a nail in the coffin I have personally built. Not only did I never see it coming, but I also didn't predict how devastating it would be. He's been working for my brother. He's been fooling Melissa and Minnie. He's been sending women back to New York by the dozen.

I was just another name on a list that meant nothing to him. A paycheck. A couple thousand dollars. I wonder how much my name was worth, but I don't want to know the answer.

Trusting Arthur was a mistake. My naivety has left me in the arms of the man I'd tried to escape. But as he holds me in this hospital room, I can't help but wonder if maybe his arms aren't so bad. Was I running for no reason? Can I truly trust Amory and all his kind words, his whispered promises, his strong arms—as sturdy as the confidence glowing in his sharp grey eyes. He is all I have left now. And even though he has every right and opportunity to become my worst nightmare, he's choosing to be my protector instead.

I thought Amory would hurt me when he took me from the steps of Gio's home. I had fully expected to wind up a patient in the hospital we're standing in. But he surprised me. And he surprises me again when he untangles himself from our embrace and takes me back home. The car ride is silent with him sending emails from his phone, but I don't miss the furtive glances he sends my way. We're avoiding and watching each other at the same time. Both of us confused, both of us wondering what just happened in that hospital room.

I have no idea.

When I had expected punishment, I got undeserving mercy. When I had expected cruel judgment, I received overwhelming forgiveness. Amory is undoubtedly angry that I tried to run away again, but he's put that aside, offering me yet another blank slate. A place to start again—this time by his side. With his help. With his protection.

I won't be a cruel husband.

Is that possible?

Is it safe to get close to this man?

I thought it was safe to love Arthur, but he was only a liar and a man using the name of God for his own gain. I had placed so much trust and faith in him *because* of his faith, but he'd been the wolf in sheep's clothing. He'd been my enemy all along.

But does that make Amory any less dangerous? He's just

as crooked as Arthur and he isn't Christian, either. Still, he has offered me more in this dark world than anyone else in my life ever has. He isn't a light. But he is a flicker—a fighting spark, like the sputtering flash of a tiny candle. But even that small glow is enough to chase the shadows away.

Carefully, with gentle steps and blushing cheeks, I might fall for him.

When we pull up to my brother's penthouse, Amory takes me upstairs and we find Junior in the living room. My brother takes one look at me and frowns, the skin between his eyebrows bunching in anger. "I thought you were going to teach her a lesson?" Clearly, he had expected me to be beaten as well. The fact that he's disappointed I haven't been abused is a little more than disturbing.

When he rises from the sofa and approaches, I instinctively take a step back, but Amory is right behind me, blocking my escape. A warm hand rests on my waist. Possessive. Daring. And I feel him kiss the top of my head before he says, "Go to your room."

"Stay where you are," Junior snaps.

A single moment of hesitation sweeps the room; me watching Gio watching Amory. Their eyes are locked, fighting without words, battling for dominance—though I am the one who decides the winner.

My father ruled my life before he passed, and when that happened, I became Gio's responsibility as my older brother and don of the Italian mafia. But now that Amory is going to become my husband in a week, he has a fair claim in this odd arrangement.

So far, I have run away from my father and defied my brother. What I do next will determine who exactly is in charge here.

I take a step, shocking Gio so much that he breaks his staring contest with Amory to shoot me a glare. Behind me, Amory chuckles. It's a small laugh, barely audible, but it's enough to send my brother into a rage.

His arm whips out to grab me as I try to tiptoe by him. I wince at his grip, but just as quickly as he grabs me, I am suddenly released with a jerk. Clumsily, I trip sideways and turn to find Amory holding Gio by his arm.

"Don't touch her," he says, voice dark and low.

"She's still my sister," Gio snarls, yanking his arm away.

"She's my fiancé."

"I'm the don here. That makes me a rank higher than you, *underboss*."

Amory takes a deep breath, straightening his shirt. "Fine." He looks over at me. "Rosa, stay."

I will admit that I enjoy getting along with Amory more than being grabbed by my hair and yelled at. But I don't like being bossed around—bouncing between my fiancé and my brother, seeing who will win their spitting contest and order me around for the rest of my life.

I fold my arms. "Are you two done?"

They both frown at me.

"I'd like to get something to eat and then lie down." I turn to leave. "So I'm going to the kitchen. And *then* I'm going to my room."

No one protests as I leave. And no one is in the living room when I emerge from the kitchen, sandwich and glass of milk in tow. I could give a hundred guesses as to where my brother and fiancé ran off to, but the truth is that I don't care. They both delivered dazzling performances, trying to show off who has more control over me, but as the sole audience member in attendance, I was not impressed. Giovanni is my evil, controlling brother. Amory is my angry, controlling fiancé. As far as I'm concerned, it's a lose-lose situation for me.

Yes, Amory is the better choice between the two, but he isn't my husband just yet. I can't run away to the safety of his protection until after we're married. For the next week, I'll be at Gio's mercy. And it'll be much easier to survive those seven days if I'm on his good side.

I quickly learn that I am *not* on his good side.

Gio leaves me locked in my room for the next four days. I don't even get to attend my own rehearsal dinner. And my last dress fitting is done in my bedroom—just me and the seamstress. My bridesmaids are nowhere to be found and the dress designer doesn't say more than five words to me.

It doesn't take a genius to figure out I am being punished for siding with Amory in that little spat. But all I've got is three days to go and I'll be free of my brother. It's not entirely comforting that I will then be at Amory's mercy, but I've learned he's a different kind of storm. A brewing dark cloud whose lightning seems aimed at my enemies more than myself. Versus Gio, an uncontrollable squall flaring up at random. When my brother strikes, he hits everyone in the area. As long as his target gets scorched, he doesn't care who else is hurt.

For a fleeting moment, I feel like Christina with her fear-filled eyes and her dark omens shrieking through the halls. She is all alone. Locked in her own home with no access to her friends or family. It's obvious Amory cares for her, but there isn't much he can do against his father.

Right now, I don't see much difference between Christina and myself. We are both locked away. We are both being kept in silence. The one person who seems to care for us isn't powerful enough to stop the man responsible for our suffering. But unlike Christina, I serve a God who doesn't answer to the don or the Jägermeister.

I spend my free time praying, writing down my words in a journal as if they are letters to my Father. It keeps me from going insane, reminds there is Someone listening. Someone who would never turn His back on me, even though I don't understand why I'm here. Why all of this has happened to me.

I thought it was part of God's plans for me to escape, but it almost seems like He wants me here. Like there's something in New York City that I'm supposed to be doing.

What is Your mission for me?

I scribble down the question and then close my notebook just in time to see Gio barge into my room. He glances down at me, quirking his eyebrow in judgment as his gaze settles on the leatherbound Bible spread open on my bed. It's on

162

Genesis, the story of Joseph and how he was betrayed by his brothers, sold into slavery, and then thrown into prison. But through it all, God was by his side, ordering his steps, giving him comfort when he needed it most, and in the end, he emerged victorious—better than he was before the betrayal of his brothers.

Genesis 50:20 is highlighted, when Joseph faces his brothers and tells them, *You intended to harm me, but God intended it for good to accomplish what is now being done, the saving of many lives.*

I have been betrayed. I have been sold like a slave. And I have been thrown into a marriage that will feel like a prison. I wouldn't dare compare myself to the likes of Joseph, but I can learn from his story, from his courage, and his unrelenting faith and trust in God—even in the midst of his suffering. I can choose to believe that there is a greater purpose to my predicament. That I'm not here because Gio has won. I'm here because God intends for me to accomplish something.

"Yes, Gio?" My words draw his attention from the Bible back to me.

He sniffs at the air. "You should open a window."

"Maybe I could open my door instead."

He smirks. "Had enough of solitary confinement?"

"Have you come to let me out or not?"

His grin vanishes. "Yes. And it's a good thing you're reading your Bible because we're going to church."

I don't question why we're going to church, I don't even care, I just run to the shower as quickly as I can before Gio changes his mind. When I finish cleaning myself and changing into fresh clothes, I find my brother waiting by the elevator. I'm carrying my purse and my Bible bag, with my prayer journal tucked inside. But I realize I won't need either of those things when Gio pulls up to the church and drops me off without following me inside.

It's a Wednesday afternoon, there aren't any services at St. Joseph's today. But I'm not here to listen to a sermon. Father Serrano greets me at the church doors and guides me into the sanctuary with a smile on his cheery face. Even though I haven't been here in months—and I'm not Catholic—I still stop to make the sign of the Cross before I take a seat on a bench beside him.

The entire place is empty except the two of us and I don't have to ask why. I'm here to discuss my wedding vows.

Father Serrano smiles at me, letting out a friendly chuckle as he pulls me into a hug. "You are glowing."

If he weren't my Father, I'd tell him to stop lying. I'm not glowing at all, I'm nervous and jittery because I haven't even thought about my wedding vows, and I don't want to. Vows are serious, at least they are to me as a Christian. *Marriage* is serious to me as a Christian. It isn't just two people with googly eyes and blushing cheeks who want to try raising a family together soon. It's a covenant before God, sealed in blood, and lasting a lifetime. Even after we die, Amory and I will be as one before the Lord.

Eternity is forever.

I can't stand at that altar and swear before God and man that I'll love and cherish and remain loyal to a man I don't even want to marry.

Father Serrano sees my apprehension and cups my chin. "Don't worry, Rosa."

With his hand on my face, I can see down the wide sleeve of his cassock. The rose tattoo is still there. Father Serrano has been at St. Joseph's since before I was born. I don't know if he was always a member of the clergy, but that ink is proof that he was once a member of the mafia. The number of petals depicts his rank, the number of thorns shows how many lives he's taken. His rose goes from his wrist up to at least his elbow. An impressive design, but I refuse to judge him. I'm in the mafia, too. Whatever I have to say about him could easily be thrown in my face as well. I may not have killed them myself, but it's my fault my own parents are dead. To me, that's a greater sin than pulling the trigger on a random hit.

Father Serrano sees me gazing up his sleeve and pulls his hand away. "I know you probably have questions."

"No." I shake my head. "I mean, I do, but not about your affiliation to the Garden."

He tilts his head to the side. "About your vows, then?"

"Well..." He smiles and it's so genuine I can't help but smile back. "Maybe about both."

"Talk to me."

I do. I tell him how much I truly love God. How much my mother wanted me to be free of this world. How I thought God wanted me to be free of this world, but how it now seems that maybe being in New York was part of His plan all along.

"How do I maintain my faith in a world like this?" I ask

165

Father Serrano.

He swallows, his hand moving to rub his other arm—the one with the rose tattoo. "I won't lie to you and say it's easy, child. But it is possible. There is a place for people like you in this world—on this side of New York."

"Is that true for you?" I ask, looking him in the eye.

Father Serrano lets out a small laugh, it's a pleasant sound that echoes through the grand cathedral. "I'm done with the mafia, Rosa. I quit the day I took the cloth."

"So, you don't do any work for the De Lucas?" As far as I know, he's been the family's Father for decades. A sweet old man with a charming, unassuming smile. If it weren't for the tattoo on his arm, I would never believe he was ever involved with the mafia. I wouldn't even believe he ever jay walked if I didn't see him do it myself.

He shakes his head. "I work for the Lord."

"But you handle business for Gio. You're here now because he asked you to be."

"I'm here because I want to help a young woman with her wedding vows. And I'll be there when Giovanni asks me to assist any of his other brothers in the business, too."

"Why?" I frown. "Why would you ever help them?"

He gives me a smile that makes me feel stupid and childish. "I don't help them by hiding their drugs and arranging hits. I help them *spiritually*. You'd be surprised how many hardened gangsters sit in these pews and weep when they think no one is watching."

When I don't respond, he pats my hands, clasped together

on my knees, and says, "Even men like Giovanni need comfort and guidance. I'd rather it come from someone who knows and loves God than the bottom of a bottle."

"So you pat them on their backs when they cry, and then send them out to wreak more havoc on the city." I fold my arms, unable to stop the anger from swelling within me. I had promised not to judge Father Serrano, but I don't know how to handle the burning frustration I feel toward him now. I feel like he's done more harm than good.

He drops his gaze a moment, like he's thinking to himself. "I can't make people change, Rosa. All I can do is give them the Word. It's up to them to decide what to do with it."

He's right and I know he is, but I'm feeling indignant, so I don't uncross my arms and I don't let his charming old-man smile get to me. It's almost like I *want* to be angry with him.

"If I pack up and leave," Father Serrano says, "who will be left to speak the Truth to the men and women I council? Who would be here to help you through this journey now?"

Now I feel his words hit me like a truck, their sincerity, their honesty, all the sense they make. If Father Serrano had escaped like I'd tried to, I would have no one in my life to offer spiritual guidance. I'd have no one to tell me God has a way and a purpose for me here in this city. I'd be left with people like Gio who laughed at my faith or Amory who openly admitted he isn't a Christian man.

My shoulders sag and I glance up at the old man before me. I can't find the apology I owe him; it's lost somewhere between the gasps and the tears I let go of, but he receives it, nonetheless, rubbing circles on my back as I cry.

"You're going to be okay," he tells me kindly. "God's got you, Rosa."

"How?" I ask desperately. "Where is He in this city? What's my purpose here? How is marrying Amory part of His plan?"

Father Serrano cups my chin again, lifts it so I'm looking him right in the eye. "God is right here." He pats his heart. "And His plan *is* your marriage. Don't you see?"

I don't. Not at all.

"He wants Amory. And He wants this city back."

I almost laugh. Amory has been raised in the mafia, just like me. He went to Catholic school, just like me. Was christened at birth and then baptized when he graduated eighth grade. He's had the same opportunities as me to give his life to Christ. And he hasn't. I don't see how I'm supposed to change that.

"You think I can deliver Amory's heart to God?"

Father Serrano nods. "I know you can."

"No, I can't. It's just like you said, I can only give him the Word. He has to decide what to do with it. If he'll choose God or not. So far, he's only ever chosen the mafia. What difference will I make?"

"You've already made a difference," he tells me.

I don't speak for a moment, and he takes this opportunity to lean forward and say, "I spoke with Amory before you came in. He drove all the way to Manhattan to discuss his vows with me instead of his own Father. Do you know why?"

I shake my head.

168

"Because he wanted to meet the man who had a hand in teaching you the Bible." He laughs. "He said there must be something special about me if I've somehow gotten you to believe as deeply as you do. But I told him it wasn't me. Mostly, it was your mother; but even so, Laura Willis and I are not special at all. We're just obedient. Laura taught you the Bible like a good Christian mother should. And I speak the truth God gives me, like a good Father should. In the end, *those who have ears to hear* receive the message." He pats my hands again. "You've got ears to hear, Rosa. And you've listened. Now, your kind heart—your *faith*—has overflowed into Amory's heart without him even knowing."

A scripture pops into my head. *The Word of God is quick and powerful.*

"If you were to marry him, he wouldn't be able to get away from your Christian influence."

I sigh. "But I don't have to marry him for that to happen. Why can't God grab his heart by having you preach to him?"

Father Serrano laughs lightly. "Everyone is different, Rosa. I didn't give my life to Christ after hearing a sermon. I got saved one night in my bedroom after listening to a Christian song on the radio. The lyrics spoke directly to my broken soul, and I cried out to God right there in the middle of my floor." He smiles. "God knows exactly what will touch Amory's heart. Apparently, it's you."

"If I marry him, I'll be unequally yoked."

The Bible is full of warnings against Christians dating outside the faith and even spending too much leisure time with unsaved people. How could I ever expect anything good from marrying the future Jägermeister?

Father Serrano nods like he understands my concerns. "Being unequally yoked is a real danger. Many think they may be able to draw their partner to Christ, but when you date outside the Faith, the reverse can also happen. Your unsaved partner can pull you away from the Lord. The Bible says bad company corrupts good manners." He sighs. "I would never advise a Child of God to date outside the church, however, marrying Amory isn't your choice, Rosa. You don't even want to marry him. And maybe that's exactly why God can use you for this. Because He can trust that you won't allow Amory to pull you away from Him."

"Perhaps," I say slowly. "But what does marrying Amory have to do with the city?"

The grin Father Serrano gives me tells me he's been waiting for me to ask this question. "Your presence here, your unrelenting faith, is an answer to my prayers, Rosa. I have been pleading with God for the last ten years to provide an opportunity for New York to return to Him so He can return it to the hands of law enforcement. The mafia has ruled long enough."

"I agree, Father, but I don't—"

He cuts me off. "Amory Jäger is a powerful man. He's the future Jägermeister. Imagine the sort of good he could do for this city if he were a Christian. Together, the two of you could dismantle the Italian and German mafia. The rest would tumble like dominoes."

Now I understand. And I feel an overwhelming sense of flattery at the very thought of God considering me worthy of this task, of helping right the wrongs of New York City, of helping clean up the mafia. All this time I'd been trying to escape, trying to run away from the crime and lawlessness, when God wanted me right here. Wanted me to help run the mafia out of New York not run from New York and the mafia.

It was hard to see the bigger picture when I was so focused on my own pain and betrayal and suffering, but I think it was probably hard for Joseph, too. When he was in the pit, praying to a God who seemed silent. When he was accused of sleeping with another man's wife. When he was forgotten by the men who promised to put in a good word for him. But God's plans were greater than Joseph's suffering. Just as they are greater than mine.

Amory's questions flow into my mind as I sit in the pews. *Will you behave? Will you stop running? Will you give me a chance?*

Yes, I will. But not because Amory asked me to, I'll stay here in New York by his side because God wants me to.

Chapter Fourteen

"Apparently, *beer* isn't fancy enough for a wedding." Wolfgang sighs as I struggle with my tie.

I hate this. For some reason, I'm nervous. I've known all my life that I would have to walk down that aisle at some point, whether it was with a woman I loved or not. My marriage was likely never going to be out of love. Men like me, with my sort of power, don't marry for love. But if I *could* marry for love, if I could have chosen my own bride … I'm not sure I would have picked someone else.

I want to slap myself for even allowing that sort of sappy thought into my head. Now is not the time to be getting emotional. Thoughts of marrying Rosa and what will happen afterward are starting to have an effect on me—on my body.

Wolfgang whistles over my shoulder, he's looking in the mirror, his gaze locked on the reflection of my beltline.

Great.

"Ready for tonight?" he jokes, wiggling his eyebrows.

I drop my tie and adjust my pants. This is beyond embarrassing. I feel like a hormonal fifteen-year-old on his first booty call. And the fact that Wolfgang is here to witness it just makes it so much worse. He is never going to let me forget this.

"Guess I should hand these over right away." He passes me a small pack—I don't have to ask what's inside. "I was going to give you them after the wedding, but you seem ready to use them now." He snorts.

I turn and punch his shoulder. "Shut up, Wolf."

"I didn't know you had the hots for The Rose."

I didn't know, either.

I go back to fumbling with my tie. "Rosa's a beautiful woman."

"A beautiful virgin." He quirks an eyebrow and steps to the display of drinks to pour himself a shot of whiskey. Once he's finished his own, he pours another glass and passes it to me as he reaches for my tie.

"Most mafia women of her stature are virgins," I say with a sigh. "It's not a big deal."

"You're right." He rolls his eyes. "I mean, it'll be great tonight, but everything after that is just boring. Virgins are only good the first time."

I let my liquor sit on my tongue, debating whether I should spit it into Wolfgang's eyes. We've always talked about women together, but he's coming dangerously close to taking things too far. Rosa isn't just some woman I rolled around in bed with

173

one random, meaningless night. She's my fiancé. She'll be my wife in less than an hour. Her talent in bed isn't a topic for discussion, not even with my little brother. But if I react violently, he'll know just how much I care for her. How much I want her. And I can't have that. Those are things that can be used against me.

I swallow the whiskey. It burns all the way down.

Wolfgang is still going on about virgin sex when Vater walks inside. He's handsome in his three-piece suit, a matching bowtie, and shoes that shine brighter than Rosa's engagement ring. If I didn't know any better, I'd say he's excited about this thing, but the frown on his face reminds me of who I'm dealing with. Vater is never happy, not even when he's getting his way.

"The Italians are here," he mutters in German. "And the Stronghold. We are outnumbered."

"It's a wedding, Vater, not a battle."

"This life is all about battles. You have to *fight* for everything—"

Wolfgang passes him two fingers of whiskey. "Please drink, Vater. You're starting to sound senile."

Vater hisses a few words at him before downing the drink, some of it dribbles down his chin as he swallows. He wipes it away with a handkerchief. "Giovanni thinks he should sit in the same row as me."

"He's Rosa's brother and the Italian don. That makes him your equal," I tell him flatly.

In the mirror, I can see the way my father's face heats with anger. He looks like he might smash his glass over the back of my head. For a moment, I think about where he's coming from. The De Lucas are seriously confused about how much power they *don't* have anymore, the Stronghold is prideful, and the Jägers are eternally on the edge of an outburst. Maybe gathering three of the five mafias in the city under one roof wasn't a good idea. But it's too late now.

Hindsight and all that.

"That mixed-breed brat is not my equal!" Vater seethes. "I was leading this mafia when he was still wiping snot from his nose!"

I sigh. "It's my wedding, Vater. And the ceremony is only going to last twenty minutes. You won't have to suffer for long."

His eyes widen. "So you aren't going to have his seat changed?"

"Would you rather sit next to King James?" I ask. "He was leading gangs when *you* were wiping snot from your nose."

That shuts him up. If there's anyone who can calm my father's stormy temper at just the mention of his name, it's Jameson Willis. The oldest mafia boss in New York, the man who singlehandedly united over a dozen petty gangs in the Bronx to form one superpower. Rosa's grandfather. Vater is a powerful man, but even he knows better than to step on the toes of the king. That's one of the reasons I'm glad Jameson decided to come.

Aside from the fact that it would be really awkward if he missed his granddaughter's wedding, I wanted King James here so he could keep my father in check. Now I won't have to keep an eye on Hans while my mother enjoys herself tonight. Uwe might hold a shamelessly tight leash on her at home in his own castle, surrounded by his own German brothers, but he wouldn't dare touch Christina with the Stronghold present. They don't treat their women the way we do. Monique Willis is nothing short of a queen, and her granddaughters, Adella and Nona, are princesses—each holding as much power in the Stronghold as Wolfgang does for the Hunters. Or maybe even the same power I hold.

If Vater or Hans dare to lay a hand on my mother at this wedding, they won't get away with it.

With an audible harrumph, Uwe leaves me and Wolfgang alone in the room. My brother lets out a laugh and reaches for the whiskey again. An image of that nameless woman in the hospital flashes in my head, and I grab Wolf's hand.

He blinks up at me and asks in German, *"Na, Bruder?"* His voice is light and airy like when he was just a kid, and I was just his older brother.

"Go easy today."

In an instant, Wolfgang shifts from my kid brother to the wolfish mafioso I know so well. "At my brother's wedding? It's a shame I'm not tipsy right now."

"Wolf, I mean it." My grip on his hand tightens until he releases the glass, it hits the table with a clatter. "There's a woman in the hospital right now, in a *coma*, because of you. I won't let you add another. Not at my own wedding."

Slowly, Wolf pulls his hand from my grasp and rubs his wrist, his eyes never leaving mine. "I understand."

From there, the wedding begins. It isn't a small occasion by any means. We have three different mafia organizations in one church and each of them has their own reason for wanting to murder the other. It feels like a very twisted game of sorts, everyone watching over their shoulders, issuing compliments through clenched teeth, smiling to reveal fangs. I should be used to this dark world of lies and deceit, but I suddenly feel very much like Rosa. Blushing and awkward and in constant denial.

When the procession is ready to begin, my uncle pulls me aside. "You look nervous."

"I am nervous, *Onkel*," I say in German.

He smiles, slaps me on the back. It's a surprisingly gentle touch for his massive size. He could stand toe to toe with Hans and give Douglass a run for his money in a wrestling match. But my uncle has always been the kind brother between him and my father. Their hot and cold demeanors remind me of myself and Wolfgang. Wolf got his violence from Vater, I took my self-control from Onkel Oberon.

"It will all be over soon, Amory," he tells me, guiding me through the double doors as the organ begins to play.

I lead the way down the aisle, walking right up to a smiling Father Serrano. Vater was livid when I told him we'd be going with Rosa's priest instead of our own, but I wasn't going to budge on that decision. Rosa is a lot of complicated and irritating things, but the one thing that gives me the biggest headache and the most confusing joy is her dedication to her beliefs. It's all she has left to cling to, the only thing in her life that hasn't failed her. I won't stick my hand in her faith, too. Not when I'll already have so much control over every other area of her life.

As I stand and wait for my bride to take her walk down the aisle, I glance out at the audience and look for familiar faces. My mother looks beautiful beside my father, especially because he's grimacing so hard, face distorted in anger. Giovanni Jr. would be sitting right beside Vater, but I know he's waiting with Rosa—since she doesn't have a father anymore, he will walk her down the aisle. For now, his seat is empty and next to it is King James. The old man smiles like we're friends, aged skin tugging back to reveal his golden tooth, his giant mink coat ruffles with his movement—a slight incline of his head. Monique is beside him, looking gorgeous in a slim black dress she has no business wearing so perfectly. I hope Rosa has her genes. The woman is in her 70s and doesn't look a day over 50.

The rest of the crowd is peppered with Germans, Italians, and members of the Stronghold. I wonder if Douglass feels awkward, but as I look around, I realize he's not here. Probably decided to wait in my car. I hate how complicated this must be for him, but it won't last forever. After today, I won't see King James in person for a while. Which means Douglass won't have to hide his face. He played his part in testing Rosa's loyalty well, he shouldn't have to hide anything. But we're on shaky ground right now. With so many powerful, ill-tempered people under one roof, the slightest offense could set this place on fire.

I'm suddenly thankful we decided to hold the ceremony in a church. The presence of God is the only thing keeping these people from slitting each other's throats right now.

The song on the organ changes and people rise to their feet.

My attention is immediately drawn to the doors as they open to reveal my young bride. Her face is covered by her veil, but it doesn't hide her body in that wedding dress. I don't know anything about women's fashion, but I make a mental note to tell Rosa how great she looks when I get the chance.

My mouth is watering, like a dog panting for more. I swallow thickly. I've had time for nothing else but work, making arrangements, holding meetings, signing deals. Everything in preparation for this day. So much of my life is going to change after I say, 'I do.' So much about my organization is going to change after we tie the knot. Three of five gangs will be united by blood. It's a monumental event that has commanded my attention since Gio first called me to his home and offered his sister's hand to me.

The burdens of this marriage have been at the forefront of my mind for weeks now. But the perks of it have never been far behind. Right now, as I gaze at my young bride, I am reminded of everything I'll get to enjoy tonight and every other night of my life. But that thought brings a new wave of worry into my heart.

I know Rosa doesn't love me. Arthur isn't a question anymore, but that doesn't mean my wife will want anything to do with me tonight. Or tomorrow night. Or any other night.

I think we ended our last date on a good note, but I can't say for sure. Rosa's had time to think, to contemplate everything she's been through and everything she will go through after this day. Whether it's a good or bad experience totally depends on her. But I've made myself clear. I want to be a good husband to her. I want to be different from my father and brother. I want Rosa to love me. When Gio first made the offer to take the withered rose, I wasn't interested in being loyal or faithful or *married*. But things have changed. Rosa has begun to change me.

When she's standing before me, my heart begins to hammer in my chest. I barely hear Father Serrano as he delivers his words and then calls for the rings. I say my vows like a kid mindlessly repeating whatever his teacher says. And then I shakily slide Rosa's wedding band onto her slender finger. She does the same for me. Then Father Serrano tells me I can kiss her, and it takes a moment for the command to sink it.

I actually gasp and say, "Oh," before I lift her veil away from her face—to the sound of laughter skittering through the room.

Rosa is smiling when I glance down at her, but it's a nervous smile, one that matches my own. I lean down and give her the most bland, chaste kiss I've ever given. And then Father Serrano announces us man and wife.

It feels surreal. Like I should be happier than this. But the only thing I can register is the pit of nausea growing in my gut.

Get it together, I tell myself, reaching for my bride's hand. We are ushered out for pictures which hold no joy, and then it's time for the reception. I can't get a drink in my hand fast enough. I feel like Wolfgang for a moment, snatching the bottle of whiskey from the waiter and waving off the glass he offers as I take my seat at the sweetheart table set up for myself and my new lady.

Rosa slowly sits beside me, her eyes glued to the side of my face. She doesn't speak. Just sits and sighs, watching the guests pour into the dining room. We're in my home, the same place where our first date happened. Where she saw both the horrors and the delights of being attached to a man like me. How my father displayed his cruelty by allowing Hans to drag my mother away, and how tenderly we'd kissed on the patio after it was all over.

I sneak a glance at her and stiffen. She's watching me. Her eyes slide down to the bottle in my hand and I cough. "Want some?"

She hesitates. "I'm not twenty-one."

I get the feeling the real reason she doesn't want to drink has something to do with the crucifix dangling from her neck, but I don't push her. It could also be a wariness of being too drunk to say no when the reception is all over.

Rosa knows I want her. I've let her know that beyond a doubt. I've even made it clear that I don't just want her body, but I want her in my life. I want to be a good husband to her. But she's never even hinted at reciprocating those desires. All she's ever given me is tears and broken promises. Even at the hospital, she never outwardly said she would give this a try. She never agreed not to run away again or not to fight me anymore.

She just cried and clung to me and let me whisper promises of a sweet marriage into her ear.

I wasn't paying attention. I was too distracted by how well she fit in my arms, by how easy it would be to lean down and claim her lips again. I should have been listening to what she was saying—or what she wasn't. Because now I have no idea what to expect from her when we leave this place.

I've got a hotel room booked nearby, the best suite in the building. But I'm not stupid, I went ahead and booked the room beside it, too. Because I'd rather be alone in my own room, suffering the shame of rejection in pure solitude, than lying on the couch while my virgin wife snuggles up to her pillows on our wedding night. That would just be cruel.

Chapter Fifteen

Dinner goes by too slowly. Rosa and I barely speak, but I'm not entirely upset about that. I'm halfway through my bottle of whiskey when it's time to cut the cake, swaying on my feet as I grip the knife and hack at the velvety dessert. The crowd laughs. I grimace and hope it's a smile. Rosa looks like she's about to faint.

We feed each other a little piece, smile for pictures, and then we're back in our seats so Wolfgang can deliver a speech I don't listen to and Vater can tell everyone stories of how he raised me into the man I've become. I ignore everything around me and focus on the bottle gripped tightly in my hand. I stare at the decorations, the floral arrangements, even count the pieces of silverware on my table. The purpose is to distract me, but all it does is remind me of how much money I've spent on this whole thing. I'm going to need another bottle when I get the bill later, but I've done a quick calculation with all the time I've spent blinking around the room.

I'm pretty sure I'm five million deep, from the gold dusted cake to Rosa's gown, and her bridesmaids' gowns, too. To the one-thousand roses arranged beneath the glass dancefloor, and the gaudy ice-sculpture Wolfgang insisted we have shipped over from Italy to impress the De Lucas. It's in the shape of a rose with hundred-year-old wine pouring from one of the thorns. I hope it's poisoned as I watch Gio fill a glass and take the mic to deliver a speech of his own.

It's at this moment that I realize how badly I need to urinate, but I think excusing myself during the statement from my new brother-in-law might be a little rude, so I stay put until he's finished and then I finally release my chokehold on the whiskey bottle. This gets Rosa's attention. She glances at me curiously, but I wave her off.

"Gotta pee."

The bathroom isn't far, but it takes me a long time to get there since I have to greet everyone I pass by and endure a flood of congratulations along the way. When I'm finally at the urinal, I gasp as I relieve myself, suddenly aware of just how close I was to wetting my own pants at my wedding reception.

I should really slow down on the whiskey.

"Sir," I hear a familiar voice behind me, and I turn with a start to find Douglass standing in the doorway.

"When did you come inside?"

"Just now to find you."

"What's wrong?"

"You have a visitor."

I frown and zip up my pants. Move over to the sink. "It's my wedding day. I have a thousand visitors out there."

Douglass steps closer and passes me a cloth to dry my hands. "Sir, it's Mikhail Volkov."

I am slapped to sobriety at the sound of his name. Mikhail Volkov, the Wolf of Staten Island. Boss of the Russian mafia.

He was not invited to my wedding. But he's shown up anyway, which could only be taken one of two ways; a deep sign of disrespect—which will be met in full force once Rosa is safely out of harm's way—or a very dramatic show of respect which will be rewarded with my full admiration and cooperation. I can only find out by going to meet him.

"Where is he?"

Douglass turns to leave. "In the parking lot, sir."

When I exit the back doors of my home, I find a black truck with tinted windows pulled to the side. The driver steps out as I approach and opens the back door to reveal a tall, slender man old enough to be my father.

Mikhail has smooth skin and silvery hair that seems to reflect the moonlight. His eyes are a shade of grey that's lighter than mine and makes him look dead. Maybe it's the flat expression on his face or the way his mouth doesn't seem to move except to frown as he greets me, but he looks eternally unimpressed.

"Amory Jäger," he says, his accent so sharp his words are almost unintelligible.

"Volkov."

We shake hands. His grip is surprisingly gentle, like shaking hands with a baby viper.

"You're mighty bold for showing up at my wedding."

"You are mighty bold for leaving it to greet me." He smiles. It is not charming.

"What do you want?"

"I came to give you a gift. Even though you did not invite me."

I don't allow any emotion to show on my face. "We are not associates of any kind. You shouldn't be surprised I didn't invite you."

"No? But I am associated with your new brother-in-law." *Giovanni?*

"Then you should call him and say congratulations." I turn to leave.

"Jäger," he says, "you will want to hear my gift before you leave."

"*Hear* your gift?" I turn back around.

He grins. "My gift is an offer."

"I'm not interested in making deals with Russians."

"No, you are only interested in kidnapping us and stealing our information."

I almost wince at his words, thinking of the Russian man Wolfgang hunted and called me in to interrogate weeks ago. That was when I'd been busy trying to work out deals with the Morenos. Those deals eventually came through, made even more profitable from the information we got from the Russian captive.

Mikhail tries hard to hide his anger. I'm not surprised he's still upset about losing a man from his gang. That Russian sang like a bird in our warehouse. I sold his secrets to the Morenos—who paid me via multiple shipments of raw cocaine, which I used to pay King James for his granddaughter's hand in marriage.

Technically, Mikhail is five million deep for this wedding. I should thank him.

"The Jägers are hunters. We've been collecting men for decades. It's how we operate," I tell him.

He glares at me, for the first time looking more alive than dead. "And the Russians have been selling flesh for decades, but how would you feel if your sweet flower ended up in one of my whorehouses?"

I take a careful step forward, lowering my voice as I say in Russian, "Watch yourself."

My use of his native language takes him by surprise, but the moment is fleeting, shock quickly lighting up his face before his normal calm chases it away. He replies in English, "I did not come here to fight you."

I nod.

"I have information I want to give you for free."

I squint. Free information is never truly free.

"Do not trust Giovanni De Luca."

"You didn't have to drive all the way to Brooklyn to tell me that."

He laughs. "Yes, I did. Because this is more than a warning, Jäger."

"What is it?"

"A revelation."

"I'm listening."

"Did you know your wife is not the withered rose? The wilted flower of the Italian Garden has always been Giovanni Junior. He has owed me money for years now. And he is using his sister to pay those debts."

I'm not stunned. With me taking over a portion of the De Luca assets—as part of my contract to marry Rosa—I'll be bringing in a lot more money once I turn their failing businesses around. I've already given Gio a handsome sum as a token of good faith. I'm assuming he handed most of it over to Mikhail.

"What's your point?" I ask in a tired voice.

"Giovanni is a dirty man. I no longer want his money."

"Then don't accept it." *I* no longer have the patience to figure out how any of this pertains to me. "You need to start connecting the dots before I walk away," I warn.

Mikhail studies me a moment. "Giovanni killed his father."

My mouth goes dry. "His father killed *himself*."

"Is that what he told you?"

I glance away, my thoughts racing.

"Gio has owed me money for years now, due to bad deals he made behind his father's back. The De Luca businesses were failing long before Rosa ran off. That was just the straw that broke the camel's back. Instead of telling his father the truth, Giovanni killed him to take over Manhattan and use Rosa as a pawn. So far, his plan has worked."

"As much as I would love to believe you, I have to wonder

how you learned all this."

"My sniper saw him kill his father."

"Your sniper," I say flatly. Then I realize the implications of that statement. "You were going to kill Junior yourself."

"He had not paid up. I was tired of waiting." Mikhail says this so nonchalantly, I can't help but nod understanding. I might not be cruel like Vater, but I'm still mafia. I understand the importance of getting what you're owed in this business.

"When my sniper was ready to take the shot, he did not pull the trigger because of what he saw through his sights." Mikhail leans closer, lowers his voice. "Gio shot his own father. And made it look like a suicide."

"You still don't have any proof."

He shrugs. "You will have to take my word on it."

"Even if I do, why are you telling me this?"

"Because I no longer want to accept money from a man who killed his own father. I want Giovanni dead."

"You definitely won't get your money if you kill him," I say.

"It is not about the money anymore. Giovanni Senior was a good man. He was foolishly blinded by the love of his son, but he did not deserve to be shot by his own child. He was a don. We deserve better than that. And Junior does not deserve to be holding his father's title."

Not that the mafia cares much for laws and rules, but we do live by a code. Murdering one's own kin is a big no-no. Even across different gangs, we uphold the importance of family. I know this better than anyone. It's because of my desire to protect Wolfgang and hide his madness from the world that's gotten me here in the first place.

But Giovanni holds no such morals. He killed his own father and sold his sister to me to pay off his debts. To save his own skin. Mikhail has no proof of this, but I believe every word he's said so far. The kind of man who would blackmail his childhood friend into marrying his kidnapped sister sounds like the kind of man who would murder his father.

"Still," I roll this information over in my head, "what does this have to do with me?"

"You are Gio's brother-in-law now. If I kill him, you will be obligated to take action on behalf of your half-Italian wife."

"I will." Even though I don't want to.

"And the Stronghold will be obligated to lend aid on behalf of your half-Black wife."

"They will."

"But you have the power to keep them at bay."

I squint. Suddenly seeing where this is going.

"You want me to stand by and say nothing while you murder the don of the Italian mafia. My wife's older brother. Grandson to Jameson Willis, the man I have inside my home right now." I grit my teeth, a muscle spasming in my jaw. "Mikhail—"

"Junior should not be allowed to get away with what he has done."

"It's not your job to avenge Giovanni Senior!"

"Mafia aside, Gio Senior was my friend." Volkov pauses to swallow, grey eyes staring at the pavement. "Why do you think

190

I lent so much money to his son and never demanded payment until it became too much?"

"You were going to kill his son," I say flatly. "He couldn't have been that much of a friend to you if you were willing to take his heir from him."

"I was doing him a favor. Weeding the Garden." I shake my head, but he speaks before I can reply. "I am going to kill Junior. I came here as a courtesy to ask for your cooperation. Junior's life is not worth a war between all of us. Let me kill him and be done with it."

I take a deep breath. "You could have killed Junior any time in the last month. But you waited until now to have your revenge. *After* I became his brother-in-law."

Mikhail smiles.

"Why?" I demand.

He shrugs one shoulder. It's a thin shoulder which I could probably dislocate with one well-placed hit, but I don't want to get into a fist fight with the Wolf of Staten Island on my wedding day. So I bite the inside of my cheek as he says, "Maybe I just wanted to see your reaction. Maybe I wanted to see where your loyalty lies—with your business or with your pretty wife."

"And what am I supposed to tell my pretty wife when she expects me to retaliate against you?"

He shrugs. "The German underboss does not owe his wife an answer."

I cram my hands into my pockets, so he doesn't see them curl into fists, but Mikhail's eyes miss nothing. He smiles impishly as he lets out a low, menacing chuckle. "When did you fall for her?"

"I'm done here," I say, turning to leave.

"Jäger means *hunter* in your language, no?"

I stop walking, but I don't turn around. "Yes."

"Do you know what Volkov means in mine?"

I do.

"It means wolf," I say slowly. I can *feel* him smiling behind me.

"Really ... who is hunting whom in this game?" He takes a step closer. Douglass responds by moving forward. I don't want a fight to break out, so I turn around to stare at the older man. He's still smiling. "You think a hunter can catch a wolf before it catches him?"

"You're not a real wolf."

"And you are not a real hunter." He waves his hand. "This is all pointless, anyway. A dog chasing a cat chasing a mouse. But what is the mouse after?"

"I don't have time for your riddles, Volkov." I pinch the bridge of my nose. "I'm not going along with your plan."

"So, it will be war? Over Giovanni Junior?"

"That's for you to decide. You don't have to kill him."

"You have a decision to make, too, Jäger."

I blink at him.

"Now that you know the truth of what your brother-in-law has done, what will you tell your wife—whom you love so much?"

I carefully turn back toward my house because I'm positive

I will shoot Mikhail if I stay out here any longer. But I can't ignore the weight in his words. He is absolutely right. I can't keep the truth from Rosa. She will never forgive me if she finds out her father was murdered by her brother, and I'd known all along. But she also won't forgive me if I sit back and allow Gio to be killed.

I'm stuck between two impossible choices. I could just tell her the truth. That her brother is a lying murderer, and the Russians shockingly want him dead for it—because they suddenly have a conscience now. But Rosa has already experienced so much heartbreak and betrayal. I don't know if she can handle the raw truth.

Whatever I decide. I'm not going to act on it right now. It's still my wedding day, and I intend to enjoy what's left of it. I intend to go inside and dance with my pretty wife who's probably been looking for me. And I intend to forget about all this until morning.

Chapter Sixteen

I was right. Rosa has been looking for me. She's almost at the door when I reenter my home, her hands holding up the front of her dress, revealing her smooth legs as she walks. I glance down at them when she reaches me, her voice filled with worry.

"Where have you been? They're waiting for us to share the first dance."

I smile, pulling her close for a second. "You want to dance with me?"

She's not expecting the question. It throws her for a moment, and she blinks, licking her red lips as she tries to come up with an answer. It isn't until she's unable to make eye contact that I realize she's not lost for words because she's shy.

She really doesn't want to dance with me.

I nod, letting go of the hurt, but also the kindness and the concern, too. Rosa agreed to behave, but she never said anything about warming up to me. Fine. A quiet, obedient wife who doesn't love me looks just as good in bed as one who can't stand the sight of me. I'll take my wife any way I can get her. As long as she doesn't fight me.

That was the agreement. And I'll stick to it. She'll behave, but not love me. And I won't hurt her. But I won't be nice, either. I've gone through too much trouble, money, and stress to let Rosa have her way. I won't make her my physical punching bag, but she doesn't get to turn me into her emotional one.

I grab her hand and march back toward the reception. Rosa senses the change in my demeanor, squeezing my hand and stumbling to match my pace.

"What's wrong? What happened outside?"

"Nothing you need to know about," I grunt, practically dragging her onto the dancefloor.

Murmurs rush through our guests as Rosa trips over her gown and I leave her in the middle of the floor to go to the DJ. "Play something slow and romantic," I snap, turning on my heel before she can even respond.

Rosa is waiting with wide eyes when I return to her. The lights dim around us and the crowd hushes, understanding what's about to happen. I glance at my watch. Two minutes should be a long enough dance, then we can leave and get the dirty work over with and I can get back to being the man I'm supposed to be. Amory Jäger. Mafia underboss. Detached, removed, unemotional.

The only man I know how to be.

One hand goes around Rosa's small waist, the other takes her hand and we dance quite formally. It isn't romantic, it isn't even pretty with my bride tripping across the stage, clumsy in her heels and long dress and unable to keep pace with my quick, hurried movements. I dip her and she grips my shoulder, almost panting for breath.

"What's going on?" she whispers, lifting her head to gape at me.

"I just want to get this over with," I say, my voice cold, my face flat.

She stares at me as we dance, pleading for answers and explanations she will never get. I don't even look at her anymore. Just stare out at the crowd as we twirl around the floor. She's doing better at keeping up—determined to get some sort of response out of me—but I ignore her until the music changes, and then I'm marching off the floor, hauling her behind me.

We pass smiling guests and excited friends, even Nona steps out to hug Rosa, but I don't give them the time to hold each other long. Thankfully, Nona thinks I'm just in a rush to have my bride all to myself, so she doesn't see any insult in the way I drag Rosa away from her. She even squeals and winks at us.

The ride to the hotel is quiet. My wife doesn't look at me. And she's given up asking questions, finally understanding that I'm not going to answer. The silence remains when I go to check us in, Douglass rushes ahead of us to take our things up to our room, but Rosa just stands idly by my side, refusing to look anywhere but at the floor. Even in the elevator, her gaze seems stuck to the red carpeting, I have to grab her elbow and guide her down the hall to our room. She seems to come alive somewhat as she enters and clicks on the lights to find a grand suite with a king-sized bed, a full bathroom, a kitchen, and a small living room with a television.

There aren't any rose petals on the bed, but there is a bucket of ice and a free bottle of champagne. I wish it was whiskey, but it'll do just fine. I walk over and grab the alcohol, bite the cork and tug it out, and suck down a mouthful right from the bottle.

I gasp and set the bottle on the desk nearby, wiping the wetness from my mouth. Rosa hasn't moved from her stance by the door, staring at me from across the room. I can see her reflection in the mirror on the wall, how her eyes scan me from head to toe, wondering who this man is and what he's done to the gentleman who held her and forgave her for her lies a few days earlier.

He's gone.

"Go change into something sexy," I rasp, turning to face her. I remove my suit jacket and toss it over the chair at the desk. "Let's get this over with."

She lets out a noise, but I don't know what it is. A cough, a sob, a *moan*? I know that's not it. Only one of us actually wants to do this. I almost laugh at myself, at how stupid it was to think a good girl like Rosa would ever want to have anything to do with a man like me. The only time we'd ever enjoyed each other's company was a decade ago, when she was a goofy kid too blind to know who I really was, too childish to understand exactly the sort of life I lived.

The only thing that's changed is her age. She still doesn't understand who I am. Why I do what I do. Why I can't be the man she wants. The Prince Charming she deserves.

But it's not my job to make her understand. Or to even care that she doesn't.

I flop into the chair, reaching for the champagne. The bubbles fizz in my throat, threatening to choke me. I burp. Lean back into the soft leather and gaze at my new bride. She's clutching her crucifix. I want to snatch it from her neck. Instead, I surprise myself by saying softly, "You look beautiful."

She wrinkles her brows, and for a second, I think she might burst into tears. Or maybe that's me choking on a sob.

"Amy..."

That name again. It almost breaks me, but I won't let it. I can't let it get to me. Not now.

I rise and go to her, invading her space, standing less than an inch away. My hand goes to her cheek, enjoying the feel of her soft, warm skin. She flinches and I realize she's afraid.

"It'll hurt for a minute," I murmur. "But I can be gentle. I can make you feel good."

She takes a step back, but the door is right behind her. I briefly wonder if she'll try to bolt, but she just takes a deep breath and stares at the floor like I'm the boogey man.

"Rosa," I whisper. "I want you. You already know that." I hate that I'm doing this, but the words are slipping from my lips before I can stop them. I'm giving her one more chance, one more opportunity to turn this around. To accept me. To let me in. "What do you want?"

When she doesn't answer, I lean down and kiss her, gently at first, but when she tilts her head back to give me more access, I'm overcome with emotion. My mouth covers hers with a groan and I press her against the wall, my hands on the door, resting on either side of her head. Her hands slide up my chest, the touch sending fire shooting through me, burning in the friction of our kiss.

I groan into her mouth, and she tips her head back, gasping for a breath. "Amy," she says again, and I feel weak in the knees. She has no idea what that nickname does to me.

"Yes, Rosa?" I kiss her neck. "What do you want?"

Her hands press against my chest. It takes me a moment to realize she's pushing me away. "I want ... to sleep alone tonight."

I stare at her, unsure if I've heard her correctly. "There's no way," I mutter.

Rosa swallows nervously.

"There's no way you want to sleep alone after kissing me like that."

"Amy—"

"No." I shake my head, grabbing both her shoulders. "You felt something in that kiss—you've felt something since the *first* time we kissed."

She inhales sharply and drops her head, unable to look me in the eye. Because she knows I'm right.

"Why are you fighting this?" I ask, and when she doesn't answer, I lean down to kiss her again, but she squirms and shoves me away.

"I want to be alone!" Her eyes are ablaze with emotion— not anger, not annoyance, not frustration. She's filled with passion, desire, need. Her cheeks are flaming red with blush, her lips swollen and puffy from our kiss. Her hair has come loose in some places, thick curls trailing her bare shoulders. She is the image of desire right now—her want is so obvious it's almost embarrassing. Yet, she denies it. Fighting her attraction to me like it's a sin.

I run my hand through my hair. "Tell me you don't want me, Rosa."

She hugs herself.

"You can't, can you?"

"Please just go, Amy."

"I'm your *husband*. It's okay for you to want me. It's okay for us to have sex."

She sucks in a long breath, squares her shoulders. "I don't want you."

Pain burns through me, her words cutting like a barb of poison. Instead of letting it show, I quirk an eyebrow and release a dark chuckle. "I'll believe you when you can say that like you mean it."

She pales, pressing herself against the door as I step forward. Her head angles away from me, like she's afraid I might kiss her again. "You promised," she whispers. "You promised not to hurt me."

I grit my teeth. Lord in Heaven, does she think I'm going to *rape* her?

"I'm not my brother or my father, Rosa. I told you that already." I brush a curl from her face. My gentleness surprises her and she blinks at me, finally meeting my gaze again. Tears have gathered in her eyes, tiny droplets of water wetting her lashes, sitting on the dark strands like crystalline bulbs. I want to kiss them away, but I know if I make a move now, she'll never stop running from me.

"I won't touch you unless you want me to," I say softly. "But I'm not going to let you get away with this act forever."

She tilts her head to the side, face crinkling in confusion.

"You do want me, Rosa. You're just afraid to admit it."

With that, I lean down and kiss her forehead. Then I scoot her to the side, so I can open the door and leave—retreat to my room alone on my own wedding night.

"Goodnight, Mrs. Jäger."

Chapter Seventeen

I know what you're thinking. I'm thinking the same thing. It's my own wedding night and I've ruined it. But hear me out; I hadn't agreed to any of this. I never wanted any of this. And even though Amory didn't either, he's made it more than clear that he *does* want *me*. If not as his wife, then at least as someone to simply warm his bed.

Our deal was that I would behave. That I wouldn't fight him. Wouldn't try to run away anymore. That doesn't mean I have to strip down and give him a show just because it's our honeymoon. It doesn't mean I have to love him. Or even care about him.

God wants me to feed the Word to Amory. I don't have to sleep with him to do that.

But ...

You do want me, Rosa. You're just afraid to admit it.

Amory's words hammer through my mind as I stare

blankly ahead, watching the door he just walked out of.

He's right. I do want him.

My heart had beat so erratically as he'd kissed me, I thought for sure he would hear it. I nearly buckled in his arms as he'd held me, as he'd touched me, caressing my cheek, whispering gentle words of seduction.

I've never felt so drawn to someone before. So wanted. So undeniably, inexplicably desired by another person. It awakened parts of me I didn't even know existed, summoned feelings I'd never felt before, threatened to wreck me even before I'd properly put myself together.

Amory Jäger is a dangerous man.

And then, just as quickly as I'd discovered the power of his gaze, he regained that chilling self-control and walked away. Leaving me hot and desperate and confused.

I wish I could say I'm too holy for all that. That I'm a Child of God, and the lust of the night didn't affect me. But the dirty truth is that I'm ashamed. *Embarrassment* is the only thing keeping me from chasing behind Amory, tearing down his door and begging him to finish what he started.

Guilt wracks me like a storm as I listen to his fading footsteps. I cannot get the expression on his face out of my mind. How dejected he'd looked when he'd asked what I wanted, and I'd given him my answer.

To be alone.

Was he disappointed that he wouldn't be getting laid tonight, or had I truly hurt him? Amory and I want each other. Desire each other. But the way his face sank was almost as if his very heart had been shattered.

Is there something else between us other than lust?

Because lust is the reason I'm holding onto the thinning strand of self-control clenched tightly in my heart. Yes, Amory is my husband. It's okay for us to have sex. But what is sex when it isn't something done out of love? What is intimacy without passion?

It's lust.

Dirty, filthy, sinful lust.

At least … I think it is.

Right?

If I'm not in love with Amory, then it doesn't matter that he's my husband. Anything we do in bed together would still be wrong because it wouldn't be done in love. It would be done in a burning, uncontrollable lust. Pure desire. Nothing more.

Shaking my head, I march over to the bedside table and yank the drawer out. There's a King James Bible inside. I snatch it up and flop onto the giant bed, madly flipping through the pages. There must be something in here to help me. Something to calm my racing heart. Something to confirm that I had every right to send Amory away.

I want him. But I don't love him. And I don't know if it's right to give myself to someone I don't love.

Tears blur the pages of the Bible as I turn them. I get so frustrated I end up hurling the Book across my bed and collapsing onto the pillows. I have no idea what to do. I have no idea why I'm feeling this way. I just want it to stop.

Throwing away God's Word is not going to help at all. So

I gather myself and crawl across the bed to the Bible, it's fallen open to I Corinthians 7:9.

But if they cannot contain, let them marry: for it is better to marry than to burn.

I've got the marriage part down. But what about this pain I have inside? Is this what it's like to *burn*? To want someone so badly that you ache for them.

I sit up straighter, gathering my wedding dress around me. Maybe it isn't wrong to feel this way. We're already married. There's no going back now. I'm just afraid I'm doing something wrong. I'm afraid that giving myself to Amory will leave me with nothing. Because once the flames of our burning desire have been extinguished, all we'll have left is ash.

I close the Bible. Ash or lust or passion or whatever, it's too late to deal with all this. And I'm sure Amory will never see things from my perspective. He's just so...

My thoughts trail off. *So ... what?*

I don't know a thing about Amory. He's distant, yes—detached, even. He's a hard worker. He's stern when he needs to be. But that's all I've got, other than a handful of distant memories that have faded over time. And even if they hadn't dimmed, his smile is different now. His eyes are colder now. Amory is not Amy anymore. He's a different man entirely.

And I'm a different woman.

I roll onto my back, staring up as I exhale. Maybe this would be easier if we got to know each other a little bit. I was taken back to New York and dragged to the altar all in three weeks. Under any other circumstances, we'd be seen as lunatics for getting married so quickly. But that's mafia life. Marrying for *love* is what's weird around here. By our standards, Amory and I are totally normal. In fact, we should be happy. We're both young, both high-ranking, both attractive. Tonight should have been a ball for the both of us. Instead, we're in separate rooms both feeling alone and confused.

But it doesn't have to stay this way. If I'm going to survive this marriage, it *can't* stay this way. I won't let Amory force me to do something I'm uncomfortable with, but I'll do my part in trying. I'll get to know him. I'll make an effort. And maybe, just maybe, that'll make a difference.

When I wake the next morning, I have every intention to eat breakfast with my husband and enjoy myself. I shower and fight my hair into a cute bun, shimmy into a dress, pick out shoes, and spray on perfume. Then I decide I hate everything and start all over. I change into a skirt and a strapless shirt, take my hair down so my curls pour over my bare shoulders, and change from sandals into nude heels. A bit of makeup goes over my face; blush on my cheeks, a neutral colored eyeshadow, and matte lipstick.

In the mirror, I convince myself I look nice enough and step into the hallway to come face to face with Douglass. He gives me a nervous smile, thick lips pressed together almost painfully, and stares at my bare shoulders for a second.

"Um, good morning, Mrs. Jäger."

The sound of my new last name almost disarms me. Amory

used it the night before, but it sounds different coming from his driver. Speaking of his driver…

"What are you doing here?" I ask.

His gaze moves up to my collarbone, then my neck, and finally finds my eyes. "He sent me to bring you home."

By '*he*,' I assume he means Amory. I frown. "Where's my husband?"

Douglass takes a deep, uncomfortable breath. "He's at his office."

"At his office?" I glance at my watch. It's 8:47am—but it doesn't matter what time it is because this is the day after our wedding. We're supposed to be on our honeymoon, not back to business as usual.

I sigh because I know there's a valid argument in there somewhere about how I made it very clear that I wanted to be alone last night, so Amory has every right to assume I still want to be alone this morning. But still…

"So, you're here to take me home," I say slowly.

Douglass nods. "Your things have already been brought to Mr. Jäger's estate."

Mr. Jäger's estate. That's right. Home is no longer Junior's penthouse or daddy's mansion. It's Amory's house.

I almost groan, thinking of the horrible night I'd had at his place when his mother had been violently dragged away by one of his father's henchmen. I don't want to go back to that place even for a visit. Now I'm going to live there.

Douglass makes a noise which makes me realize he's expecting some sort of response. Amory's left him with orders.

Even though I know he can't drag me bodily to my new home, I also know it isn't right to make his life worse just to get back at my husband for skipping breakfast this morning. If I give Douglass a hard time, it'll only hurt him. And it'll push Amory further away.

He *should be trying to win* me *over*, I grumble internally, but even that idea fizzles out because I know—deep down—that's all he's tried to do since we were reunited. Even after I tried to run away, he gave me yet another offer. Start over fresh. Wipe the slate clean.

That was much more than his mother got from his own father. And all she'd done was get tipsy at a party.

I shudder and take a step forward. "I guess we should get going, then."

Douglass nods and then holds his ear as he glances off and says something in German. It takes me an extra second to realize he's speaking into his earpiece. When his focus returns to me, he heaves a sigh and says, "Someone will come up to get your things from the room."

I nod. "Ready?"

"Just follow me."

A tiny, little part of me half expects Amory to be waiting in the car, but when Douglass opens the door for me to get inside, I find only leather seats. Life is breathed back into my expectations when we pull around the circle at Amory's estate and I realize this isn't the home I visited for his family dinner. This mansion with stone pillars and elaborate detail in the sculpted finishing, with two floors and enough space to comfortably house a family of twelve, is Amory's estate. His private home.

It's grand in a very subtle way. Dark and menacing like a small fortress—not a castle. Everything about the house screams Jägermeister, from the evergreen shrubbery casting shadows over the side of the mansion, to the vines curling up over the front windows, to the cracked stone pillars holding up the home. It's as if the house itself is brooding, a stony extension of my husband.

Douglass brushes past me and goes to the door. I'm right behind him when he uses his key to unlock the door and let me inside. It's everything I expect, given the outside. Old wooden furnishings, cold, stone floors that echo as I walk through the open foyer, a grand double staircase winding up to a second floor. I crane my neck and spin around as I pass into the massive hallway, there are paintings lining both walls. Scowling old men with pale skin and dark hair stare down at me from their framed cages.

Oddly, the figures all look similar, and I realize with a shock that they are portraits of Amory's family members. Great grandfathers, uncles, cousins—every Jägermeister to ever hold the title.

I'm in awe, walking slowly down the hallway, my heels clicking against the tiled floor. I never realized how much history—how much culture—had been preserved in Amory's family. Yes, these men were mafia, but they weren't animals. There is a code that exists within the business, if you can believe it. I can see the remnants of that code in these paintings, in the furrowed brows, the hard lines in all those serious faces, the eyes void of emotion and warmth. Just like Amory's eyes. That code is dedication. Complete loyalty to the family name and the legacy it upholds.

Someone clears their throat behind me, the noise bounces off the high walls and thrums in my chest. I turn, hope blooming, heart swelling—begging God to let it be Amory come home for a visit.

I find Douglass standing a few feet away.

"I can show you to your room," he says. Then he raises his eyebrows, and the gesture almost confuses me. I suppose he could simply be gazing at me, he could have even gotten dust in his eyes, but I can only interpret his expression as a sign for me to hurry up, so I gather myself and march back down the hall in a hurry.

Douglass leads me up the giant oakwood staircase in silence; we round two corners before he stops in front of a room at the far end of the hall. When he opens the door, my heart truly sinks.

A queen bed waits inside with a double sized dresser, a walk-in closet, a connected bathroom, and all my things from my room in Gio's penthouse. But nothing more.

There are no suits in my walk-in closet, no ties in the drawers beside my scarves and other accessories, no boxers thrown in with my panties.

This is my room. Just mine. Not Amory's. Not ours.

I don't even know why I feel so upset by this fact. I should be happy he's giving me the space I asked for. But somehow, in his quiet absence, I feel like this solitude is some form of punishment. Whispers of Amory's anger echoing through the house, the emptiness of it all.

When Douglass leaves me, I quietly walk through the house, barefoot and nervous. The mansion is silent as a tomb and almost looks like one, too. High grey walls of stone, dark tiled floors, ominous looking paintings and hundred-year-old sculptures. The curtains over the windows are pulled shut, letting in just slivers of sunlight to slice through the ashen darkness inside.

Almost every door is locked, except the one leading to the massive, industrial style kitchen, and the library. After an hour of walking, I return to my room totally defeated. I don't know what I was looking for or what I even wanted. *Well ...* I wanted to find Amory, but I knew I wouldn't when I'd first arrived. Douglass said he was at his office. So it wasn't like he'd pop out of a wardrobe or storage bin somewhere in the house just because I was walking around searching for him.

I don't even know what I would have done if I'd opened a door and found him in one of the rooms. Maybe I'd talk to him? Maybe I'd apologize for the night before? I didn't exactly have a reason to say sorry, I felt my feelings were justified, but I was trying to extend the kindness to him that he'd shown to me when I'd tried to run away. It's my turn to say, let's start over. Let's get to know each other. And maybe things would eventually lead to what should have happened last night.

All these thoughts swirl in my head as I return to my room and lie down. Maybe it's a good thing I didn't find Amory. He's already proven himself dangerous, with those eyes, and that low, husky voice, and the disarming gentleness he always uses. It never fails to catch me off guard; in the middle of an argument, when I'm expecting an outburst, I get a kiss. When I think he's going to yell, he whispers that he wants me. When I'm sure he's going to break his promise to never hurt me, he uses the hand that'd been drawn into a fist to brush a curl from my face. In this world of death, violence, and crime, I don't know how to respond to such gentle behavior.

Encountering Amory without a plan would be foolish.

So I curl up in bed, close my eyes, and, despite the grumbling in my stomach, I fall asleep.

Amory still isn't around when I wake, but there's a platter of food on display in the dining room when I wander inside.

I eat. Unpack some things from my room. And then prepare myself to see Amory at dinner.

He still doesn't show.

I smell food in the dinning room again around 6:30. But no Amory.

And no Amory the next day, either.

Or the day after that.

After a week of solitude, I start to believe that maybe this is *my* house and Amory lives somewhere else, but then I come in for breakfast and find a half-eaten plate of eggs and sausage and I realize what's really happening.

He's avoiding me.

"Fine," I grumble, crossing my arms as I glare at the plate. "I asked to be alone. I should be happy about this."

"You should," I hear a deep voice say over my shoulder.

I turn and find Amory standing in the doorway. He isn't smiling, but I catch a hint of humor dancing in his eyes as he studies me. All six feet and two inches of him is on display, his dark suit and white shirt, grey tie slightly askew as he leans to the side. His arms fold over his chest, making his shirt crinkle around his abdomen. I fight hard to keep my eyes level with his instead of dropping to stare at his body.

I'm … suddenly very thirsty. And I don't know why.

My mouth dries at the sight of my husband and all I can do is take a slow, deep breath as I wait for him to speak. His eyes quickly scan me over, but he does it in a way that almost makes him look bored of me, not the lusty way he'd watched me on our wedding night. Eyes half-lidded and lazy, focused on every part of my body, drinking me in from head to toe.

Amory's slightly accented voice catches my attention. "Are you settling in?"

"Where have you been?" I ask.

He chuckles. "Miss me?"

"I don't understand—"

"I've been busy," he cuts me off, walking past me to the breakfast table. "Besides," he says, taking a sip from the cup of coffee resting next to his half-eaten food. "Isn't this what you wanted? To be alone."

Actually, I had asked to *sleep* alone. But I feel like pointing this out will expose more of me to him than I want right now.

"I was hoping we could spend some time together," I say as bravely as I can.

"Why?"

"So that maybe," I pause, "maybe things will be easier between us."

Amory sets his coffee down and crosses the room. He's standing right in front of me in a moment. His grey eyes aren't on mine, they're focused on every other part of me, slowly dragging from my neck down to my collar to my breasts to my waist. I shift beneath his scrutiny and his focus snaps back to my face.

"What sort of *things* are we talking about?"

I swallow which makes him chuckle again.

His hand is on my face, brushing a curl behind my ear. Too quickly for me to stop, his other hand finds my waist and pulls me against him. "What sort of things, Rosa?"

I can't breathe. But I know he won't let me go without giving him an answer. I look up at him, trying hard to meet his gaze and desperately praying he can't see the wariness in my eyes.

"A—Amory," I say, my voice a whisper.

His hand slides down from my waist … lower, to my backside.

I stiffen.

"Yes, Rosa?" His voice is husky. His eyes ablaze with desire.

"I—I—" I squeeze my eyes shut, suddenly overwhelmed. He said he wouldn't touch me until I asked him to, yet his

214

hands are all over me.

"Amory, you promised," I say breathily.

His deep laugh fills the dining room, and my eyes fly open to find him smirking down at me. "*Amory, you promised*," he mocks, voice high and teasing.

Anger bubbles inside me and I shove him away. "Don't make fun of me."

"Don't make it so easy," he snaps back, straightening his shirt. He checks his watch and then moves past me to the door. "You wanted to be alone, darling, now you've got it."

I stare at him in disbelief. I was right. This *is* punishment.

"When you want things to change, just let me know," he says with a wicked grin and a wink that makes my traitorous heart flutter. Then, without another word, he turns and walks out.

Chapter Eighteen

I *know*. I'm being such a drama king right now. In my defense, this is what Rosa asked for. And in Rosa's defense … No, it's not.

I have good hearing and a great memory. I am well aware that she asked to *sleep* alone, not spend eternity in solitude. But I'm angry and I'm irritated and I'm letting my emotions get the better of me right now.

What did my wife think would happen after issuing a request like that? She wanted to sleep *alone*? On our *wedding night*?

Fine.

If she can't make good decisions on her own, I'll teach her how to make them through swift punishment. Whether I have the right to punish my own wife is questionable—I *know*—but I'm frustrated, and I don't know what else to do.

I've … never been rejected before.

And it's even more cutting because I had been so honest with Rosa. And she'd taken that honesty and tossed it out the door. Then told me to follow it. All while basically salivating over me.

How dare she.

I tore my heart out of my chest and served it to her on a platter and her only response was to tell me to leave? She was so hot I could have taken her right there and she wouldn't have fought me—*for once.*

I'd felt the tension in the air. I'd held her trembling frame in my arms. I'd drowned in her desire as we'd kissed. And she pulled away with wide eyes, blinking away those few moments of pure bliss as she returned to her façade.

To her credit, she wore her armor like a champ. Kept up that innocent little Christian girl act right until the door closed behind me, panting all the while.

I know wanting when I see it. I know desire when I hear it. I know desperate need when it's standing right in front of me. But, like the perfect gentleman, I tucked my tail and scurried off. Granting my wife her single request.

Now I'm acting out. Throwing a tantrum to punish Rosa for hurting me. Which makes me feel very sad and pathetic— but I'm allowed to throw myself at least one pity party in my life, okay?

To be fair, I *have* been busy lately.

It's been three weeks since I got married and every day since then, Vater has been bugging me to get things moving with our newly acquired territory in Manhattan. Giovanni isn't far behind with his pestering; he's already nagging me for payment from the businesses I took over—payments I *don't have* because I *just* took over the properties. But Gio cannot understand that because he's an idiot.

To top it off, the Volkovs are breathing down my neck.

They have been the thorn in my side since I said, 'I do.' Maybe I'm just paranoid, but I swear I've seen more Russians walking the streets of Brooklyn, dancing in our clubs, drinking beer at our bars, and eating at our restaurants lately. They have become my shadow. And it's starting to weigh on my nerves. Something is going on; I know it is. But I can't do anything about it because action on my part would give the Wolves permission to start a war with me.

So I have to sit and wait.

Wait for them to kill Gio or kill me or both. Meanwhile, precious little Rosa has no idea what's going on. And I can't even tell her. She will never forgive me for letting her brother die, but she also won't understand why I cannot intervene. I might not even live to explain things to her. The anxiety is eating away at me. I half expect my head to be blown off by a sniper every time I step outside—or Rosa's head to get blown off. Which is another reason I've been keeping her at home. I'm not just being cruel, I'm being protective. The Volkovs are unpredictable and with my rejection of Mikhail's offer, anyone is up for grabs. He might just put a hit out on me out of spite.

So … *Yes*, I've been a jerk to my wife. But I've also been handling a lot of rubbish. I don't have time to deal with Rosa and her religious dilemma right now. She wants me. I want her.

I'll sex her down when I'm done with all this. Until then, this is how it's going to be. It's how it's *got* to be. I cannot afford to be distracted right now. Not when death is hanging over my head. Not when it's right *in front* of me.

I had the Russian grunt we took in executed this morning.

It wasn't right. But I couldn't take the risk. With the Wolves on the move, any Russian in our ranks is a potential spy. So I killed him. His blood still stains the cuff of my white shirt. I had the decency to pull the trigger myself. That's how the Germans do it.

I wipe at the red smear on my shirt cuff as Douglass takes me to my father's estate. He wants a report on our books since taking over more than two dozen new businesses and properties. It's only been three weeks since Giovanni handed over the titles and deeds, but, for some infuriating reason, everyone expects that to be more than enough time to miraculously turn all those failing companies around.

I am not looking forward to this meeting.

"I'll wait by the car," Douglass announces as I exit the vehicle. He knows Vater doesn't like him very much. I nod and stroll up to the house, stopping only for the guards who open the double doors and let me inside.

Vater is in a small conference room just down the hall from his office. My Uncle Oberon is there, along with my cousin Conrad, and my stupid little brother. I can't help but notice Hans and Morgen are missing but I don't say anything. Morgen's recently engaged, so I don't expect him today anyway. But if Hans isn't glued to my father, then he's out somewhere murdering someone or just being annoying. I don't care.

Vater is sitting at the head of the table when I walk inside, he's eating a fried bologna sandwich, the seared meat burnt black around the edges. "Amory!" he shouts over the food in his mouth. He's happy to see me because he thinks I've got a great report. The briefcase in my hand suddenly feels much heavier than it did before I walked in, despite being relatively empty.

I smile at him and take a seat, waving off the shy woman who walks over to see if I'd like something from the kitchen. "Afternoon, Uwe," I say.

My use of his first name catches his attention. His eyes narrow on me. "You have a report?"

"Not a good one." I figure it's better to be upfront instead of sugar coating anything. "I'm going to need more time to—"

"We have acquired thirty percent of Manhattan," Uwe says slowly.

"Thirty percent of Manhattan is failing, Vater."

This news takes him by such surprise, he nearly chokes on his sandwich. Oberon leans over and offers him water as he blanches and then turns red. I sneak a glance at Wolfgang, he's staring at his plate, avoiding eye contact with me. A wise decision.

I will never forget the fact that it is his foul temper that's put me in this situation. And I'll never let him forget, either.

Vater regains himself, dabs at his mouth with a

handkerchief. "What do you mean thirty percent of Manhattan is failing?"

They don't know. No one besides myself, Giovanni, and Mikhail Volkov knows how bad the De Lucas were doing before this. The only reason Mikhail knows is because Gio owes him so much money—which is why he's pestering me for his percentage of the profit he's convinced himself I've brought in. Even though I've taken over a portion of his businesses, our contract gifts him ten percent of all revenue. But ten percent of zero is still zero.

I take a breath, trying to buy myself enough time to think of what to say. How do I explain to my father that we will need to sink millions into these ventures before we can expect to just break even? He knew the Garden wasn't what it used to be, but he had no idea it had totally withered in the last year or so. And he's going to kill me once he learns that I knew and still decided to marry Rosa.

I didn't have a choice. But he doesn't know that. He will never know that because I'm a good big brother. Aside from the fact that this whole situation is far beyond me being a good big brother. Mikhail Volkov already wants to kill Gio and anyone who tries to stop him. If he finds out I had a hand in covering up the murder of his own daughter, he will skin me alive and make Uwe watch.

"It looks like Giovanni stuck me with his worst businesses," I say, placing my briefcase on the table and laying out some papers. They're documents detailing exactly how bad some of the storefronts and other organizations are doing.

Jägers have diamonds, the Morenos have their cocaine, the Russians sell their women, the Stronghold deals weapons, but the De Lucas handle property. They deal real estate like it's crack—trading square feet for thousands of dollars over the property's true value. In a place like New York, the Garden thrives by overcharging for buildings. There are millions of people in the city, each needing a place to live, or wanting to open a business, or trying to buy land. The De Lucas own Manhattan, which means almost every boutique, every hair salon, every trendy little coffee shop pays rent to them.

But with Gio's bad deals, Manhattan is spiraling out of control. He doesn't even have the cashflow to get a loan from his own bank. The entire borough is essentially in its own depression.

Vater would keel over right now if I say all this, so I simply pass a few papers down the line and wait for him to examine them. They're papers from some of the businesses that aren't entirely failing. Ones I could actually save. Still, the reports turn my father's face from beet red to bruised purple and I know I'm about to get an earful.

He starts cursing in German and then shreds the report and points a thick finger at me across the table. "Fix this, Amory! *Fix* it! If you weren't my son, I'd send Hans after you!"

I press my lips together. This is what I have to deal with when I'm not home being annoyed by Rosa. I don't know which is worse.

I endure ten more minutes of aggressive German yelling before Vater's blood pressure gets the better of him and he leans back in his chair, wheezing. Uncle Oberon looks at me with a somber expression, like he's afraid I'm going to cry.

"Perhaps we should call it a day for now," Onkel says.

I nod and stand before anyone can stop me, leaving my briefcase and heading straight for the door. Conrad is quicker than he looks, already by the door when I approach, his eyebrow quirked like he wants to say something but knows he shouldn't. He jerks his head toward the door before opening it and I follow him into the hall.

"That was entertaining," he says with a laugh.

I shrug. "You know Uwe."

"I used to be jealous you were his heir when we were kids," Conrad says casually. "Now I'm glad to only be his nephew."

Wolfgang moseys over and leans against the wall with his hands in his pockets. He smiles weakly at me before he says, "You look tired, brother."

Conrad snorts. "The man's a newlywed. I'd be surprised if he wasn't tired." He wiggles his eyebrows and grabs his crotch, as if we somehow missed his joke.

"I'm mostly tired from work," I mutter. Honestly, being a newlywed sucks.

"Oh? You should come with me, then. Grab a drink."

It isn't until I glance up and find Conrad staring at me with an expectant look on his face that I realize I'd said that last statement aloud.

"My wife drove me crazy the first year of our marriage," Conrad says. "The sex was great, but everything else—" he rolls his eyes, "I'm glad I had the club to keep me busy. Or else

I would have lost my mind." He pats my shoulder and turns me toward the front doors. "Let's go have a drink. I'll tell you all about it."

Conrad runs a club in Brooklyn blandly named 'The Club.' It's a 24-hour establishment that doubles as a casual cigar lounge while the sun is up. We head there and settle into one of the VIP booths with a sigh. I lean into the creamy leather seats as my cousin goes over details of his marriage that I don't need to hear. I also don't think his wife would appreciate him sharing some of these stories, but I don't say this. The more Conrad talks, the less I have to.

A waitress comes and takes our drink orders—Wolfgang asks for a woman to come dance on the pole in the middle of the table. I glare at him, but he just shrugs and leans back with a stupid grin on his face.

"Come on, brother. Might as well enjoy yourself since you aren't getting any action from Rosa."

I squeeze my glass of whiskey just to keep from climbing over the table and poking his eyes out.

Conrad nudges me. "Things are that bad?"

"She's religious," I say, though I'm sure this only confuses them even more. I'm confused by it, too. I went to Catholic school; I remember learning that sex was for married people. But Rosa and I are married. So I don't get it.

I even downloaded a Bible app onto my phone and searched up every scripture on marriage just to see if I was missing something, if maybe I was doing something wrong, and Rosa was too afraid to tell me. But I don't think that's the case.

"I don't know *what* the case is," I mumble, taking a sip of my drink.

Conrad's hand is on my shoulder. "Maybe she's just shy."

The woman Wolfgang asked for walks over in nothing but a G-string and stilettos. She steps onto the table and grabs the pole, stealing my little brother's attention. I'm somewhat grateful for her presence, now Wolfgang won't hear how my marriage is already falling apart. For some reason, I don't want him to know. I don't think he deserves to know the relationship he got me forced into is crumbling faster than it began.

"She's not shy," I tell my cousin. "She's in denial."

"Are you sure?"

I nod and then throw back the rest of my whiskey. "We've been married almost a month and she still won't let me touch her."

I don't mention the fact that we've only encountered each other four times since getting married. I don't bring up the fact that I've been busy and actively avoiding my own wife for the last three weeks. But Conrad's eyes bulge all the same.

"You mean ..." he leans forward, "you haven't consummated the marriage?"

I shake my head, sneaking a glance at Wolfgang. He isn't listening, too distracted by the dancer's booty shaking in his face.

I'm right to be cautious with sharing this information. I shouldn't even tell Conrad about it, but I don't know what else to do or who else to talk to. If I tell Vater I haven't deflowered my bride yet, he will personally hold Rosa down until the job is done. Or he might rejoice. Without a consummation, I could probably get out of the marriage—especially if I present the reports from Gio's failed businesses. I could argue he gave me a bad deal and a crazy wife—which isn't too far from the truth.

Conrad whistles and takes a sip of his drink; I absently stare at the bullseye tattooed onto the knuckle of his middle finger. "Who's been keeping you busy, then?"

Ugh ... I knew this question would eventually come up. I shake my head almost in shame. I haven't had another woman in my bed. It wouldn't be a crime if I did—in fact, by mafia standards, it's quite shocking that I *don't* have a mistress. I can see that shock on Conrad's face as his mouth falls open and he makes a face I can only describe as pure horror.

I understand the feeling.

I haven't had a woman since the night before Gio invited me to his house and told me about this stupid marriage proposal. Over six weeks ago. This is the longest I've gone without sex since I was a teenager.

I should be losing my mind. I should be dragging this topless dancer away to a backroom for a private show. But the truth is, I don't want anyone else. I want Rosa. My wife.

I'm aching for her. But I made a promise not to touch her until she wanted me to, and I intend to keep it. There was never a promise not to keep myself busy while I waited, but what can

I say? I love her.

I gasp as the thought rushes through me. *Do I love Rosa?*

That's the only logical explanation for all this. All the promises I've made to her, the fact that I *want* to honor my wedding vows and be faithful to her, even after she's done nothing but lie and break her promises and try to leave me. Even though it's only been a few weeks since we were reunited after spending ten years apart.

When I look back, I think I've always loved Rosa. I fell for her a decade ago on that fateful day. At the time, it wasn't a *romantic* love—but it was love, all the same. A deep desire to protect the little girl who looked at me as if I was her world— her hero. As an innocent kid, Rosa didn't see me as a gangster or a mobster or a murderer. She saw me for the man I could be. Now, years later, that longing to be her rock has turned into a desire to be the man of her dreams. And it's paired with a hope that she could somehow love me for the man I've become.

I'm actually relieved to realize I'm in love. Because now it all makes sense. Now, I don't feel so crazy anymore. There's a reason behind all the suffering I've put myself through. I'm not a pathetic boy whining about not getting laid. I'm a man trying to find a way to get his own wife to love him back.

Conrad is leaning toward me, his eyes full of dread and shock. His words catch my attention and pull me from my thoughts. "I don't know what to say, cousin."

I frown. It shouldn't be this surprising that a man doesn't want to cheat on his wife. I can't be the only one. I'm sure

Onkel Oberon is loyal to his wife. He's a decent enough guy, mafia affiliation aside.

"I don't know how to change things," I say.

Conrad nods. "You guys got married fast. Maybe you should try getting to know each other a little bit? It might help make things easier."

I have a distinct memory of Rosa suggesting the same thing and me shooting her down out of spite and pettiness.

I let go of a very deep sigh. "Maybe you're right."

"I'm always right." Conrad laughs and slaps my shoulder. "Bring her to dinner tonight. My place."

"Why on Earth would I do that?" I roll my eyes. I like my cousin, but I don't feel like going to dinner with him. I've already spent an afternoon in his club. And trying to spend time with Rosa might fix my marriage but it also might backfire on me. Caring for people in this business is dangerous. Loving people is a deathtrap. It makes you weak and vulnerable—two things I cannot afford to be as an underboss.

Look what loving Wolfgang got me into. If I patch things up with Rosa, I will lose every part of me that I hate. But it's the hatred that makes me strong.

The scars on my back begin to ache as if to remind me of the consequences of weakness. To remind me of what will happen if I lose that hatred, if I let go of all the pitch-black anger I keep hidden inside.

I adjust against the seat, discreetly trying to stretch the muscles in my back so it doesn't hurt so much. Conrad is smiling, but not at me. His eyes have shifted to the dancer who is now on her knees shimmying in Wolf's face.

"You guys need to go out on a date," he says, still not looking at me. "Start with this dinner."

"I don't know."

He finally pulls his gaze from the dancer to look at me. "The Flower will need a German friend now—a *lady* friend. Perhaps my Gisela can teach her how to be a proper mafia wife."

I laugh because I'm sure Gisela is a doll. Conrad is the one staring at a stripper's boobs right now. He needs to learn how to be a proper *husband*.

"All right," I say, standing. "I've got to head home to let Rosa know we're going out."

"Dinner is at seven." Conrad winks.

Chapter Nineteen

Conrad's home is very bland compared to the grandeur of Amory's house. It's a two-story home with a two-car garage and a spacious front and backyard. When we first pull up, I'm surprised by how normal it looks, but Amory catches me staring and his chuckle draws my attention from the window.

"My cousin is a simple man. Prefers to pour his money into his business instead of his home."

I glance back out the window, eyes tracing the frame of the very plain wooden door, the wind chimes singing in the breeze, the welcoming potted plants on the porch. You would never guess the cousin of a mafia underboss lives here. I suddenly feel like I need to look my best for these people. Without thinking, I reach down and button my blouse all the way up to my neck.

I'm as nervous as I was the first time I sat down across from Melissa and one of her advisors for her women's shelter.

There was an interview process I went through before getting accepted into the program. I basically had to prove that I was, in fact, homeless and not just a swindler there to steal their free food, clothes, and lodging.

I remember being anxious. Wondering if I deserved their charity.

A similar feeling works its way over me now as I stare up at Conrad's home. These people are the closest I've seen to normal human beings since I was dragged back to New York. Everyone else lives in luxury, diamond rings on their fingers, expensive watches on their wrists, and guns holstered on their hips. Mafia life.

I'm glad they seem so normal; I just hope I come off as normal and welcoming, too.

Douglass opens Amory's car door and then mine, but he doesn't walk us to the door. we march up the porch steps alone and I nervously ring the doorbell, expecting a meek, little housewife to appear on the other side. Instead, a woman in six-inch stilettos and a skintight strapless dress opens the door. Red-painted lips part into a toothy smile, as she says, "Hey there!" and black acrylic nails extend toward me as the woman pulls me into a hug.

She smells of expensive perfume and feels like an expensive boob job as her fake breasts press into me in our crushing hug. When she pulls back, I can't keep myself from staring at her overflowing cleavage. There is a single diamond hanging on a silver chain around her neck, the glimmering rock is stuck between her pale breasts.

"Hi," I say to her boobs.

She giggles and shimmies her shoulders, making them jiggle. I cannot control the possessive wifely instinct that latches onto my *soul* in that moment. With speed I didn't know I had, I turn and look up at Amory to see if he's staring, too.

He isn't.

Amory is absently looking over this woman's shoulder and into the house, a very vacant expression on his face, like he isn't even aware of what's going on in front of him. Let alone interested.

He sniffs. "Evening, Gisela."

Her smile falters somewhat. "Evening, Amory."

For the first time, Amory's eyes drift from the inside of the house to land on Gisela, a woman I can only assume is Conrad's wife. She beams up at him, jerking her head to the side to move her black bangs from her face.

"Where's Conny?" Amory says, his bored gaze shifting away and into the house again.

He's ignoring her so hard I'm starting to feel embarrassed.

Gisela takes a breath, her voice coming out less cheery than before. "He's inside. Come on, you two, let's go in and get dinner on the table. You're letting my air out."

Gisela leads us into the small mudroom and explains that the kitchen is just ahead, and the dining room is off to the left. Then she mumbles something about a blueberry pie in the oven and leaves us there to remove the coats we aren't wearing. It's the middle of Spring, we don't have any outerwear to take off, but I'm grateful for the moment alone anyway.

I can't believe I was expecting a meek housewife. Gisela looks like a 1950s pin up model. Meanwhile, here I am in a stupid knee-length skirt and a blouse I'd buttoned all the way up to my chin. I look like some sad and eternally single Sunday school teacher.

I let out a sigh, catching my reflection in the mirror on the wall. Amory must have heard me because he steps closer and places his hand on the small of my back. "You look beautiful," he says, kissing the top of my head.

The only response I can muster is a slow blink. I think I might have nodded, too. That's the nicest thing my husband has said to me in the month we've been married. Not necessarily because he's mean, but because I can count on one hand the number of times I've seen him since leaving the altar. We have been maintaining our distance under the unspoken agreement to give me space. Space he knows I didn't ask for, but we're both being stubborn about it.

He goes out of his way to leave me alone—like I asked. And I go out of my way to enjoy the solitude he's given me.

I'm sure we're both miserable.

But this is an opportunity to possibly change things. Other than telling me we were having dinner at his cousin's house; Amory hasn't spoken to me much today. And I haven't said much to him, either. But we're here together and Gisela seems like the type to never leave a lag in the conversation for long, so even if we don't exactly speak to each other, at least we won't be left in the miserable silence that's been echoing through our home.

Amory steps away and gently tugs on my elbow to guide me from the mudroom through the kitchen and into the dining room. Gisela is pouring water from a crystal pitcher into giant goblets. At the head of the table is Conrad Jäger, leaned back with his phone in his hand as he idly scrolls. He glances up when we enter and a smile crawls over his handsome face. Conrad looks exactly the way you would expect Amory's cousin to look.

Brown hair so dark it's almost black, smooth pale skin, sharp grey eyes, a square jaw. He's nice to look at, but not as handsome as Amy—or as tall. He looks *up* at his cousin as they shake hands, and when he turns to me, pulling me close to kiss both my cheeks, I can see the scar on his chin that mars his otherwise impressive beard.

"Welcome," he says in a German accent that's thicker than Amory's.

I smile back and take my seat beside my husband. Any nerves I had before dissolve as Gisela dishes out food and sits across from me with her big, flashy smile. Since our husbands remain locked in conversation during the appetizers and main course, we are forced to giggle and smile at each other at the proper intervals until Conrad sets down his fork and eyes me closely.

"Rosa, how are you settling in? Is married life treating you well?"

I'm not sure how to answer that. I could be honest and say I was better off being locked up in my brother's penthouse— but that would only be partially true. I couldn't even leave my

234

bedroom in Gio's home, at least with Amory I have the house all to myself. Except with Amory there is an ever-present threat to our relationship that's slowly getting beyond our control. And the fact that most of our problems center on the lack of *love* in our love life makes everything that much more complicated.

I stare at my plate, pushing around my rice and grilled veggies as I reply, "I think I'm settling in okay."

Amory shifts closer to me. I'm not sure if it's a warning or an act of comfort but it makes me nervous all the same. When I look up and find him gazing down at me, my anxiety fizzles into anger. The look on his face is not anger or shock, it's gratitude.

To think that I would ever try to cover up the failure of our marriage to protect his reputation makes me burn. He hasn't cared at all about me or *my* reputation since we met. He hasn't even tried to speak to me since our wedding night.

"I think I'd be settling in better if Amy was around more," I add to my statement. "In fact, this is our first date since we got married."

My confession earns me two pairs of raised eyebrows from Conrad and Gisela. But Amory's brows have flattened on his forehead, edging away his previous gratitude.

Silence storms through the room as we all glance at each other. I look at Gisela who nervously glances at Conrad who smirks at his cousin. Amory's gaze is fixed on his plate, like he's thinking deeply, trying to figure out how to escape the unease swelling around us.

"Where have you been, cousin?" Conrad says with a bit of humor on his tongue. "Sounds like you've got a needy wife who misses you."

I don't like the way he says *needy*, but I don't comment on it. I feel like I've said enough for the night.

Amory finally tears his vision from his plate. He takes a deep breath and scoots half an inch away from me. It could easily be seen as an adjustment in his chair, shifting to focus on his cousin, but I catch the movement and I know what it means. Amory doesn't want to be near me anymore. He's angry.

Well, so am I, I think, fighting the urge to cross my arms like a petulant little girl.

"I've been working," Amy says flatly.

"Business has been difficult lately." Conrad nods.

"Especially since the wedding." Amory's voice edges on anger and I know that statement was directed at me.

"Giovanni stuck you with all the failing businesses, eh?"

Failing businesses?

Conrad laughs but Amory doesn't. He casts a subtle glance at me, which Conny catches right away and then clears his throat.

"Babe, why don't you get dessert?"

Gisela nods and reaches across the table for my hand. "Help me out, sweetie? Carrying four plates of pie by myself isn't easy."

Like a good little mafia wife, I stand and follow her to the kitchen. Once we're inside, Gisela kicks her heels off and goes straight for the fridge, completely ignoring the blueberry pie on display in the middle of the pristine white countertop.

"Drink?" she asks over her shoulder. "Conny likes beer when he's eating something sweet. Weirdo."

I shake my head, though I know she doesn't see the action with her back facing me. "I don't drink."

"That makes two of us." Gisela giggles as she turns and catches the shocked look on my face. "What? You think you've got a monopoly on manners and good behavior, *Christian* girl?"

I roll my eyes. "How do you know I'm Christian?"

She nods at the crucifix around my neck as she sets down a pitcher of what I assume is lemon iced tea. My hand instinctively goes to the jewelry. It was a gift from Melissa, the only thing I have left from that part of my life. Other than my faith itself.

"Oh," I whisper, watching Gisela pour me a glass.

She slides it across the table to me and takes a sip from her own glass. "Plus, you're dressed like some lonely woman fresh from Bible study." She motions to my blouse. "Those buttons are making me sad."

"They're making me sad, too," I mumble, moving to unbutton the first three.

With a long sigh, Gisela sets down the cup and swipes her bangs to the side, black nails clawing at her face. "You look nice for a Christian girl."

"You say that almost like it's an insult."

She holds her hands up in defense. "I would never make fun of my own beliefs."

Is Gisela …?

She nods, confirming my thoughts. "You're not the only Christian in the mafia."

I don't speak, because the first response that pops into my head is too judgmental for me to share.

She doesn't *look* Christian at all.

Gisela must be able to read minds because she tosses her head back and laughs loudly. I see a flash of silver in her mouth and realize her tongue is pierced.

"Sweetheart," she says, "we come in all shapes, sizes, colors, and *style*."

I take a dramatic look at her. At her heavy makeup, her long fake nails, her big fake boobs with the diamond stuck in her cleavage.

"What?" she asks sincerely.

"I—I just … well—"

She sighs. "I know my clothes are a bit much, but I wouldn't dress this way in church, okay? Right now, I'm in my home, having dinner with my husband and extended family." She shrugs. "I can let my hair down today."

I don't comment on the fact that she seemed intent on catching my husband's eye when we first arrived—which wasn't a very Christian thing to do, but whatever.

Gisela leans against the counter, her expression turning serious. "No matter how I dress, I know what's in my heart. And God does, too. There is a place for women like us in this environment, Rosa. You don't have to compromise your faith. I sure don't."

I chew the inside of my cheek. "Does Conrad believe, too?"

For a moment, she just watches me, then she lowers her head and says, "He believes in God. But he isn't committed."

"Does it affect your marriage?"

"Of course it does," she says earnestly. "How could it not? We are *fundamentally* different from each other."

"How did you manage to stay with him and get along, despite your differences?" I can't help thinking of how horrible things have been in my own marriage.

She laughs, though it sounds sad and longing. "We don't always get along. In fact, if I could have left like you and found myself a Christian man, I would have. But this is my cup. I know it was a mistake to marry outside the faith, but I'm in it now. Short of divorce, all I can do is feed Conny the Word and let God do the rest." She shrugs. "The Lord changes me more and more every day. I know He can do the same for my husband."

"I don't know if I can do that for mine," I mumble. "Even though I think it's what God wants me to do. I just don't know how."

"I used to wonder the same thing," Gisela admits. "The Bible is clear on Christians marrying other Christians. But what do I do if I make the mistake of marrying outside the Faith? What happens if one spouse gets saved before the other?" She raises her eyebrows like she's waiting for an answer. "Praying about this issue brought me to First Peter."

I press my lips together, trying to remember what the Book

of I Peter says.

"For women in our predicament," Gisela explains, "the Bible doesn't tell us to divorce our unsaved husbands. It tells us to focus on God so that our spouses will be won over by our behavior. In other words, we lead by example."

That makes me feel a bit better. Maybe instead of fighting Amory, I can show him what it means to be a Christian wife—and how much better it is versus being a mafia wife.

"Thank you," I tell Gisela.

She winks and steps back into her heels, then click-clacks to the cupboards and grabs plates for the pie. "Don't worry about it."

"I thought my marriage was doomed," I admit with a nervous sigh. "It was like the more I prayed the worse it got."

She smiles, setting a thick slice of pie on a plate. "Now your prayers have been answered."

"They have. Things will be different with Amory if I try a different approach."

"A different approach," she repeats with a naughty grin on her face. "Like maybe giving him a little *something-something* tonight?"

I take a very deep breath. Sex isn't as simple as stripping down and getting it on. Not for me. I can't just lay with someone I'm not in love with—let alone the fact that I barely know Amory.

I'm trying to figure out a way to explain this to Gisela when she passes me a plate of pie and says, "Come on, girl. It's been a month and you still haven't given it up. He's your husband!

Sex with him isn't a sin." She leans closer to me, her boobs coming dangerously close to brushing the crust of her pie. "Don't you want to know what it's like?"

I can't answer. Not because I'm embarrassed or too holy for this sort of talk—I can't answer because I don't understand how Gisela knows I'm still a virgin.

"He told you..." I whisper, my heart breaking. "Amory told you we haven't slept together."

Gisela straightens and clutches her heart. "Oh, sweetie..."

Betrayal is the only thing I feel. Not anger, not disappointment, not even frustration. I am utterly betrayed. There is a line, a barrier of privacy and intimacy, you simply do not cross as a married couple. That means not giving details of your love life to people who aren't involved in it. At least that's the moral code I have decided to live by as a wife. Apparently, Amory doesn't feel the same.

"Why did he tell you?" I ask Gisela, and then it hits me. "Is this his way of getting me to sleep with him? Did he bring me here so you can convince me to climb into his bed tonight?"

Before she can answer, I whirl around and march back into the dining room, betrayal turning into anger, edging on rage.

"Your little plan didn't work," I hiss, rounding the corner.

Amory's brows crinkle, but I'm yelling before he can utter a response.

"You think some girl-talk and pie is going to get me in bed with you?"

Conrad coughs, earning a quick glance from Amory.

"What?" I snap. "It's only okay for you to tell people about

241

our sex life but not me?"

"That's enough," Amory says darkly. He rises from his chair and buttons his suit jacket. There is a sense of calm to him that seems to amplify my anger. His smooth demeaner, the way he turns to pat his cousin on the shoulder, muttering goodnight. How he calmly waves goodbye to Gisela who's cowering by the kitchen entrance. His calm makes me feel so childish and petty that I want to tear my hair out and scream. But that will only make me look worse, so I hold my tongue as he walks over to me and places his hand on my shoulder.

"My wife is tired," he announces, his eyes locked with mine. "Thank you for dinner, but we won't be staying for dessert."

No one speaks as I am escorted through the house; once we're on the porch, I pull my arm away and pivot so I can look Amory in the eye but he's already brushing past me like he doesn't care what I have to say.

I yell at his back. "How dare you! How could you tell Gisela?"

Calmly, Amory waves off Douglass and opens the car door himself. "Get inside."

"No."

He shrugs and ducks to get in. "Then walk home."

With a huff, I march down the stairs and slide into the car, making it a point to slam my door as hard as I can. Amory is unfazed. He's already on his phone, scrolling messages and sending emails—probably about the failing businesses he inherited through his marital contract with my brother.

I don't have time to wonder how some of the De Luca businesses could be failing; I need to know why my husband has betrayed our privacy.

"Did you really think having Gisela talk to me would get me in bed with you?" I spew venom as I speak, taking at least thirty minutes to chew him out on how I value my privacy. Amory says nothing through all of this, which only makes me more furious as we ride through the city. By the time we reach the house, I'm fuming.

"And having Gisela give me that little 'Christian lady' spiel in the kitchen—*really*?" For all I know, she could have made everything up—she might not be Christian at all. "Are you that desperate to get laid?" I nearly shout.

For the first time, Amory glances up from his phone. His eyes are pools of a rage so carefully contained, I shudder as I stare into them. Grey orbs of flowing anger and emotion stare back, they are paired with a clenched jaw and heavy eyebrows that have flattened into one dark line.

His voice is threatening. "Are you done?"

I don't answer.

"I spoke to Conrad about our sex life because I didn't know what else to do," he explains with a mirthless chuckle. "I've even started reading the Bible because I'm so confused, I have no clue where else to turn."

My jaw hangs open. Amy's been reading the Bible?

"First, you agree to behave and then run away *days* later. After I get you back, you agree to behave *again* and then swiftly remind me that behaving is not the same as getting along. You won't have sex with me—fine—I'm not going to force you to, but I am going to try to find out why, Rosa. That's why I spoke to Conrad about everything. And that's why I brought you to his house for dinner. He suggested we go on a date to make things easier for you. Exactly what you suggested earlier."

I ... don't know how to respond.

Amy sighs, but it sounds more like a hiss. "You embarrassed me today."

"I'm sorry," I say quietly.

"I forgive you." He opens his car door. "But you will be punished for it."

Punished?

Before I can ask what he means, he walks around the car and opens my door. "Get out."

I shake my head. "No."

"Rosa—"

"You promised not to hurt me."

"And you promised to behave." He dips his head and from this angle, half his face is bathed in moonlight, the other half is covered in shadows. It's a hauntingly beautiful sight. "It isn't fair that you keep breaking your promises when I've never broken a single one, is it?" he asks.

"I'm not going inside with you."

He laughs. "Not by choice." And in one swift motion, he grabs my wrist and hauls me out the car and over his shoulder.

I kick and scream as he marches to the front door. "Let me go!" I shout, pounding my fists on his back.

"That's *enough*, Rosa," he says in an annoyed voice. Then I

feel a swift swack to my bottom and I freeze. Did he just ...
spank me?

Amory's chuckle fills the corridor as he enters the house and walks toward the staircase. "Not that it hurts," he says, adjusting me on his shoulder, "but if you keep hitting me, I will hit you back."

There's another slap to my butt, sharp enough to make me yelp.

"I didn't hit you again!" I cry.

He hums. "I know. That was for my own pleasure."

I go limp on his shoulder, slightly amazed by how easily he carries me around. Then I realize we're halfway up the stairs and I exhale a question. "Where are you taking me?"

"To my room," he answers.

"For what?"

A very dark yet charming laugh vibrates through his chest, a hand slides up my skirt to squeeze my upper thigh. "You'll see when we get there."

Terror seizes my heart. Every dirty scene from every dirty romance I've ever read rips through my mind, sending me into a panic. I cannot let Amory take me to his room.

With a gasp, I reach for the handrail and cry, "Let me go!" My fingers grasp wood and I latch on, yanking hard.

Amory curses, and I feel gravity shift as we teeter and then topple backwards down the stairs. I should have taken the brunt of the fall, but when I open my eyes, I realize Amy has shifted his body and I've landed on top of him at the base of the steps.

He groans and then snaps his eyes open; they instantly lock on me. The rage he'd exuded in the car is on his face again, but this time it is not controlled. His lips pull back into a snarl as he hisses, "You little—"

I bolt.

I haven't even registered the fact that I'm sprinting up the stairs until I reach for the rail and use it to propel myself around the corner without losing momentum. Amory is not far behind. His heavy footsteps tear down the hall, echoing off the walls as he chases me.

I am running for my life through my own home from my own husband. I have no idea what he plans to do when he catches me, but I plan to never find out. I steal a glance over my shoulder as I round another corner, using the stone statue to boost me so I don't lose any speed. Amory does not follow my tactic and ends up skittering across the tiles and slamming into the door. It happens to be the door to the library, one of the few rooms left unlocked in this house, so when his body rams against it, the force knocks the door open, and he falls inside.

That gives me the extra few seconds I need to get away. But I halt when I realize Amory isn't chasing me anymore. For one dreadful moment, I think he hurt himself when he fell into the library, and then ... over the pounding of my heart, I hear footsteps.

Slow, deliberate steps carry my husband down the hall. His shadow appears before he does, like a phantom coming after me.

"Rosa…" his voice sends a chill down my spine.

I turn and start running again. I need to find my room. I need to get away.

The sound of Amory's footsteps never ceases. He might as well have been slamming bricks onto the tile with how loud they are. I cannot hear anything but his slow, torturous pace. He follows me through the house, somehow knowing exactly where I'm going, which room I'm going to duck into in search of a shortcut, which way I will run after turning a corner.

All the while, he never picks up his steps or slows down.

"Rosa…" he says again, but I'm finally at my door and I don't hesitate to shove it open and then slam it behind me.

I nearly burst into tears when I click the lock into place, heart pounding, chest heaving. Even though every part of me wants to lock myself in my closet for extra protection, I can't get my feet to move. I stand there and listen for the sound of Amory's footsteps, but I no longer hear them.

In his anger, I'd expected my husband to kick down my door and burst inside to deliver my *punishment*. But he never does. For thirty minutes, I stand and listen—even pressing my ear to the door—but he never comes.

I am left alone. Safe. But alone once again.

Chapter Twenty

The next day, I avoid leaving my room at all costs. I shower, write notes in my journal, finish the mystery novel I've been reading, and then I walk circles in my room. My growling stomach keeps trying to convince me to go down to the dining room, but my heart and my mind know better.

What happened last night?

I can't make any sense of it.

Amory chased me through the house in a fit of rage. I will admit I pushed him to that rage, but … what was he going to do once he'd caught me? I don't want to know. I don't want to think about it, but my mind keeps drifting back to the outrage on his face when we first crashed to the bottom of the stairs. My brain keeps replaying the sound of his haunting voice as he'd called my name, the echo of his footsteps as he'd followed me through the mansion.

That was not Amory—not *my* Amory. Not Amy.

That was the underboss, son of Uwe Jäger. The same man who sent a henchman after his own wife.

Have Amory and I fallen to that level? Are we beyond repair now?

I shake my head and rub at my arms as I hug myself. Father Serrano's words whisper through my memories. *God wants this city back....*

And He plans to use Amory to do it.

Whatever state we're in right now is temporary. It will get better. It has to. The salvation of New York relies on this. And not just New York. Arthur might have lied and turned his back on me and God, but he'd been telling the truth about the mafia. Their influence stretches far beyond the Big Apple. They might even have a grip on the entire country.

That's got to stop.

Amory can stop it. A Christian underboss would ruin the mafia from the inside out. But before we get there, we've got to first save our marriage.

Ignoring the pangs in my stomach, I pull up the Bible app on my phone and grab my journal. I sit at my desk as I scroll through chapters to find the scripture Gisela mentioned last night. A swirl of guilt hits me hard. I had accused Gisela of lying to me, of not even being a Believer to begin with. And then Amory told me the truth, that she wasn't part of some grand scheme to get me in bed. And that he'd only been doing what I'm doing now. Trying to find a way to save our marriage.

I had judged Gisela. Mostly because of the way she was dressed. And also because I was angry, but the reason behind it doesn't matter. She didn't deserve to have her salvation questioned by me. I might not have chased her screaming through the house, but my actions toward her weren't any less insulting than what Amory did to me last night.

We're just alike, I realize with a painful gasp.

We both jump to conclusions. We never give each other the time or the chance to explain. We both judge others. We both lose our tempers and end up doing ridiculous things. I ruined our first date as a married couple and Amory ruined the night.

"We're a horrible pair." I laugh bitterly.

All this time I thought Amory wasn't good enough for me when, in fact, we were made for each other. Perfectly imperfect.

"So how do I fix this?" I ask the Lord. "How do I lead by example?"

I know I won't find the answer overnight, but, glancing down at the Bible app, I know I will find it here.

Hours pass. I read and write until my eyes blur, and I feel like I'm going to pass out from hunger. I haven't eaten all day or left my room.

With a groan, I stand and stretch my horribly sore limbs. My nerves race through the roof when I finish and stare at my still-locked door. I don't want to leave, but I won't get food any other way.

The house is quiet. My bare feet make no noise as I make

my way to the dining room. Amory has staff somewhere inside. I've never seen them, but I have heard them vacuuming nonexistent dust in other rooms and mopping the already immaculate floors in the hall. An array of food is always set out in the dining room for breakfast, lunch, and dinner. A small buffet of German, Italian, and Soul food for each meal. I don't know if the gesture is the chef's idea or Amory's, but I appreciate it, nonetheless.

Today, there is no buffet waiting for me in the dining room. Instead, there's a man in a suit standing by the table wearing an apron. He freezes when I walk inside and then lets his features settle into a tense smile.

"Mrs. Jäger, are you ready for dinner?" he asks.

"Yes," I answer, staring in surprise. "Is something going on?"

He laughs and then moves toward the door like he's in a hurry. "Just a moment."

I take a seat at the table and decide to count the silverware just to keep myself distracted. Thankfully, I'm not left alone for long. True to his word, the chef returns in a moment, opening the large dining room doors to let in my husband.

Amory spies me at the table and presses his lips together in a very thin line. Then he walks over and sits across from me, places his napkin over his lap, and swallows thickly. "Ready for dinner?"

I blink. Did I miss something?

"I didn't know we had plans," I say.

He shakes his head. "We didn't. I was waiting for you to

come down and eat."

"All day?" I gape, noticing his loose tie and ruffled hair. He looks like he just walked in from a long day at work or just rolled out of bed from an extremely long nap.

"I didn't think you'd come out if I knocked on the door."

"Yeah..."

He stares at the tablecloth, fiddling with the silver fork by his empty plate. "I'm ... I'm sorry for last night, Rosa. I shouldn't have behaved that way."

"I'm sorry, too."

"No," his voice is deep and raspy. "I was way out of line." He leans forward and places his elbows on the table, buries his face in his large hands. "After I promised I would never hurt you."

"You didn't hurt me." I frown, somewhat shocked at how personally he's taking this.

"Not physically," he says through his fingers. "But I know I scared you. I know I'm the reason you didn't come out to eat at all today."

How does he know this?

As if he's read my mind, Amory lowers his hands and sighs. "I stayed home from work. Waiting for the chance to speak with you."

Wow. The man couldn't find the time for me the day after our wedding, but now he's skipping work for a *chance* to speak with me? I prayed things would turn around, but I have to admit, I wasn't expecting a turnaround this fast.

Thank you, Lord, I pray inside. Then I study Amory a

moment, trying to plan out my next words. I have to take responsibility for my actions, too.

"You're being too hard on yourself. I interrupted dinner and embarrassed you in front of your cousin. I accused you of hitching up a plan just to lure me to bed. And then I threw us down a flight of stairs." I chuckle. "So, it's not like you were angry for no reason."

"But did I have the right to chase you through the house?"

"Did I have the right to do any of the things I did last night?"

He holds my gaze, that Jäger stubbornness refusing to allow him to lose even in this foolish spat.

I smile, defusing him a moment. "Fine. You were a big jerk. Is that what you want to hear?"

"No," he grumbles. "I don't know what I want anymore."

"Well, I want us to get along."

His eyes narrow into slits. "I've been trying to get us to do that since before we got married."

"And now I'm trying, too. I promise."

He holds up a hand. "I'm not asking for any more promises from you because it inevitably leads to you breaking them. Like it's a goal or something."

I cover my mouth to laugh which makes him quirk an eyebrow. Some of the tension in the room chips away as he smiles, and it feels like a weight has been lifted from both our shoulders.

"I'm normally not this bad at keeping my promises," I say sheepishly.

He rolls his grey eyes, but there is humor in his voice as he says, "I don't believe a word you say."

I want to shoot back a witty response, but the doors behind us open and the chef returns with a cart and two trays. He wheels the food over to us and then serves two cheeseburgers and a load of fries.

I actually snort in laughter, glancing up to find Amory watching me. There is a look of uncertainty in his eyes, but it's washed away as I laugh like a dork and nod at the food.

"Cheeseburgers?"

He shrugs one shoulder. "I had a craving. And ... I thought this would be more casual than last night. More relaxing."

I pick up a fry. "Is this a date?"

"Will you run off to your room if I say yes?"

I almost snort again. "Not unless you start chasing me."

He leans forward, palming the back of his neck. For a second, I think he's going to apologize once more, but he seems to change his mind at the last moment and says instead, "How was your day?"

I don't believe what I'm hearing. Amory is actually spending time with me. Trying to get to know me.

"I spent the day reading and taking notes."

"Reading what?"

"The Bible."

He pauses, his mouth full of cheeseburger. After gulping down half his glass of Coke, he clears his throat and replies, "What did you learn?"

I don't realize I'm holding my breath until I exhale everything in my lungs. I had almost expected Amory to make a joke about me reading the Bible, but the look on his face seems genuinely interested. He did say he'd been reading it himself lately.

I set down my fries, wipe the salt from my fingers, and reach across the table. "Actually, let me show you. It's something I learned a while ago. When I was with my church family in Norman."

He gives me a puzzled expression but drops his food and takes my hands anyway.

I bow my head and begin to pray. "Dear Heavenly Father, thank You for this food You've given us. Forgive us for our sins, Lord, and also forgive us for starting to eat without saying a blessing first." I laugh. "Thank You for moving in our lives and giving our marriage another chance. Bless the food we eat and the chef who prepared it for us. In Jesus' name I pray, amen."

When I look up, Amory is watching me. He retracts his hands and reaches for his burger again. "Do you do that before every meal?"

I nod. "At least I try to. Sometimes I forget."

He laughs which makes me blush. "When we eat together, I'll try to remind you to pray. For both of us."

"Thanks," I say quietly.

My nerves get the better of me and I fall silent for most of the main course. Amory doesn't seem to mind the quiet, he's busy stuffing his face so hard I start to wonder if he waited to

255

eat all day, too. I contemplate asking him about it but decide against it, unsure if his answer will make me feel guilty or not.

When dessert is served, I laugh again. It's a vanilla ice cream cone. Mine has sprinkles; Amory's is plain.

"This is kind of perfect," I say.

Amory lets go of a sigh. "I really wasn't sure what you'd think of the food."

"I grew up eating at five-star restaurants. Burgers, fries, and ice cream is a welcome change."

"What about pizza?"

"As long as it's four-cheese."

His eyes double in size. "No toppings?"

I shake my head. "I love plain cheese pizza. Toppings are an insult."

He snorts so hard ice cream flies from his mouth. I erupt into a fit of laughs which makes him turn red with embarrassment, but I can't help it.

"Sorry," he mutters, dabbing his mouth with a napkin.

"Don't apologize." I lick my ice cream. "It was funny. But now I've *got* to know, what's your favorite pizza topping?"

He grins. "Ham and pineapple."

"You're a monster!"

He lifts his shoulders, cheeks dimpling as he tries to hold back his laugh. "It tastes good. I can't help it."

When our laughing fades, we're left in a very awkward silence. I can't even get myself to look at Amory because I know he's watching me. Those grey eyes focused so sharply, staring like I'm the only woman in the world.

I hear movement and realize he's standing now. He walks over to me, hand extended. "Come with me."

I let him guide me from the dining room to a sitting room with a sofa and fireplace. It's too warm to use the fireplace, so he turns on the lamp by the bookshelf in the corner, it casts a red hue over the room the way the fireplace would have.

"I have something for you," he says when I settle on the couch beside him.

My eyebrows shoot to the top of my head. I don't have an apology gift. Then again, I didn't expect to eat dinner with Amy or join him afterward for … whatever this is.

Amory produces a small box from his pocket and holds it out to me. I take it and hesitantly open it. I'm already wearing a wedding ring, so I'm honestly unsure what to expect, but my breath leaves me when I realize what it is.

A rose-shaped hairpin.

Everything falls into place. The cheeseburgers, the vanilla ice cream cone, and now the rose-shaped pin. He's recreated our fateful day together ten years ago. We walked through the park, had lunch at a greasy burger place, then he bought me an ice cream, and we went window shopping on the strip. I spotted the hairpin on display at Tiffany's, totally unaware of how expensive it was, but Amy had bought it for me anyway. Like it had cost two dollars.

I can't stop the tears from swelling in my eyes. My hand clutches at my chest as I very clumsily suck for air—an attempt to keep myself from crying.

Amory smiles beside me. "I'm guessing you figured it out

now."

I nod, practically blinded by my tears. One blink and they all go racing down my cheeks, dripping from my chin. Amy wipes them away and pulls me into a hug. "I know I said I wouldn't do this," he whispers into my hair. "But there's one last promise."

I nod, face rubbing against his shirt. I can smell his masculine cologne up close; it leaves me dizzy and gasping for a whole different reason. I've never noticed how firm his chest is, never realized how broad his shoulders, or strong his arms as he wraps me in them. We've never been this close before—yes, we have kissed, quite passionately, but we've never been *intimate*. We've never shared an emotional moment—well a moment where the emotion wasn't blaring anger.

This is different, and it scares the living daylights out of me.

"Promise we'll never give up," he says. "No matter how bad it gets between us."

I can't promise that I'll be a quiet little mafia wife. I can't promise that I'll just sit back and not ask questions or challenge Amory to be the man I know he can be. But I can promise that I will fight for this—for the man I know he can become, and the wife I know I'm meant to be.

I pull away to wipe at my tears, whispering, "I—"

Promise would have been my next word, but Amory's lips cover my own and I'm instantly silenced. My eyes flutter shut as my barrier is broken and I melt into his embrace. He moans into my mouth as he deepens the kiss, pulling me into his lap, pawing at my clothes like a starved animal. The desperation in our exchange restores my resolve, and I pull away, wiping at my mouth.

"Wait, Amy—"

"For what?" he murmurs, dipping his head to kiss my neck. His lips brush against the tender skin, sending tingles over my body.

I shiver. "I—I'm—" He adjusts me on his lap, and I suck in a sharp breath as I feel something press against my inner thigh.

Amory chuckles at my surprise. "See what you do to me?" he asks huskily, leaning in to kiss me again.

His hands go under my dress, and I grab his wrists in a panic, blurting, "I'm on my period!"

Amory stills.

The room is silent for an eternity with us just sitting there, unsure what to do next. I hear the crinkling of leather as he leans back into the couch. His hands go limp in my grasp, and I release his wrists, letting his arms drop to his sides.

He sighs. "You're on your period."

I nod, unable to meet his gaze because I'm afraid he'll know I'm lying.

All at once, the room tilts and I'm thrown on my back and my dress is flying up all around me. Amory has laid me out on the couch and thrown my skirts up, exposing my underwear. He uses a finger to snap the band on my lacy panties.

"If I pull these down and check, will I find a tampon?"

My eyebrows lower, my teeth grind together, I let out a low

growl—as bold as I've ever been. "You wouldn't dare."

Amory laughs like my anger means nothing to him. "I wouldn't." He pulls my dress back down. "But I'm also not going to let you off the hook that easily, Rosa." Before I can reply, he scoops me into his arms and walks out the sitting room, headed toward the stairs.

"Hey!" I shout, wriggling in his grasp.

He holds me close to his chest. "Calm down."

"Where are you taking me?"

"To my room."

Another stroke of terror shoots through me, but this one is not as frightening as the last.

"What's going to happen when we get there?" I ask.

I can hear the rumble of his laugh in his chest. "You'll see."

If Amory's house is a fortress, his bedroom is a dark chamber. Everything is matte black, the spread on his bed, the curtains over his floor-to-ceiling windows, the thick carpeting, the massive wardrobe and dresser.

Even after he sets me on the bed and flicks on the lights, the room still feels somewhat dark. Like all the black is sucking away the light. I blink around the room in awe; it's beautifully decorated, in a very simplistic, manly sort of way. I had no expectations before entering, so I'm not exactly surprised, but I am impressed.

The rustle of clothing catches my attention and my eyes snap to my husband across the room. He's standing at his wardrobe, getting undressed.

"What are you doing?" I ask, narrowing my eyes.

"Changing into my pajamas," he says matter-of-factly. He turns and pulls off his shirt and I realize with a start that he's tatted.

Bold designs cover his back, wrapping around his torso and shoulders. He has quarter-length sleeves on both arms, tattoos ending just below the elbow so he can roll up his shirt without revealing his gang affiliation. There's a bullseye tattooed onto his chest, right over his heart, with thick black markings crawling over the rest of his ribs and dipping below the hem of his black boxers.

Amory clears his throat and I realize I've been staring. With my mouth open.

"Like what you see?"

My jaw snaps shut. "I just didn't know you had all those."

"Well, you would have known on our wedding night," he shrugs, "but you sent me away."

"Did you bring me here to finish what you started?"

He laughs, but it's unkind and teasing. "I brought you hear to *sleep*, Rosa. It's late and I'm going in to work tomorrow. Which means I've got to get up early."

I choose not to remind him that he'd still be wide awake and busy if I hadn't told him I'm on my monthly.

The bed shifts as Amy tosses the covers back and climbs in. He reaches for me, and I fight him, but he's so much stronger. I end up pressed against him, my back to his chest so he can spoon me. I've never been held like this before, so I

261

shift and wriggle, trying to get away and get comfortable at the same time. I'm torn between the awkward urge to flee and the aching desire to stay.

"Stop squirming," Amory says, voice muffled by my curly hair puffed in his face.

"I—" I don't want to tell him that his nearness is making me blush and sweat and shiver. "I don't have any pajamas," I mutter. "It's hard to get comfy."

He sighs and then the room gets cold as his warmth suddenly leaves. He stands and goes back to his dresser. Something lands on my head, and I snatch it away to find one of Amy's shirts. He'd tossed it to me.

"You can wear that for now," he says, returning to the bed.

"Why can't I just go get my own pajamas?"

"Because if you leave this room, you won't come back."

He's right about that. But tonight was a good night, all things considered, and it's not like snuggling with my husband is bad. I don't want to ruin things. Again. So I change into the shirt and leave my dress on the floor. I do it with my back toward Amory, too embarrassed to face him as he watches me like a hawk.

Strong arms return when I climb back into bed. Again, I start squirming around, feeling awkward in this strange new position.

"*Rosa*," Amory says sharply. "I'm actually trying to sleep."

"So am I," I say.

"Doesn't seem like it."

"Do we have to sleep so close?"

As if to prove some point, he wraps his arms tighter around me and presses a kiss to the back of my neck. "I think we're fine just like this."

"Amy—"

"Rosa." His voice is annoyed. "Just let me hold you for one night. I'm your husband, I shouldn't have to beg to spoon you."

Spoon, the childish part of me almost giggles at the word.

Amory adjusts so I'm totally wrapped up in his arms. "Doesn't this feel good?"

It does. But I'm too embarrassed to admit it. A lifetime of being hammered over the head with abstinence, modesty, and purity has left me crippled. I never had a problem waiting for marriage, but now that I *am* married, I have no idea what to do.

My teachers, parents, and elders made sure to teach me the importance of being chaste, but no one offered any insight on what comes afterward. Once the vows have been spoken and the bride has been kissed. How do I handle myself then?

I've spent my life being 'good' and 'innocent,' now, all at once, I'm expected to just drop my drawers and bend over backwards for my husband like some porn star?

I can pretend all this discomfort is because there is no love between us, but the truth is that I don't know how to enjoy this simple moment. I don't know how to be a wife. I don't know how to move forward from this.

"You think too much," Amory speaks into my thoughts.

I gasp, unaware of how long I've been staring into the darkness.

"Just relax and close your eyes," he says, voice low and tired.

"How do I know you won't try anything while I'm asleep?"

His laugh sounds like he's half asleep already. "I'm a gentleman. And I'm also too exhausted to try anything."

He must be telling the truth because moments later, I hear his soft snoring and it sets me at ease. He'd meant what he'd said. He brought me here to sleep. Nothing more. So I close my eyes and try not to focus on how weird this feels. Instead, I think of everything that's right with it. How warm it is against his body, how firm his chest feels pressed against my backside, how large his hands are as they hold me close.

It isn't long before I drift off, too.

When I blink back into the realm of consciousness, Amory's arms are still around me. I inhale deeply and shift against him, which must wake him up because he groans and starts to move his arms. I think he's pulling away until I'm pressed against his chest again.

"Good morning, Rosa."

I squirm, trying to get away. "Let me go now, Amory."

"Keep moving just like that," he says with a laugh dancing through his words.

I freeze as I notice something hard pressed against my lower back. A heartbeat of silence passes through the room, and then I shriek and jerk forward, breaking free of Amy's grasp to scoot halfway across the bed.

"What's wrong with you!" I shout, clutching the blankets to my chest—despite being fully clothed in his giant t-shirt.

Amory scowls at me. "Calm down. It's only there because it's the morning. It has nothing to do with you."

"Yeah right," I grumble. "You've been trying to get me in bed since we met."

He scoffs. "Get over yourself, darling."

I glare at him. "It's the truth."

"I want you. Yes. But that's because you're my *wife* and I'm attracted to you. Not because you're some hot little piece." He tosses the covers back and marches toward the bathroom, not caring to hide the very obvious swelling in his underwear. He stops and leans against the frame of his bathroom door. There is no hatred on his face—there's barely any anger. But there is plenty of humor. Like he's mocking me.

His words come out edged with bitterness, but he covers it with a dark laugh. "You think I haven't had better sex than what you can offer? You're a virgin. That makes you tight, but it doesn't make you good in bed. I know for a fact you won't be the best screw of my life."

My heart turns brittle at his words. We're actually having a fight right now. About how good I am in bed. Or, apparently, how *bad* I am in bed.

This isn't even fair! I've never had sex before. How can he make this comparison?

"If I'm so bad at sex, then why are you trying so hard to get it from me?" I clench the covers as I try to temper my emotions. Anger, embarrassment, and confusion fight for control. No matter which one wins, I feel like I'm going to cry. I've never felt so humiliated in my life … But Amory doesn't need to know that. I don't have to give him the satisfaction of seeing how upset he's made me.

"We've still got to consummate the marriage," his voice is like ice sending chills over me. "Until it's sealed in blood, the contract I have with your brother is just words on paper. Wet ink that won't dry until red is added to the mix."

"So it's about money," I say, dropping my gaze. "How much is our marriage worth?"

There is a heavy pause and for a moment I think Amy might return to the man who had dinner with me last night. I think he might tell me he was only kidding and that he'd spoken out of anger. I think everything might go back to the way they were just eight hours ago. But none of that happens. Amory simply goes into his bathroom and shuts the door behind him.

Chapter Twenty-One

I can't begin to describe how messed up things have been lately. The things I said to Rosa ... They weren't the kindest words I've ever spoken; I will admit that. And I'll admit I should apologize, but my stubbornness won't let me. I let my anger get the best of me and in a moment of bitter rejection, I opened my mouth without thinking.

The insults I spewed at Rosa leaves a fire burning between us for three weeks. We immediately fall back into the same miserable routine we'd been going through before that horrible night. Avoiding each other at all costs.

Most days, I wake up first. I go for a run and then spend an hour lifting weights or trying to murder my punching bag—lately I've been favoring the punching bag, leaving my knuckles raw and bloody by the time I'm done. Then I shower, eat breakfast, and head to my first meeting. All of that is done in the dark hours of the morning before my brooding wife awakens.

We have gotten used to living our separate lives, despite sharing a home together. Sometimes it feels like things are better this way, like the raging storm of fire has somehow calmed to just a few dying embers.

We have both given up.

I know it cannot go on like this forever, but whenever I think about trying to make things better, I am reminded of how many times I've tried to do that already and just ended up getting rejected. I am tired of being cast aside by my own wife. I am tired of being tangled up in her confusing mess of emotions. I am tired of being her emotional punching bag.

Which is why it's so messed up that I turned her into mine.

I won't forget the look of hurt and defeat on her face. How utterly dejected she appeared in the moments after my great outburst. I had closed myself off then. Refused to allow any remnant of guilt to pierce my dark heart because I was enjoying the sweet taste of vengeance. Rosa had rejected me twice by then—once on our wedding night and again with that pathetic lie about her period. It was finally time for her to know what it felt like to be denied and cast aside without a second thought.

Did I take things too far?

Yes. But I was pissed off and I couldn't take the words back once they'd left my mouth. No matter how much I regretted them. And now it's too late to try to fix things. I'm up to my neck with work and drama from my father, my brother, Gio, the Russians—things have only gotten worse since that terrible night. I don't have time to beg Rosa for her forgiveness. I haven't even forgiven myself.

I have not gone without punishment for the things I said to my wife. I don't know if I believe in Rosa's precious God yet, but there is one thing about Him I have read in the Bible that has always sent chills up my spine. He defends His own. And real or not, Rosa *is* a Child of God.

I have been nothing short of miserable and stressed since that night. Whether this is divine judgment or unfortunate circumstance, I don't know. But I'm not surprised when I step out the shower this morning and find eleven missed calls from six individuals. Vater, Conrad, Onkel—even Hans has called me, which immediately lets me know whatever is going on isn't good. What's more disturbing, however, is the fact that Wolfgang hasn't called me.

I stare at my phone an extra moment before deciding to dial Klaus's number first. He's my father's best friend and will be father-in-law to my cousin Petra in a matter of months. He also happens to be as fierce as Uwe and as levelheaded as Onkel Oberon. He seems the best person to call while I'm standing naked in my bathroom.

"*Na?*" I say when he answers.

Klaus breathes deeply for a moment, instantly setting my nerves on fire. "It's bad," he says.

"How bad?"

"The woman in the hospital—" *the one Wolfgang put his hands on?* "—she's awake."

"That's a good thing," I say, trying to be optimistic. Wolf had hurt her so badly she'd been in a coma since I dropped her off at the hospital. I still remember when I took Rosa to see the nameless woman; it was a tactic to scare her into submission. Show her that she could have been shackled to the abusive brother. Make her appreciate my kindness a little more.

Rosa had been so scared she'd agreed to behave again and had even said a prayer for the woman. I guess her prayers have been answered. Somehow, that's bad news for me.

"It's not a good thing at all," Klaus says with a sigh.

"I don't understand." Now that the woman is awake, we can find out who she is and get her back to her family, who's undoubtedly been looking for her for the past two months. I feel like we should be happy this lady has finally pulled through; now she won't be our problem anymore. But this is the mafia. Nothing is ever that easy or smooth for us. Especially not where my little brother is involved.

Klaus's voice is heavy and deep as he tells me, "She's Russian, Amory."

Ice runs through my veins, chilling every part of my body. I'm charging out my bathroom and searching for clothes before I can even process a plan. My only thought is to get to the hospital. Now.

The woman in the coma is Russian. And all this time, we never knew. She had been unrecognizable when I first brought her to the hospital. And since she was in a coma, she obviously couldn't talk, so we had no way of knowing or finding out her identity. Wolfgang should have told us. But I doubt he knew. My brother is a screwup, but even he wouldn't make the same mistake twice. Not a mistake like this.

We got away with it once, but Gio isn't here to hide evidence this time. Especially not since this woman is still alive to tell her story. My stomach starts to cramp up with anxiety as I shove my leg into my pants. Klaus was right. This is bad. No one else knows about what really happened to Sofia, but things between us and the Russians have been so tense lately, they are likely to start a war with us even if this hospital woman turns out to be no one significant within the Volkov mafia. They are desperate for an excuse to attack us, and Wolfgang might have just handed them one.

"What's the woman saying?" I ask desperately. "How do we know for certain she's Russian?"

"She woke up this morning around six o'clock. A nurse found her trying to get out of bed. She told the nurse everything that happened to her. How Wolf treated her that night."

"Who exactly is she?"

He breathes into the phone, taking long, heavy breaths. "I don't know. The Wolves showed up and took her away before our men could move in."

"What?" My heart hammers in my chest. They already know. They've already started making moves. "How did they find out so fast?"

"The nurse," Klaus answers. "I don't know what the Russian woman told her, but it was enough to get her to make a phone call to Mikhail himself. The hospital was flooded with Wolves less than an hour after the call was placed."

"You got her phone records?" I ask.

"Morgen's been collecting the data."

"And the nurse?"

Klaus curses. "We didn't find her. The Wolves likely took her just to keep us from getting to her."

Now it makes sense that Wolfgang is the only one who hasn't called me about this mess. This is *his* mess. Again. Of all the women in New York, he had to pick up another Russian. And nearly kill her. If the Wolves weren't after him, I'd kill the kid myself.

Speaking of my stupid brother. I yank a tie from the stand on my dresser and sling it over my neck as I leave my bedroom, I switch my phone off loudspeaker in case Rosa is around. This is the last thing I want her to hear. "Where is Wolfgang?"

"He's safe," Klaus assures me. "The Jägermeister had him sent to Stonehall."

Stonehall. A house that's been in my family since they first arrived in the United States from Germany over 100 years ago. It was only a tiny brick house when it was first purchased, but my great-great-grandfather turned it into the fortress it is today. It is one of our grandest homes, the place we use for major events like family reunions or weddings—ones that aren't rushed—or even the birth of an heir. It is big enough to draw attention to itself and should be the last place anyone will run off to if they want to hide, but its grandeur is also its greatest defense.

The Russians would be fools to think they could walk into the home of my ancestors. Stonehall is sacred ground for the Hunters of New York. It is our top priority when we are faced with threats of war. We can lose the diamonds, we can lose the businesses, but we will never surrender Stonehall. Uwe would rather die screaming than let it go, and I'd be bleeding out right beside him.

"Who's on his security?" I grunt to Klaus as I descend the stairs and shove open my front door. Douglass is already waiting by my car, door open. I slide inside and lean into the leather seats, trying to focus on Klaus's words.

"Oberon went with him," he explains, "along with a dozen first-class guards and six Hunted men."

"Contact Onkel. Tell him to make sure Stonehall is secure and then execute all the Hunted men tonight. We'll send German guards out tomorrow as replacement."

Klaus doesn't speak for a long moment.

"I'm on my way to the hospital. I want to see if I can get any information from the staff."

He takes so long to respond; I glance at my phone to see if he hung up without saying so. Then his voice drags over the line, dark and gloomy and full of the turmoil I know he'll never acknowledge aloud. "Understood."

Klaus doesn't agree with the bloodshed. But we cannot afford to have any loose ends right now. Every Russian in the city wants my brother's head, our Hunted men might be desperate enough to give it to them.

I can't believe how much of a traitor I've become. After years of standing up for men like Douglass, preferring their company and their hard-earned loyalty over that of my German guards. Now, when it matters most, I'm choosing my own brothers. My blood brothers.

I'm just thankful Douglass wasn't part of Wolf's security team. I don't think I could have made the same call if he was at Stonehall.

I glance up and catch him watching me through the rearview mirror. I know he heard me give the order to execute the Hunted grunts. As a reminder of who he is and what he's done to earn his place by my side, he speaks to me in German. His voice is hollow, but the words ring through my chest and threaten to penetrate my heart.

"I am with you."

I nod. Glance away. "I know, brother. That will never change."

When we get to the hospital, I don't tell Douglass to wait by the car. There are too many vehicles in the parking lot, vehicles that undoubtedly belong to Wolves. I don't know what to expect once I enter the hospital, so I'm happy to have Douglass by my side. Though he is angry with me, he doesn't protest my request. In fact, before we leave the car, he checks his weapon and makes sure its fully loaded before returning it to the holster on his hip. Then he grabs another handgun and shoves that one into the holster under his arm. I have a gun at my hip and a knife I keep up my sleeve. We're not a walking arsenal, but we've got enough to put up a fight if anything bad happens.

Inside, the place is crawling with Wolves. They are in the lobby, in the hallways, standing guard outside random rooms, stuffed into the elevators. Douglass and I immediately stand out in this sea of snow-blonde hair and milky pale skin. There are cold eyes staring all around me, piercing my backside as I make my way to the woman's room. I ignore them all and keep walking, glancing back only to make sure no one is bothering Douglass. Not that he needs my help. He's a giant Black guy who was kidnapped, branded, and forced into the German mafia. Despite all that, he still managed to climb the ranks and become one of my most trusted men. There is nothing the Russians can do to him that some idiot from the Hunting Grounds hasn't tried already.

When I look at his face, I see no emotion, no concern, no worry. Douglass is not afraid. He has nothing to lose—not even his own life. I took that from him six years ago.

That sounds cruel, doesn't it? Because it is.

Have you finally realized I am the monster I've always been? How much longer will it take.

I finally reach the woman's room and am pleased to find no guards standing outside. When I shove open the door, I realize they've taken the party inside.

Mikhail Volkov and six other men are standing in the room. I almost stumble backwards, but Douglass is right behind me, so I end up catching myself and forcing my feet to go forward.

Mikhail smiles wickedly at me, and I begin to wonder if he's been waiting for me. "Jäger," he says in his sharp accent.

"Volkov."

"You have some nerve showing up here."

"I could say the same about you."

His eyes never leave mine as he uses Russian to order his men out. All except one leave the room, a big bald guy who hovers beside Mikhail like an ominous, pale shadow.

I glance at him. "Why does he get to stay?"

Mikhail nods at Douglass. "Why does he?"

Fair enough.

"The last time we met," Mikhail begins, "I asked you for permission to murder your brother-in-law. Now I am here for another brother. But I am not asking for permission. I am demanding his head."

"You aren't getting it," I snarl.

"Is he worth a war with us?"

"If you touch my brother, you will face the full wrath of the Hunters and the Stronghold and the Garden. That is not a fight you can win."

Mikhail waves an uncaring hand. "I am not worried about the Garden. They are weak and insignificant now."

"They aren't our only ally," I remind him, to which he simply laughs and says with a singsong in his voice, "Are you sure the Stronghold is your ally?"

I squint at him.

"King James is a powerful man," Mikhail admits with a reverent nod, "but he did not gain all that power by making stupid decisions."

"It wouldn't be stupid to defend his own granddaughter. Rosa's life will be in danger just as much as mine if war breaks out."

"You are right. But there are rumors going around." His thin lips stretch into a teasing grin. The sight sends tingles of pain crawling down my back, making my scars throb in anxiety. "I have heard you have not clipped The Rose's thorns just yet." Mikhail cannot stop himself from laughing. He even glances up at the guard standing beside him; they share a chuckle and then his pale eyes are back on me, sharply focused and intent on watching me boil with anger.

I have no idea how he found out about my sex life with my own wife, but it takes everything in me not to walk over and knock every tooth out his mouth for daring to mention it in front of me. To joke about it.

But I know better. Mikhail is baiting me. Knocking that smirk off his face would start a war with the Wolves just as easily as Wolf beating the daylights out of some nameless Russian woman. I refuse to give this man the satisfaction of drawing me into a fight with him.

He tries to bait me again. "You have not plucked her petals in almost two months. I have heard you are a patient man, but that is impressive." Mikhail leans forward and drops his voice to a rumbling whisper, like we're friends sharing secrets. "I bet it drives you crazy. I do not know if I could control myself with such a pretty girl. If she were my wife, I would have her *begging*—"

"*Watch* your mouth," I snarl.

A strong hand on my arm jerks me backwards and I realize, suddenly, that I've taken a step forward. My right hand is on my holstered gun and my other is balled into a fist so tight, there are little crescent moons of blood left in my palm when I uncurl my fingers.

Douglass loosens his grip. "Don't fall for it," he tells me in German.

I know he's right. I need to control myself. But my patience is reaching its limits.

Mikhail is standing now, leaning slightly closer to his guard, a cautious look on his face. Even he knows he's gone too far. But he plays it off, pulling his eyes from the gun at my hip to laugh and say, "No matter what The Rose means to you, if you have not consummated your marriage, the Stronghold owes you nothing. They might intervene to protect Rosa—but that is only if King James is feeling especially kindhearted." He shrugs. "Everyone knows he blames her for the death of her own mother, Jameson's only beloved daughter. For all we know, he may not believe the life of a mother-killer is worth the war that will unfold. And I do not blame him."

I don't exactly blame him, either. But I don't want Mikhail to know how much sense he's making right now. So I keep my mouth shut and resign to simply glaring at him from my stance beside Douglass. I even cram my hands deep into my pockets to keep them away from my gun.

Mikhail runs an aged hand over his silvery hair. "The Garden is weak. And the Stronghold is not a guaranteed ally. The way I see it, this war will be a very fair fight." He presses his lips together like he's thinking deeply, even nods to himself. "But we can avoid all this, Jäger. We can make a deal."

"I'm not interested," I say tartly.

278

He laughs. "You should be. Because I do not make second offers very often."

I don't speak, waiting for him to lay out the terms I know I'll end up rejecting. There's only one thing Volkov wants— my brother's head. And he's not going to get it. No matter what.

"Let us avoid war, Jäger. Give me Wolfgang and I will leave Giovanni alone. I will also leave your pretty wife out of it. We will not shed any more blood than his."

I start shaking my head. "My brother is off limits, Volkov, you know that."

"Is his life worth all this trouble?" he asks disappointedly. "He is poison. Just cut him loose and be done with it."

"Who is the woman? Is *she* worth all this?"

He shrugs. "She is a girl from one of my whorehouses. I do not know why she was in Brooklyn or how your brother met her. Maybe she was entertaining a client. Maybe they met at a club. It really does not matter."

"*Yes*, it does," I correct him. "You think my brother's life is worth some nameless hooker's?"

"It is not all about the girl!" he snaps, then he spews a string of nasty Russian words. "It is about our honor. And about our dignity. I am tired of Russian blood being shed and no one answering for it!" He takes a bold step forward, his eyes never leaving mine. "And every time there is blood spilled, your brother happens to be at the center."

I step forward too, meeting him face to face. "I wouldn't care if he hacked that woman to pieces and mailed them to you. I am not giving you my brother."

"Then you ask for a war you are not guaranteed to win. Or survive." He tsks. "You will not get a better offer than this, Jäger. I am asking for one man in exchange for the lives of hundreds that will be lost if there is a war. I will even forgive Giovanni's debt."

"I don't care about Gio's debt."

"Yes, you do." He chuckles and takes a casual step back. "I know he has been pestering you for payment. That is because I have been pestering him—just to watch you squirm as you try to suck money from his dead businesses."

I take a deep breath, trying to calm myself down. "This is a waste of both our time."

"Do not make hasty decisions," Volkov warns. "I will give you seventy-two hours to think about it."

"Don't bother," I hiss. "My answer will be the same then as it is now. We have no deal."

He gives me a wolfish grin. "You are tired, Jäger, so I will let that slide." He jerks his chin at the door behind me. "Go home. Talk to your father. Make love to your pretty wife. Then get back to me."

I walk out of that room feeling like a child who's just been dismissed. I hate it. But leaving is the wisest decision I can make right now. I'm more angry than worried. But, despite Volkov's confidence, he isn't as right as he thinks he is. His entire plan hinges on nothing but assumptions.

He *assumes* the Garden is weak. He *assumes* the Stronghold is not dependable. While there may be some truth to those statements, nothing is set in stone. Especially not the Stronghold. The Italians might be insignificant right now, but the Willis Kingdom certainly is not. And the only thing standing in the way of our alliance is the consummation of my marriage.

I could go home and rectify that issue right now. But I made a promise to my wife, and I intend to keep it. The last time we tried anything sexual, she freaked out and lied about being on her period. She isn't even comfortable with cuddling yet. Asking her to sleep with me just to get soldiers from her grandfather is an unspeakable cruelty. She will leave my bed with emotional scars, forever viewing sex as a business transaction or a demonstration of my power over her.

I don't want that for her. Because of her faith, Rosa views sex as something sacred. I don't share her faith, but I would never do something to taint her beliefs or the image of love she keeps in her heart. I want her to hold on to her views as long as possible. I want her to see sex as an act of love or passion. Asking her to sleep with me to fulfill a contract would shatter her.

I won't put her through that. I know my options are limited. I know the lives of hundreds of soldiers shouldn't amount to one woman's discomfort toward her own husband, but I'm not willing to go down that road with Rosa until I've exhausted every possible option. Which means I've got to speak to King James myself. In person.

Chapter Twenty-Two

I don't bring a gift when I go to see King James. Unlike my last visit, I'm not here to charm him. Rosa is his granddaughter, and she will be in danger when the Wolves strike. Either he's going to help me protect her or he's not.

Jameson Willis is not a man to be tested. He is a king and rules his carefully constructed kingdom from a throne that has stood the test of time and devastation. I have no desire to poke the sleeping bear, but I'm also not here to play games. We are running out of time and options. I need his help and from the way he doesn't smile at me when I enter his home, I know he's more than aware of that fact.

"Amory Jäger." His voice bellows from his thick chest, filling the entire room and echoing off the sleek, black and gold painted walls. Monique is right beside her husband, sitting tall in a chair that looks oddly similar to a throne. Her thick hair is pulled back into a low bun, revealing her entire face; full lips painted a deep burgundy, perfectly arched eyebrows, and wide blinking eyes I'm sure Rosa inherited.

Jameson's children are here; Tyrese and Trenton Willis. As the heir and the eldest, Trenton has brought his wife along; Diamond is as proud and as beautiful as Monique—just twenty-five years younger. Her two daughters are familiar faces, and they both greet me with a smile. Adella and Nona. Even Adella's husband, Jared, is here.

It's a family event.

I'm instantly on edge, but I swallow my nerves and replay Volkov's nasty threats in my head to help strengthen my resolve. I've got to get Jameson's help, no matter what.

"King James," I incline my head, "Grandfather."

He laughs and it almost sounds like something is genuinely funny, but the chuckle is cut off too quickly, his smile is wiped away, his face suddenly serious. Echoes of his laughter swell around us, the last fragments of kindness that I will get from him. As they fade and hush, my hopes go with them.

"*Grandfather?*" He adjusts in his big chair, looking at me from across the incredibly long table sitting between us. We're in some kind of conference room, not the same one we used the first time I came. I can't help but feel the change of atmosphere means something, like this room is only used to murder people's hopes—if not outright kill them. "Are you trying to butter me up?" he asks incredulously. "Because that won't work here. Not in this predicament."

I swallow. "King James, the Wolves are coming for us—"

His laugh cuts me off. "They're coming for *you*. And you're stupid, violent brother."

Adella adjusts in her seat at the sound of his words. Her face gives no hint of what she's thinking or feeling, but I know she's worried about her cousin. I want to somehow assure her that everything's okay. That I would never let Wolfgang touch Rosa. If he ever did, Stonehall wouldn't be enough to keep me from him.

But all I can do is release a sigh and plead with her grandfather. "If the Wolves come for me, they will inevitably come for Rosa, too. Your own granddaughter."

Jameson glances over at Adella and Nona. "I have two others."

He can't be serious.

"You would let Rosa die?"

"Of course not." Jameson leans forward. "My granddaughter is my own blood. I would never sit by and watch her suffer."

My nerves seem to calm somewhat. For the first time since I stepped out my shower this morning, I feel like I can breathe again.

And then Jameson speaks.

"You, however, I have no obligation to protect or defend."

"King James—"

"No. My mind is made up."

"How do you plan to protect Rosa without helping me?" I challenge, leaning forward, elbows on the table.

"Send her here. Send her home." King James says so casually, I'm not sure I've heard him right away. Once the words settle into my frozen brain, I suck in a sharp breath and stare at him in the taut silence.

He wants me to send Rosa to the Bronx to live with him while I stay in Brooklyn and fight this war. Without his aid. Without any more soldiers. Without any more weapons than what we already have. He isn't offering help, he's offering sanctuary—for one person only.

I have to admit, it is a tempting offer. Rosa will be safe with her grandfather, and as long as the Stronghold doesn't get involved, the Wolves will leave them out of this war. Volkov wants to keep this between us, he knows he can't win if I have them on my side so I have no doubt my wife will be safe here.

But I also have no doubt I will not win this war without the Stronghold's help. It's not enough to just send Rosa away to hide in the Bronx; I need men, I need weapons, I need a plan to slaughter every Wolf I see and burn their island while I'm at it. That's not going to happen without help.

I try a different approach. "If I send Rosa here, will you give me men and weapons?"

"I am not negotiating my daughter's life as if she is cattle to be traded."

Even though I'm stressed and desperate, I appreciate how much respect he has for his granddaughter. That's something unique about the Stronghold; they're still old-fashioned enough to raise their daughters to be chaste, they still have arranged marriages, and King James might not have named his late daughter as his heir, even *if* she had been the firstborn. But the Stronghold doesn't treat their women the way the other organizations do. Maybe because Monique was right there beside Jameson through it all, maybe because Jameson himself has five sisters and was raised by a single mother. Whatever the case, the Stronghold treats their wives as treasured prizes to be earned, not pretty, little dolls to be taken.

Still. I'm desperate right now. If Rosa's life is a bargaining chip I can use, then I'm going to use it. If Jameson doesn't like it, then he should do the right thing and help his grandson-in-law win this war.

"Rosa is not cattle," I say slowly, "I'm not trying to make a trade with her—"

"Then what are you trying to do?" he asks me.

I exhale hard, nostrils flaring. "I'm trying to protect her and keep the German mafia afloat. Can't you see that?"

He laughs at me like I'm a fool. "I heard the rumors about what your brother did to that poor Russian woman. You think I care if Volkov wants his head?" He leans back in his chair, taps a finger on the oakwood table. "I'm sure I'm not alone in saying Wolfgang deserves what's coming. And anyone who tries to protect him deserves the same fate."

"He's my brother," I say quietly.

I know what he did was wrong. *Everyone* knows what he did was wrong. But Wolfgang is mine to deal with and mine to punish. Not Volkov's, not Jameson's, and not anyone else's.

My thoughts must be evident in my somber expression because King James adjusts in his chair and lets out a slow sigh. "I understand the desire to protect one's family. I don't judge you for trying to keep your brother alive."

"What can I do to get your help?"

He tents his fingers on the table. "There are rumors about your marriage."

I almost groan. I know exactly where this is going.

"As it stands," King James continues, "you are not actually my grandson-in-law. But if that were to change, then our alliance would be sealed in blood."

Sealed in blood. There is no need to ask him what he means. Somehow, news of my nonexistent sex life has made it all the way to the ears of Jameson Willis. I'm embarrassed, but I'm not surprised. If Mikhail Volkov found out, it was only a matter of time before Jameson did, too. Which means my father very likely knows as well.

I'm going to kill Conrad. He is the only person I've talked to about my marital problems. For whatever reason, he decided to share this information with Gisela—probably because they actually get along and tell each other everything, like a normal married couple. But one of them opened their mouths to someone who didn't need to know that information and now all of New York City knows I haven't slept with my own wife yet.

King James is looking at me with no hint of joking on his face. "You have two options: send Rosa and fight alone. Or consummate the marriage and I'll give you all the help you need."

It's simple, but it's not easy.

I can't win this war without the Stronghold's help, but I'm not going to force my wife to sleep with me to get the help I need. In a way, Rosa is still being traded like cattle. But in Jameson's eyes, this is a necessity—the natural signing of a contract which must be sealed in blood.

I get it—I do. But...

I bunch my shoulders and lower my head, burying my face in my surprisingly sweaty hands. *There's got to be another way.* One that doesn't involve violating my wife or sending her off to hide and wait for me to die. I'm not even sure she would miss me. I'm not convinced she would care.

"We can meet at your estate tonight, if you decide to consummate," King James says.

I sway in my chair, suddenly dizzy. He means to witness the act.

I'm not surprised. Jameson might see Monique as his equal, but he's still an old-fashioned man. And he's a smart man. He's not about to hand me extra manpower and weapons, putting the lives of his soldiers at risk, without being absolutely certain it's for his blood-bound family.

I nod slowly. My voice comes out as a raspy whisper. "I'll give you a call."

My phone buzzes as Douglass drives me home. I answer without looking at the caller ID. At this point, it doesn't matter who's calling, I'm equally annoyed with every soul on this earth. But no matter how stressed I get; the line of communication needs to remain open now more than ever. Volkov said 72 hours, but I can't ignore the rising paranoia that he won't honor that promise.

Vater's voice rumbles over the phone as I answer. "You little ingrate," he growls, "you've been lying to me all along."

He knows.

"What have you been doing all this time?" Uwe's voice rises. "Humping your pillows? Sleeping with hookers? You had *one* job on your wedding night, and you didn't do it!"

"There is a way to fix this—"

"You had better thank *Christ on the Cross* there is a way to fix this!" he yells so loudly I have to pull the phone away from my face for a moment.

"I'll get us the manpower we need, Vater," I say calmly. All the fight has been squeezed out of me now. I'm not angry, I'm not upset, I don't feel anything at all except a pit of black dread in the middle of my stomach.

Rosa will never forgive me for this.

"Jameson Willis called me," Uwe says. He lets that hang between us for a moment. "We've decided we want this done as soon as possible."

I close my eyes and lean my head against the window. I have no words to offer in response.

"We will be at your estate in an hour. Be ready."

Uwe hangs up without saying goodbye, not that I would have heard it over the pounding in my ears. I feel a headache coming on, which I treat with aspirin and whiskey as soon as I get home.

The house is quiet, like always. Every step I take sounds like a gunshot going off in the still silence that screams around me. I make my way to Rosa's bedroom and knock on the door, but she doesn't answer. After my third attempt, I crack the door a sliver and peek inside. It's empty.

I call her phone and she answers on the fourth ring. "Hello?" She sounds confused, like she isn't sure if she should be happy or worried that I've called.

"Hey," I say, then I clear my throat when I hear how sad and shaky my voice sounds. "Where are you, love?"

The pet name throws her for a second. I almost miss it, but there's a pause and a sharp intake of breath. Rosa is always shocked by the smallest gesture; caressing her cheek, taking her hand, even issuing a compliment earns me a wide-eyed stare. I wish I could see her eyes now, could see her blinking up at me and biting her lip the way she does when she gets nervous.

"I'm out with Gisela and Petra," she says cautiously. "Is something wrong?"

I shake my head, though I know she can't see that. "No—it's just … when will you be home?"

"I can come now—"

"*No.*" My voice comes out stronger than I mean it to, and I'm not surprised when Rosa doesn't immediately respond. I sigh into the silence. "Are you enjoying yourself?"

"Yes."

"Tell me about your day."

She launches into a story of how she met up with Gisela who invited Petra to join them, but I am not listening. I still can't get over the shock that Rosa even answered my call. It nearly breaks me that she would be willing to drop everything and come home. After all I've said and done, after how cruel I've been to her, Rosa has every right to chew me out and hang up in my face. But she doesn't do that. Because she's nothing like me or any of the other monsters of the mafia. She is too kind for this dark world; the fact that I am about to rip that kindness from her torments me.

When she should be angry with me, she is concerned. When she should cut me out of her life, she welcomes me with a gentle forgiveness that makes my heart ache. I know her faith plays a role in this—it is the source of her quiet strength, something that I secretly envy. Something that keeps me up at night, wondering if her faith would change me the way it has refined her.

Would I be kind like her? Gentle like her? Forgiving like her? Would the light of her foundation be enough to chase away the darkness in my heart?

It's a tempting thought I've spent too much time pondering lately. Flirting with salvation.

All I know for certain is that every time I'm around Rosa, my interest in her beliefs grows stronger. I've already started reading the Bible, if only to try to find out what makes her so confusing and crazy. But I don't need to read the story of David to learn anything about my wife. I don't have to huddle up with the Bible app at night, staring at the verses, willing them to make sense, just to figure out why Rosa is so hesitant with me.

I do all that on my own.

Because it's interesting, the strange similarities in my life to that of the King of Israel's. How he was faced with a strong enemy, one he had no chance of defeating, yet he overcame him anyway.

David declared that God would give him strength to fight Goliath. I'm not so sure I have the faith to make such a bold statement. All I've got right now is a gun on my hip and a contract that needs to be fulfilled. This is my cup. And it's filled with blood—not hope, not joy, not mercy.

I plan to drink every drop.

Rosa is still going on about her awesome day. I take a breath when she pauses, waiting for me to offer some sort of input. "Keep enjoying yourself. Come home whenever you're ready."

She pauses. "I'm getting worried, Amy."

That name. I run my hand through my hair and pull the phone away from my face. I don't want her to hear me as I double over, hands on my knees, and heave three deep breaths to keep myself from choking out a desperate sob.

"Don't worry," I rasp into the phone. "I was just expecting you, that's all."

"You had plans?" she asks.

"Yes, but they can wait. Just enjoy yourself, Rosa. Get home when you can."

Another long pause.

"All right. I'll see you when I get home."

"See you then."

She hangs up, and I'm left in the blaring silence of my miserably empty home.

I sit on Rosa's bed and glance around the room. It's neat and feminine; bottles of perfume on display on the dresser, makeup sitting out on her vanity, her laptop on sleep mode on her desk. There are pictures of mystic-looking jellyfish, beautiful shots of seahorses, and romantic sunsets flashing across the device as screensavers. It's the opposite of my dark, melancholy room, and I'm not surprised. Rosa is the opposite of me.

Good while I'm evil. Kind while I'm mean. Innocent while I'm the worst of sinners.

Tonight, I will snatch that innocence away and claim it for myself. I have no right. I have no desire to, but it cannot be helped. Unless I give Rosa to her grandfather.

That's not going to happen.

I will spend the rest of my life making it up to her for this selfish decision, but I cannot let her go. Not because I love her to the point of obsession, but because I cannot afford to. I need Jameson's help. I need his manpower. I need his weapons. If I don't do this, the Hunters of New York will fall. Uwe will tie Rosa to my bed before he lets that happen, especially now that he knows what needs to be done.

Speaking of the devil, my doorbell rings while I'm still sitting in Rosa's room. I have no idea how much time has passed but I blink from my thoughts and slink down the stairs as soon as I hear the noise.

One of my guards has let Uwe into my house by the time I enter the main foyer. He's standing at the drink display in the lounge, pouring himself a shot, when he looks up and sees me.

There is no joy or anger on his face. All I see is disappointment.

He downs his alcohol and pours himself another before he speaks to me. "I don't understand why you would wait this long to take care of business."

I don't respond.

"You were raised in this life, Amory. You know what marriage really means for men like us. Why would you risk your contracts with the De Lucas or the Stronghold?"

"It's complicated."

He downs his second drink, probably just to keep from throwing it at me, then he slams the glass on the tray and seethes, "We could have lost everything we'd gained and *then some* if Giovanni or Willis had found out before now! How could you be so stupid?"

"It's complicated," I repeat dryly.

He walks to the other side of the room and sits on the sofa. "Explain."

It will only make me seem like more of a failure, but all I have to offer is the truth. Mercifully, the doorbell rings again and I'm let off the hook.

"Jameson has arrived," I mutter, waiting for a guard to escort him inside. He appears noiselessly, disturbingly quiet on his feet for a man of his size in a house made of echoey tile.

"Afternoon gentlemen," he greets in his smooth, deep voice.

I nod. Uwe grunts something in German.

"Where is my granddaughter?"

"She's not home yet," I answer.

"Well, get her here," Vater demands.

I shake my head, boldly eyeing him from across the room. "She's out with her friends. I will not interrupt that for this."

Uwe rises from the sofa. "We have seventy-two hours to rally an army and you want your wife to finish having *fun?*"

"I got her into this. I'm not going to make it any worse for her."

His face turns purple as he begins to yell, but someone walks into the room and his anger dies in his throat.

Giovanni De Luca Junior.

Vater jabs a thick finger at him, but his words are aimed at me. "What is *he* doing here?"

I'm just as shocked as he is. "I have no idea."

"I invited him," Jameson explains, striding to the center of the room. Gio walks to stand beside him and for a moment, they almost look like coconspirators. "He is the don of the Italian mafia, he is Rosa's older brother, and he is my grandson. He has a right to witness the consummation."

Gio nods. "I have as much riding on this union as any of you."

Uwe disagrees. "The Garden is worthless!" he shouts. "You are the only one who will gain something from this act. The rest of us will lose—do you hear me?" He wipes spit from his mouth before going on. "We have men who will die in this war. We have homes we may lose—property that will be destroyed. What do you offer except debt?" Vater sneers those last words, still simmering over the load of failing businesses we were handed through the marital contract.

Gio lets his words roll down his back. He even offers Uwe a small smile, though it isn't as confident as the one he normally wears. "I don't have as many men as you. Or as much money. Or as many weapons. But I do have land. The Garden still owns Manhattan."

"What can a bunch of buildings do for us now?" Vater demands.

"Your women and children can take shelter in my estates. They'll be kept safe during the war. That's what I can offer." Gio stuffs his hands into his pockets, tilts his chin up. "Unless you think Stonehall is large enough to fit all of the German mafia and the Stronghold."

It isn't. And even if it were, Wolfgang is hiding there now. Stonehall is heavily guarded, and I doubt the Wolves would be bold enough to launch an outright attack on it, but I still don't want to send Rosa there for shelter. I don't want her anywhere near my brother—he's too big of a target and I'm not risking her being collateral damage.

"Let us work together in this," Jameson says calmly. "It would serve us nothing to bicker amongst ourselves."

Uwe doesn't take his eyes off Gio as he jerks a nod and grumbles something rude in German.

"Now," Junior says with a grin, "where is my sweet sister?"

"She's out with her friends," I answer.

He frowns, but Jameson speaks and cuts off whatever response he was going to offer. "Let the girl enjoy herself," he says firmly. Then he walks over and pours himself a drink, downs the whole thing, and moves to stand by the unlit fireplace. "Where is it happening? We can sweep the room while we wait."

"Sweep the room?" I repeat.

He nods, folds his big arms over his barrel chest. King James is in his 70's but he doesn't look a day older than my 58-year-old father. There are slight wrinkles in his face, but they are hidden beneath his thick beard, and he hasn't lost any of his muscle in his old age. His custom-made suit stretches over his massive bulk; fine, ebony garments accentuated with gold trim and gaudy gold chains like he's a gangster from the 80's. He *is* a gangster from the 80's—even before then.

"Uwe, Junior, and I will remove any sharp objects from the room. That way we'll know you didn't just stare at each other for an hour and then slit your finger and smear the blood over the sheets."

I swallow thickly. That idea hadn't even crossed my mind. And neither did the decision of where this would be taking place. If Jameson plans to sweep the room, that means he won't be inside to watch.

"You're giving us privacy," I say almost to myself.

From my peripheral, I see Jameson nod. Uwe shoots him a look and then reluctantly nods his agreement. "But we will be just outside," he says firmly.

They won't watch, but they'll make sure they can still listen, and they'll check the sheets once it's done.

"This is sick," I mutter through gritted teeth.

Uwe scoffs. "This is how it's done. We are mafia. There is nothing fair or pretty about our lives."

"Need I remind you this is happening because you didn't do things right the first time around—on your wedding night," Jameson says, a small smirk on his large, dark face.

I walk over and grab the entire bottle of whiskey from the display. "Follow me, I'll show you the room."

I choose a random guest bedroom to get it over with. I don't want my father poking around my bedroom, and I sure don't want anyone 'sweeping' Rosa's room. Once this is over, she will hate me. She won't want to have anything to do with me. I need her room to be left untouched. I want it to be her haven. An escape from me and the nightmare I'm about to drag her into.

I make it through almost half the whiskey before they're done in the guestroom. They leave with a letter opener from the desk, a few random safety pins, and a loose screw from the backside of the dresser. Gio even unscrewed the lightbulb from the lamp beside the bed.

"In case you get desperate and decide to use broken glass," he says, a triumphant smile on his face.

I don't have the energy to respond. I just stare at the items as they leave them on the little table beside the chair I'm sitting in. We dragged chairs over for them to sit and listen in while I break every promise I ever made to my wife. I've been staring at the wall for the last hour while Uwe, Gio, and Jameson searched the room. Now, they sit beside me and Vater reaches for the bottle in my hand.

"Take it easy," he says. It almost sounds comforting until he replaces the bottle with a condom.

I glance down at it resting in my palm.

"It's unlikely she will get pregnant on the first time, but we don't want to take any chances. No one wants to deal with a pregnancy during a war."

I can only nod and stuff the stupid thing into my pocket.

"So, what now?" Gio asks.

I stand. "Now we wait."

"You aren't going to call your wife?" Uwe is staring at me, anger taking over his face. "It's been over an hour. She should be back by now."

"I am *not* interrupting her for this," I growl. "She will get home when she gets home. In the meantime, we wait." I turn and open the door to the guestroom. "I'll be waiting in here."

Chapter Twenty-Three

It wasn't my idea to meet up with Gisela today, but I'm glad I decided to go. We went out shopping and then ended up at the Jäger's main estate. I felt a sense of unease unroll inside me when we first arrived, but she assured me everything would be fine. So far, it has been.

Petra came down from her room to join us in the small lounge and we had such a great time, she even went back and got her aunt to join us. Christina Jäger. Amory's mother.

Coincidentally, I did not mention her being here when my husband called. I wasn't quite sure how he would react and, also ... Christina told me not to tell him. When I got his call, she was sitting in her chair with her feet on a cushion, the rest of us girls were gathered around her. Petra sat on the warm carpet, smiling up at her, I was in a chair with my feet tucked under me, and Gisela lay sprawled on the fainting couch, casually painting her toes with a fiery red polish.

Christina had motioned for me to put the phone on loudspeaker when I mouthed that it was Amory, and then she motioned again when I'd glanced up at her in search of an answer when Amy asked what I'd been up to.

When I hang up the phone, she lets out a heavy sigh and tells us to listen closely. This is not the Christina I remember who swayed on her feet and had a drunken outburst at the dinner party months ago. She is sober, no drink in sight except a sweaty glass of club soda she hasn't touched. It sits on the tray beside her, along with a decanter of wine that Petra has singlehandedly worked her way through. Gisela and I enjoyed lemon iced tea.

In this calm state, I can see how pretty Christina is. She has the same grey eyes as Amory, but they are not void and distant. Instead, they're filled with an intensity I cannot explain, and they swirl with wisdom and intrigue. Her hair is loose and falls around her shoulders like balls of soft cotton. I'm not sure if she is blonde or severely grey, but it's beautiful all the same.

Christina has treated me with nothing but kindness since I entered her home. She even made a joke about our last encounter, asking if I have understood what she truly meant about being a mafia wife.

Diamonds are just pretty shackles...

Her warning sends a chill over my spine. Of course I've learned the meaning of her words. In a way, I feel I'd already known that in my heart. It's one of the reasons I tried to run away.

"He sounded worried about something," I say quietly. All

the women are still watching me in silence, but it isn't a silence heavy with concern—it feels tense, like they all want to say something but aren't sure how.

Christina sighs again. "A storm is brewing, ladies."

"I don't understand," I say.

Petra pulls her knees to her chest. "Eike cancelled our lunch date today. We were supposed to pick out designs for the wedding invitations together."

Petra Preuß is engaged to Eike, the son of Klaus Brandt—best friend of the Jägermeister. I'm guessing her fiancé is high-ranking in the German mafia, but even if he weren't, the news of his absence today is troubling.

Gisela only adds to the mounting anxiety. "Conrad got a call around seven this morning. I don't know what was said, but he bolted from the house without even kissing me goodbye." She sighs, absently stroking paint onto her toes. "He *always* kisses me goodbye."

"A storm is brewing," Christina repeats. "And we must be ready."

"What sort of storm?" I ask uneasily.

"A war."

I gulp. There hasn't been a mafia war in this city since before I was born. My grandfather was part of the last one; when I was younger, he would tell me the stories of how he lost his brother, two of his sisters, and his own eye in the war. I shiver as I realize this sort of violence may be knocking at our doors.

"Why would there be war?" Petra asks.

302

A very solemn look takes over Christina's face. "My son. Wolfgang."

Amory told me about Wolfgang and his violence. How he would hurt women when he was drunk and uncontrollable. I don't want to focus on the gruesome details for too long. I don't want my mind to wander into places it doesn't need to be. Like the dark thoughts that Wolfgang went too far this time. Maybe he hurt the wrong woman. Maybe he's finally getting what he deserves.

"I don't know all the details," Christina says. For the first time, her voice is shaky and filled with emotion. She wipes her pale hands on her dress and glances nervously at the decanter beside her, but she doesn't reach for it. I remember what happened the last time she had too much to drink. Uwe isn't around to issue silent threats, but Hans is here—standing just outside the door of the lounge. He's supposed to be guarding us, but I think he's mostly here to keep Christina in check.

Christina's eyes shift from the decanter to the door where we know Hans is waiting on the other side. Her tongue lashes out to wet her bottom lip just before she drops her voice to a whisper. "Something is happening with the Russians and Wolfgang is at the center. That is all I know right now."

"Whatever is going on, it's bad," Gisela adds.

"Will we be sent away?" Petra scoots closer to Christina, tiredly leaning her head against her aunt's knee. "I don't want to go away."

"Only time will tell if we have to leave. Maybe things will work themselves out." Christina pets Petra's blonde head. "No matter what happens, we must be strong, ladies. All of us."

I shift uncomfortably, feeling like she is speaking directly to me.

"I cannot offer you much beyond advice, but please do not take my words lightly," Christina says, voice no longer shaking. "Now is the time to stand together. Not just as members of the German mafia, but as mafia wives."

I try to ignore the strange feeling of guilt that shoots through me. And I also try to ignore Gisela who is staring right at me. Her eyes are so focused on me that it draws the attention of the other women.

Christina glances between us and asks, "Is something going on?"

I sigh. This is the first time I've seen Christina sober and somewhat happy. I don't want to ruin things by lying to her. "Things between me and Amory are not great right now."

"But he just called and said you guys had plans," Petra reminds me.

I decide not to tell her that was the first time we've spoken in three weeks. "Yes, but I don't think those plans are good."

"What is going on in the marriage?" Christina pries.

Sheesh. She leaves no room for privacy.

"We haven't been spending much time together." That's all I'm willing to give her right now. I respect Christina as Amory's mother, but she doesn't need to know every little detail about our marriage. Especially not these details. Oddly, I think this is one thing Amory would actually agree with me on.

"Go," Christina says sternly.

I glance up to find her pointing at the door.

"There is war at our door. Go spend time with your husband while you still can. Be the wife he needs you to be right now."

I stand and gather my purse. I'm halfway to the door when I stop and turn back around. "You said all you had to offer us was advice."

Christina nods.

"May I offer comfort as well?"

Her face brightens. "Of course."

I walk back over to the ladies and hold out both hands for them to take. "Will you let me pray for you?"

For a moment, no one speaks. I'm not sure if they're trying to figure out a way to shoot me down or if they're just stunned, but the silence is grating, nonetheless.

Finally, Gisela moves from the fainting couch to stand by my side. She takes my hand and extends her other to Petra who's still sitting on the floor beside Christina. "Let's do it."

Christina reaches for her hand, but Petra frowns. "You really believe prayer will do anything?"

Gisela nods. "Of course I do. Or else I wouldn't bother."

"Well, I have my doubts."

Christina rises from her chair and takes Gisela's hand. "I have not prayed in many years. But what have we got to lose?" She glances down at Petra. "Come, Petra. It either works or it doesn't. Either way, it certainly doesn't hurt to try."

Petra grumbles but gets to her feet and joins our circle

anyway. Gisela squeezes my hand to let me know I should lead us. It was my idea, after all. She even starts humming a song whose name I can't remember, but the tune is familiar and comforting and seems to give me courage.

I take a shaky breath, bow my head, and then begin to pray.

I ask God to be with us and with our husbands. I ask Him to help them avoid a war at all costs. But if conflict is inevitable, I ask God to keep everyone safe on both sides of the fight. This request doesn't sit well with Christina, I can sense her getting uncomfortable with my wishes, but I won't back down on it.

I don't want anyone to die. Not even Wolfgang. So I ask the Lord to forgive him and I ask the Holy Spirit to work on his heart, to soften it to Him, so that he would accept Christ in his life someday. I give the same request for Uwe as well, thinking of how differently he would treat Christina if he were a man of God. And I ask the same for Conrad, remembering how much trouble their different beliefs cause between him and Gisela. She squeezes my hand when she hears this. I ask for Eike and Petra—that both of them find room in their hearts to welcome God. And I ask for Amory, somehow feeling that was a request two months in the making.

When I finish the prayer, Gisela and Christina have tears glossing their eyes. Petra doesn't, but she's no longer scowling like when she'd first gripped my hand.

"I should get going now," I say shyly.

Christina nods. Gisela pulls me into a hug. Petra just gives me a half-smile.

When I leave the Jäger estate, one of Amory's drivers is waiting outside to take me home. The drive is long and unnerving. Unease has relentlessly taken control of my heart. I can't stop thinking that something is terribly wrong. I just don't know what. And I certainly don't know how to fix it.

The unease sitting in my gut seems to grow when we pull up to my home and I see three cars sitting out front. One of them I recognize as Gio's, and my heart begins to hammer. I don't even wait for my driver to get my door. It flies open as I shove my way out the car and run to the front doors, heels clacking all the way.

Something's wrong, I tell myself, bursting through the front door. Sure enough, my brother is waiting for me in Amory's open foyer as soon as I cross the threshold. His presence both stuns and warms me at the same time. It's a confusing mix of emotions that leaves me speechless and dumb. I haven't seen my brother since the wedding. I'm not sure I miss him. But I'm not entirely unhappy to see him now.

He's in his classic white suit with a tie that's greener than his eyes. He smiles at me, and it makes my skin prickle with goosebumps. "It's about time," he says, glancing at his watch. "We've been waiting."

"Who's been waiting?"

"All of us." He turns and leads me through my own home like he owns the place. We turn down a hallway I've rarely travelled, I try not to make it obvious that I'm nervous as I keep pace with him. "She's here," June announces, approaching one of the guestrooms. Sitting in chairs outside the room is Uwe Jäger and my own grandfather, Jameson Willis.

Again, I'm left speechless.

Gio says, "We're just here to listen. Amory is inside."

Instead of greeting my father-in-law and my grandpa, I turn toward the door and rush inside. Amory is sitting in a chair by the desk, a bottle of whiskey beside him—half empty. He doesn't look at me as I approach, his half-lidded eyes are focused on the floor. This whole scene feels like a repeat of our wedding night. This time, I'm twice as nervous as before.

We're just here to listen.

I swallow at the implications of Gio's words, but I let my questions die there. I don't want to know what he really meant by that. Even though I'm sure I already do.

"What's going on?" I squeak.

Amory stirs, lifting his eyes from the carpet to meet my gaze. "I'm so sorry, Rosa." His voice is hoarse and low. "I don't want to die."

The words take me by such surprise, I take a step back and clutch my purse like it's a weapon. "What's going on?" I repeat.

He clears his throat. "The Russians want to start a war. We can win the war if we are allied with the Stronghold and the Garden."

Both sides of my family.

"But neither mafia will lend aid."

"They're my family, why wouldn't they help?" I ask.

308

He sighs. It's long and gloomy. "They are willing to take you in and give you shelter. But they are not going to offer me any soldiers or weapons."

"But you're my husband."

He chuckles darkly. "Only on paper."

Everything clicks now.

My purse falls from my grip as I stumble to the side. Amory is on his feet, right before me in a second. His hands stable me, and I grip his arm just to have something to hold on to.

"I'm so sorry," he repeats.

"They want us to consummate the marriage."

"You don't have to." He holds me at arm's length and looks me right in the eye. It's almost overwhelming to have his stormy gaze focused so intently on me, but I won't look away. Not for a second. "I promised I wouldn't touch you until you wanted me to. And I plan to keep that promise. But..." his voice falters and he lowers his head, ashamed of what he's about to say next. Of what he's about to ask of me. "I don't want to die, Rosa. I cannot win this war without an ally. I need your family's help. And this is the only way I know to get it."

I don't want to, but I can't help thinking of the last time we did anything sexual. How I had gotten scared and squirmy and how he'd gotten angry. His bitter words felt like a razor peeling away the layers of my exposed heart.

"You said I wouldn't be the best screw of your life," I say quietly.

He makes a noise. With his head lowered, I can't tell if it's a sniffle or a gasp. "I said a lot of things I shouldn't have.

Because I was angry and hurt."

"Hurt?"

He laughs—this I can hear clearly, and I can see his shoulders bunching as he finally lifts his head to look me in the face again. "You have rejected me every time you've had the chance."

I won't let the guilt inside. I never meant for Amory to feel hurt by my rejection, but I refuse to let his pain make me regret my decisions. All this time, I avoided his advances because I felt it was wrong. That it was sinful.

I will never be ashamed of the choices I make for my faith.

But ... It was never sinful for me to share a bed with Amory. It was never about lust. Never about perversion. We are married and our bed is undefiled.

I avoided intimacy because I was afraid. Fearful that I wouldn't be enough to please him. Scared that he would realize I was not worth all the sacrifices he'd made just to call me his wife. And his horrible words that night solidified my worries.

That I wasn't good enough for him. That my limited experience was something he wouldn't enjoy and had no interest in.

Deep down, I feared being rejected by him.

So I ended up rejecting him in turn. And I hid behind my faith, using it as an excuse to run from my own husband. The one man I have free will to enjoy as much and as long and as passionately as I want.

"I don't want you to die."

Amory swallows so loudly I can hear it. "You don't have

to do this, Rosa."

"I don't want to," I admit. "Not like this. But…"

Christina's last words roll through my mind. *Be the wife he needs you to be right now.*

Amory straightens, keeping his eyes on me. I look away.

"Are we doing this?" he asks.

I nod slowly, sucking in a little gasp when I feel his hand in my hair, tugging at the pin keeping my coils in place. Thick ringlets of dark hair fall over my light brown shoulders and upper arms. Amory examines the pin. It's the one he gave me three weeks ago, silver and rose-shaped.

He smiles, turning it over in his fingers. "You already know how I feel about you, Rosa. I've been open about that since we got married." When he looks up from the pin, his eyes are molten pools of grey. "You're a beautiful woman."

"Thank you."

He takes a step, coming even closer than he already is. "Don't be afraid," he says in a husky whisper.

But I already am.

"I can take it slow. I can be gentle for you." He turns the pin over. "Like I would have been that night. And every other night you wanted me."

I feel like I can't breathe.

"Or we can just get this over with. I won't make it last any longer than it needs to."

I have a choice in this. I could walk out of this room. I could go home with Grandpa or June and leave Amory to fend for himself.

But I don't want him to suffer.

Does that mean I want to turn this into a romance? Do I want him to give me the wedding night I ruined months ago?

I'm not sure.

We can't pretend this is happening out of love. We aren't here right now because we want to be. Our own family is waiting outside the room, trying to listen to make sure the deed is done. Sinful or not, this isn't how I wanted things to unfold between us.

Maybe it is best to be quick about it. Tear the bandage off and deal with the bleeding later.

"What do you want, Rosa?" Amory asks.

When I don't answer, he sighs. Then he turns and sets the pin on the desk behind him. "We'll get it over with."

When his eyes meet mine again, they are no longer molten. The desire from before is still there, but it's joined by a detachment so deep I can't help but shudder.

This is not going to be romantic, I realize with a tinge of fear clawing up my throat. *He isn't going to treat me as his wife.* A sudden jolt of regret fills my heart and I want to tell him that I've changed my mind, but he opens his mouth and cuts me off.

"Take your clothes off," he says gruffly. "And get on the bed." He turns away and splays his hands on the desk, hunched over.

I can see the tension between his shoulders, even through his wrinkled jacket. A thousand worries weigh him down. It's an image so clear and painful, I can't stop myself from reaching out to him. Maybe it's out of regret. Or shame. Or the aching need I can no longer control. But I grasp his arm and he whirls so fast, I don't register his mouth over mine until I'm gasping for breath.

The kiss is fire on my lips. It burns and grows, hungry for more. Eagerly, I feed its wanting. Desperately, I fall into its craving. My hands latch around Amory's neck, and he backs me into the wall, never breaking our exchange. I lose my blouse. He loses his shirt. I drag my hands over his chest, digging my nails into his flesh. He pulls back with a hiss, but I grab him, and our lips connect again.

When he needs air, he pulls away and kisses my neck, tearing at my skirt. I help him and shimmy out of it, then I kick it away and gasp as he cups my face and kisses me so deeply, I can't breathe for a moment.

He pulls away, panting. Burning. "My name. The one you call me."

"Amy," I whisper against his soft lips.

He devours me, groaning as he lifts me from the floor and walks to the bed. As soon as my body hits the blankets, I am torn from this dream and awakened to the nightmare of reality.

This is it. We're doing this. For more reasons than one.

Amory senses my sudden apprehension and pauses. The flooding romance is slowly drained from the room, replaced by the dark truth. By the realization that this will change everything—for good and bad.

"We don't have to do this," he reminds me.

I nod understanding, but I don't stop him as he rids me of

my underclothes and then stands to remove his own. His eyes are locked on mine the entire time; I cannot stop myself from squirming. I have never been completely naked before a man in my entire life. I have never been so exposed. So vulnerable.

Amory is careful, slowly climbing into the bed like he's afraid I may bolt if he moves too suddenly. I try to stay focused on his face, but my eyes betray me, and I drop my gaze down his body. Heat runs through me as I look at my husband. He is just as bare as me. But he is not ashamed ... and he doesn't have a reason to be.

He leans forward and kisses me, gently pushing me back into the blankets. When he sits back on his heels, I grip the covers and stare at the ceiling, not knowing what else to do. Silence lingers through the room, only interrupted by the sound of a packet being torn open. Blush works its way over my face as I realize he's putting on a condom. Then I feel his hand on my thigh and I gasp, involuntarily jerking my leg away.

My name is a sigh on his lips. "Rosa..."

I don't reply.

"You're trembling," Amory whispers.

"Just do it," I say with a gasp. "We have to."

When I don't hear a reply, I lift my head from the pillows and find him kneeling between my legs. I'm so exposed right now it's almost shameful, but all I feel is confusion.

"Just do it, Amy," I insist.

He shakes his head and touches my thigh again. For the first time, I realize he's right. I *am* trembling. All over. Uncontrollably. The blankets are still clenched tightly in my shaking hands, and my breaths are coming out in shuddering little pants.

Amory stares at my body, but not with lust in his eyes. He's watching me shiver. Witnessing the extent of my discomfort, despite the passion we'd shared moments before.

A large hand reaches out to caress my cheek. "Not like this," he says quietly.

"There isn't anything else we can do."

"I'll find a way."

He moves to get out of the bed, but I grab his shoulder. "I'm sorry."

With a gentle laugh, Amory leans in and kisses my cheek. "Just knowing you were willing to do this means the world to me. I love you, Rosa."

Then he pushes off the bed and collects his clothes before walking out the door, leaving me staring behind him in absolute shock.

Chapter Twenty-Four

I stumble out of the guestroom in a daze. Before any of the men can see inside, I quickly shut the door behind me to give Rosa some privacy.

"That was quick," Jameson says, letting out a rumbling chuckle.

Uwe holds his hands up in question. "Are you finished?"

Junior quirks an eyebrow and takes a dramatic look at me from head to toe, stopping at my crotch. "You don't look finished to me."

With an exasperated sigh, I cover my lower half with my bundle of wrinkled clothes. "I didn't do it."

Shock, confusion, and anger flashes across their faces. You can guess which emotion belongs to which face.

King James says, "You understand what this means, right?"

I nod. "I need your help, but I'm not going to buy it with Rosa's body."

"You aren't buying it. You're solidifying it."

"It's all the same if it comes at the cost of her virginity. I'm not doing that to her."

Jameson eyes me a moment. There isn't any anger on his face, none that I can see, at least. He is almost too big for his chair, thick, broad shoulders spreading wide to make room for strong arms and a full, barrel chest. King James is the image of intimidation. Everything about him demands respect, but as his eyes narrow and his head inclines the slightest bit, he extends some of that respect to me. He's impressed with my decision.

But he's still mafia and he makes that very clear to me. "My first offer is still available. Rosa is welcome to take shelter at my estate. But I will offer no aid to you in this war beyond that. Without consummation, we are not truly related, nor are we concretely allied." He stands and smiles wide enough for me to see his gold tooth. "I would shake your hand, but I have no idea what you really did in there."

I exhale a bitter laugh. "Thank you, King James."

"I wish you the best, Jäger."

Gio stands and buttons his suit jacket. "As happy as I am to *not* have to listen to you bang my baby sister, I am disappointed. My stance is the same as my grandfather's. My doors are always open to Rosa, but until the marital contract is sealed in blood, I cannot offer you aid."

Giovanni is so full of it. He and I both know he wouldn't have offered aid even if I had finished the job. He doesn't even *have* aid to offer except a bunch of empty buildings to hide

317

people in—not to mention the fact that they're empty because the businesses occupying them failed and closed down.

"Thank you, don Gio," I say respectfully. As much as I'd like to bust his lip, I manage to keep my hands to myself. If only to hold up the armful of clothes I'm using to keep myself halfway decent.

Once Junior is gone, Uwe gets to his feet and glares at me with enough anger to scare the devil. His eyes look more black than grey and there's a thick vein throbbing on the side of his head. I stare at it a moment, wondering how close it is to popping.

"You have just sent this family to hell."

"We're already in hell," I tell him. "I've just decided not to bring Rosa there."

He spits on the floor. "Pathetic. Is she really worth all this?"

It will be nearly impossible to get my father to understand. He doesn't love my mother. He's never really loved anyone. So I don't bother trying to explain, I just let out a sigh and move to walk past him but he shoves me back against the door and growls, "You're not a man."

I laugh in his face and drop my bundle of clothes so he can see all of me. "Wanna check?"

He grabs my crotch.

All the air rushes from my lungs in a sudden shout. The only thing I can register right now is pain so intense it drops me to my knees, except my own father has literally got me by the balls, so I end up slumping into him. Desperate for

318

something to hold on to, I grip his shoulder and try to breathe.

"So you *do* have a pecker," he hisses into my ear, tightening his grip.

I think I'm going to faint.

"You just don't know how to use it."

Just as stars begin to dance at the edges of my blurry vision, Vater lets me go. I crumple to the floor with a gasp, sweat dappling my forehead, hands trembling as the pain swells and spreads through my abdomen and legs. I don't think I can walk. I can barely even breathe right now.

Vater's shadow makes everything dark as he steps closer. "Fix this, Amory. Or next time I'll cut it off." He laughs. "It's not like you're using it."

I had forgotten.

Spending so much time ruling in place of my father as the underboss, I had forgotten that he *is* the Jägermeister. And he didn't earn that title by playing nicely—not even with his own kin. Being Uwe's son will only get me so much mercy from him. I'm sure I've reached my limit now.

It was Vater's men who gave me the scars throbbing on my back. Beat me until he told them to stop. And then started again when he gave the word.

It was Vater who sent me my first woman at age fifteen. Told me it was time to turn me into a man. He sat in the room and watched just to make sure I got it done.

And it was Vater who stood beside me the first time I performed an execution. Blood from the victim sprayed us both once I pulled the trigger. I was only seventeen at the time.

Now it is that same man who is threatening to castrate me if don't fix this issue. I believe he would do it, but that isn't why I stagger to my feet and hobble back to my room. I force myself to ignore the ache between my legs as I shower and look for clothes because there is a woman in this city—in this mafia—who doesn't deserve any of the cruelties that are about to come.

I cannot shield Rosa from everything. But I can certainly protect her from myself. I will not be the monster in her nightmares anymore. If that means facing my father's wrath and taking on the Russians alone, so be it. My story may not be as heroic as David and Goliath, but like the King I so admire, I am not going down without a fight.

Honestly … As long as Rosa is safe, I feel I've already won.

It's the middle of the night when I exit the shower and gingerly ease my legs into a pair of briefs and then a pair of pants. I slip on a simple t-shirt, step into some comfy shoes, and begin a slow limp down the hall.

Despite the hour, I can see a sliver of light stretching from underneath Rosa's door when I reach her room. She snatches it open almost as soon as I knock.

"Amory," she breathes, looking me up and down. In this t-shirt, she can see some of the tattoos on my upper arms. Her eyes linger on them before she pulls the door open further. "Come in."

I shake my head. I don't plan to be here long.

Rosa seems disappointed, but she nods and leans against the door frame. She's wearing a short nightdress with her thick curls spilling around her shoulders. Her makeup has been washed off and she's not wearing shoes so she's three inches shorter than normal, barely reaching the middle of my chest. Her legs are bare and her feet free of stockings. I'd never noticed she painted her toes a peach color. Against her brown skin, it almost looks pale pink.

I like it.

"We need to talk," she says, drawing my attention from her thighs—or at least the few inches of them I can see. Her nightdress stops above the knee, leaving me enough flesh to appreciate and hiding enough to make me wonder.

"There's nothing to talk about," I reply.

Rosa seems stunned by my words.

"We have to sleep together to get Jameson and Gio to help us. I'm not doing that." She starts to protest, but I shake my head and cut her off. "No, Rosa. You might be willing, but you aren't *ready.*"

My words hit home. She takes a step back and fiddles with the hem of her dress. "But we promised not to give up, no matter how bad it gets between us."

"Things are the best they've ever been between us," I say, reaching up to stroke her cheek. I don't know if its subconscious or not, but she leans into my touch, and I almost lose my train of thought for a second. "I'm sending you to your grandfather." I don't bother telling her Gio also offered to keep her safe. She was never truly safe locked up in his penthouse. More like a pampered prisoner than anything.

Rosa pulls away from my caress. "I'm not leaving you. We're in this together."

"Do you remember the last thing I said to you in that room?"

She nods, beginning to blush.

"Can you say it back?"

Silence. But I'm not hurt by it. I still don't fully understand my own feelings, I don't expect Rosa to have hers all worked out. Love is a dangerous thing. And she's never been a fearless girl. Running away is something she seems to specialize in, but it takes true courage to stay put and face things head-on.

I can see her struggling with her answer as she bites her lip and drifts into her thoughts. The silence is almost stifling. I decide to break it as I step forward and say, "Think on it. And think about the consequences of loving a man like me. Then tell me your answer."

I turn and leave before she can speak. It's not that I'm afraid of her answer, it's that her response doesn't matter. I know how *I* feel. I may not understand every emotion she evokes from me, but the love is there all the same. So, my mind is made up, no matter what her response is.

___.X.___

I skip my usual workout routine the next morning. There's no time for the punching bag. I'm down to 48-hours before chaos is set loose on the city and I still have no more men, weapons, or allies than when this all unfolded.

I'm dressed and ready to go earlier than usual, an extra precaution to make sure I don't bump into Rosa on my way out. She is my weakness, the one threat to my resolve. Thankfully, she's nowhere to be found when I leave my room.

Douglass is waiting by the car with a sleepy look on his face as I emerge from the house. I've already texted him where I want to go so we don't exchange words as he opens my door and then goes to his own. It takes us more than an hour to reach Queens, my stomach turns in anxiety once an elegant villa comes into view outside my window. I've only been to this estate three times in my entire life, but it was always on good terms so I'm not too overwhelmed with nerves.

Guards approach Douglass and I once we make it up the front steps. We are searched and have our weapons confiscated, but no one is scowling or cursing at us, so I start to feel hopeful. This could go perfectly right or totally wrong.

"Amory Jäger," my name almost sounds like a song on the lips of Señor Emilio Moreno, capo of the Spanish mafia.

There is a smile on his face as he approaches, hand extended to offer a friendly shake. It quells my anxiety somewhat, but I'm still on edge. King James was laughing when he turned down my request for aid.

"*Jefe*," I say in a horrible Spanish accent. Normally, my German accent is quite attractive over languages like English and Russian, but when I try to blend it with Emilio's native tongue, I sound absolutely ridiculous.

He agrees as he laughs and slaps my shoulder. "It's the

effort that counts. Come, I know we have much to discuss."

Emilio takes me through his house, winding through chilly hallways made of cracked stone, the echo of our shoes muffled by the soft carpet beneath our feet. Portraits of his family members hang all over the walls, dozens of expertly painted images portraying beautiful people. His picture is last, at the very end of the hallway. Beside it is a portrait of his wife and then his children standing together in a flower garden I've never seen before.

We end up in his office, Douglass stands guard just outside while I take a seat across from Emilio's large desk. A picture of his immediate family sits on display. I get the feeling he's a loving husband and doting father, rare attributes in this business.

"You know what I'm here for," I say, getting right down to business.

"I do." He nods. "I heard about what your brother did."

"Everyone has."

"And everyone has also heard what you haven't done yet." He leans closer. "With your wife."

I grit my teeth and take a long, slow breath. Emilio's words interrupt my anger.

"I have been waiting for you to show up."

"You have?"

"It's all been arranged."

Now *I* lean forward, unsure if I should feel angry, cautious, or intrigued. Mostly, I feel confused. There's no way Emilio could have planned for Wolfgang to beat up a Russian woman and for the Russians to find out. But, somehow, he's planned for me to end up here. The warmth he'd extended upon my arrival suddenly feels cold and dangerous. The stone walls around us look more like a lions' den now.

"I let the cat out of the bag about your marriage."

I squint at him. "What did you use to bribe my cousin?"

"Your cousin is loyal to you. He had nothing to do with this."

"Care to explain what's going on, then?"

He leans back in his chair and exhales a happy-sounding sigh. "I have women at The Club."

I deflate. If anything, I'd suspected that maybe Wolfgang might not have been as distracted by the topless dancer as he'd seemed, but I never gave a second thought to the dancer herself. I don't remember her face or her features, but I'm not surprised she turned out to be a Spaniard. Conrad has a host of clients with a variety of tastes, so he doesn't restrict his staff to just German women. I've personally left The Club with a number of Spanish women, Black women—and one time there was this Asian lady who left me sore and exhausted for two days.

But I don't remember that dancer.

"Was she a spy?" I ask.

Emilio's face gets serious. "We are not allies, but we have never been enemies. I did not feel the need to plant a spy in your midst, Amory. She happened to be a prostitute who was picked up by your cousin. Nothing more." He takes a breath. "When she overheard your conversation, she came to me with

325

the information."

"And you spread that information throughout the entire city."

He shrugs.

"I thought we weren't enemies? You had to know that info would make things difficult for me."

"That was what I needed."

"Why?"

"To get you here."

"You could have called. You knew I would have answered."

He can't deny this. The Morenos and the Jägers have a history of sharing nothing but mutual hatred for each other, but Emilio and I have managed to carefully craft something of a friendship. As close to friends as opposing mafia heads can be.

We're on a first name basis, something I don't even have with King James—my own grandfather-in-law, and we've done good business together in the past. I sold him the information I got from the Russian we'd Hunted. He gave me all the cocaine I needed to charm King James into allowing me to marry his granddaughter. I even frequent his nightclubs, and he buys our German beer by the barrelful.

Emilio looks troubled for a moment, like what he's about to say somehow pains him. "I needed you here with no other options."

"I don't understand."

"As it stands, you are being targeted by the Russians. It

isn't a one-sided war, but it isn't a guaranteed win, either."

He's right about that.

"You need allies. And you don't have them."

"How do you know that?"

"Because you're here."

I don't respond.

"If I had kept the information about your marriage to myself, the Stronghold and the Garden would be rallying soldiers as we speak."

I don't see how that's a bad thing. The Spanish mafia would have been left out of this war entirely. Queens would be free to sit back and watch as four boroughs tore themselves to shreds. Then they could pick our bones clean and collect whatever prizes we'd be too weak to defend. But for some reason, it seems like Emilio *wants* to be in this war.

He grins at me, like he knows what I'm thinking. "If I wanted to simply help out a friend, I could have offered you aid from the get-go. But it isn't enough to just fight by your side, Amory. It must be worth it on my end as well."

"What do you want?"

His grin widens. "I want you."

This feels all too familiar.

Emilio explains, "If I become your ally, it must be a permanent arrangement."

The only way to be permanently tied to another mafia family is through marriage.

I nod slowly. "Once it's safe for Wolfgang to leave Stonehall—"

"*No*," he snaps. "The Hunting Grounds is facing war because of Wolfgang. I will not give one of my daughters to that monster."

"Well, you can't give them to me," I say. "I'm married."

"Only on paper."

"What makes you so sure?"

A long pause stretches between us as Emilio studies my face. "You would not be here if you had taken your pretty wife to bed by now. You'd be with the Stronghold or the Garden, arranging troops."

He's right. And he knows it.

"You have nothing else to offer me but yourself, Amory. You knew that when you walked through my doors. You knew this would end up being the deal."

"What exactly is the deal?"

He raises an eyebrow, then reaches into his desk drawer to retrieve a fat stack of papers. I don't even have to look at it to know it's a marital contract.

"Marry one of my daughters and unite our families."

"I'm already married—"

"Have it annulled," he demands. "It hasn't been signed in blood, I'm sure you won't have a problem getting that worked out."

"Why do you want this?"

"We work together well," he says casually. "This war might be long, but it won't last forever. Life will go on once the dust settles. I think it will be a wise investment to give you aid."

Investment.

In other words, once everything is over, the Jägers will be in such bad condition we will still require the Moreno's help. We'll be indebted to them for a long time. Longer than we want to be.

But that's just speculation. We could end up sweeping the Wolves without a problem. We could end up burning all of Staten Island. But Emilio knows I'm not willing to take that risk. I need his help, here and now, and this is the only way I can get it.

He turns the photo of his family around on his desk so I can see it. "I'll even let you pick which of my daughters you want to marry."

Eliana and Belén Moreno. Both of them are beautiful. Eliana is the oldest at 26, with olive skin and long dark hair. Belén is her opposite with light brown skin, curly hair, and a brighter, more innocent smile. It has a youthfulness to it which I'm not surprised by, she's only nineteen. One year younger than my doe-eyed wife.

"I don't care which one," I grind out.

He shrugs. "Not a picky man. I understand."

"Emilio... There must be another way."

"No. I like you, Amory, but that is my offer. Unite our families. Earn yourself a strong ally in this war. And let your wife go."

I can't, I want to tell him, but I'm afraid revealing that to him will eventually backfire. Instead, I shift in my chair, trying to find the appropriate words to say.

Emilio notices my discomfort and laughs. "I don't believe

it."

I don't respond.

"I knew there was a chance my plan may not work. How difficult could it be to sleep with your own wife, right?" He places his elbows on the desk, steeples his fingers. "I wasn't sure if you had waited so long because you didn't care for her or because you respected her wishes to wait. But now I know…"

I swallow thickly, waiting for him to put the pieces together.

"You would rather sell yourself to another mafia than violate her wishes," Emilio says with what I assume is a nod of respect. Then a curious smile spreads over his full lips. "You truly love her, don't you?"

I stiffen in my chair, unable to meet his charming gaze. He's asking the wrong question. It isn't a matter of whether I love Rosa.

The question is, do I love her enough to let her go?

Chapter Twenty-Five

Can you say it back?

Amory's words ring in my head as Gisela goes on about how upset she is over Conrad rushing out early again. I decided to go to her house for breakfast this morning; we were supposed to discuss *my* troubles but so far, our conversation has been solely focused on Glizzy. I'm not entirely bothered by that, considering how upset Gisela seems. She still had the mind to doll herself up, but even I can tell she didn't put in as much effort. Her makeup is light, and her hair is pulled into a messy ponytail; despite her blaring red dress, this is the simplest I've ever seen her dressed—though she's still wearing six-inch heels.

"If it weren't for Christina telling us about the possible war, I would think he's cheating on me," Gisela says, wringing her hands.

"I don't think he would do that to you. He loves you."

She makes a face. "Conrad does love me. But I don't let his charm fool me."

"What does that mean?"

"It means he's the owner of a mafia strip club." She sniffles. "I have never let myself forget that."

"I'm sure he's so used to seeing half naked women that it doesn't faze him anymore."

I'm trying really hard to cheer her up, but even I have my doubts about Conrad. I was raised mafia. I grew up watching women hang all over my father. There was never a doubt that he loved my mother, but I wasn't so naïve as to believe that love was strong enough to keep him from peeking under the skirts of other women.

Gisela stares into her glass of lemonade and slowly closes her eyes. I reach for her hand when I notice the single tear running down her cheek.

"I have never set foot into The Club. I refuse to go there," she whispers.

I nod, silently wondering if Amory's ever been there.

"With a war brewing, I don't think The Club is on his mind at all."

She tries to laugh. "At least I know if he doesn't have time for me then he certainly doesn't have time for that place, right?"

"Right now, we've got to focus on the positive things."

She nods, dabbing at her cheeks with her fingers. "Look at me, I'm a mess."

"You're gorgeous, Glizzy."

332

"Let me grab a tissue." She slips off the stool at the kitchen counter and walks off before I can offer her one from my purse. "Should we order lunch?" she calls from the bathroom down the hall.

"Is it lunchtime already?" I glance at my phone and press my lips together. How long have I been here listening to Gisela's worries?

She pokes her head out the door. "If you want to head home instead, I won't be upset. I'd want to eat with Conrad if he were here."

"Actually, I don't know where Amory is," I confess.

"He hasn't called?"

I shake my head, watching her slide back onto the stool beside me. "I haven't seen or heard from him since last night."

"You sound disappointed." She nudges my arm. "Did last night change anything between you two?"

I couldn't stop myself from blushing if you paid me. Heat rushes over my entire body until I'm sure I look like I need medical attention. My ears burn red, my cheeks flush, despite their brown color, and my fingers turn red as I squeeze my hands together in my lap.

As if to torture me, my mind summons images of Amory in his most natural state and I nearly tip off the stool in cardiac arrest. I thought I couldn't breathe from the way he'd kissed me, but I almost died of sudden asphyxiation when I saw him—*all* of him—for the first time. His image is seared into my head, the heat of his gaze trapped in my mind, the whisper of his last words stamped on my heart.

I love you, Rosa.

Had he been serious? Or was that a heat-of-the-moment confession?

My heart is beating too loudly at the memory of it to try to analyze any part of that scene.

"Rosy?" Glizzy touches my shoulder and I jump in surprise.

"Yes? Sorry."

"Are you all right?"

I nod vigorously and she smirks in response. "*More* than all right."

"*Glizzy*," I say in a whine. "Please don't tease."

She gasps and starts shaking me by the shoulders. "Did you finally do it!?" she squeals. "Did you?? How romantic!"

"No!" I blurt. "It didn't happen."

She frowns and releases my shoulders. "The Rose still has all her petals."

"Sorry to disappoint," I say.

Gisela crosses her arms. "Wait a minute, Flower, if you didn't get jiggy with it, why are you all red and squirmy?"

I'm sure I turn even redder.

Glizzy squeals again. "Something even better happened!"

Because I can't keep it to myself, I nod and crack a smile. "Something better did happen."

"Don't tell me..."

"He said he loves me."

A manicured hand flies to Gisela's chest while the other one frantically fans herself. "You're kidding!"

"I'm not!"

She pulls me into a hug. "That's so wonderful, my little flower!"

"It was wonderful. I still can't believe he said it."

Gisela pulls away and cups my chin. "He fell in love with you without ever touching you. Don't you let this man go."

My smile falters—Glizzy sees it right away.

"What's going on?" she asks, sharp eyes narrowing.

"He told me he loves me, but I didn't say it back."

"That's okay. You can go home and say it now."

I laugh, pulling my chin from her gentle grasp. "That's just it. I'm not sure I can say it back."

"After everything you two have been through?" She sounds more confused than I am.

"I can admit that I want him. That I'm attracted to him. And that I want our marriage to work. But … do I love him?"

"I don't understand."

Of course she doesn't. Gisela fell in love with Conrad, fully aware that they weren't equally yoked. She's never had the joys and thrills of dating a Christian man. She has no idea what sort of difference it makes in the relationship.

I know Arthur turned out to be a liar, but, while I was in Norman, I believed he was Christian. I was convinced that we held the same standards and beliefs. Even though we technically weren't together, I was well on my way to falling for him. Our careful relationship hadn't been built on lust or desire; it was constructed on the solid rock of our faith. Brick by brick. And if he hadn't turned out to be the man he's

335

become, our relationship would have been strong enough to survive the trial I'm facing now. I would have found a way out of New York. I would have made it back to him. And I know he would have waited.

With Amory, it's different. For the first two months of our marriage, sex was the biggest problem between us. We were fueled by our desires, unable to see beyond our lust for each other. The only thing that gave me comfort when heat blushed my cheeks in response to his advances was the fact that we *are* married. That our exchanges weren't wrong in God's eyes.

Now, that lust has turned to passion. Desire has become love. Want is now need. But some part of it still feels … wrong.

Gisela takes my hands. "Is it because he isn't a Believer?"

I can't look her in the eye as I whisper, "Yes."

"Mmm, I see."

"My faith is the most important thing in my life. If I can't share that with the man I'm married to, then what sort of connection do we really have?"

A flicker of emotion crosses Glizzy's face but she blinks it away and forces a smile.

I suddenly hate myself.

"Gisela, I'm sorry. I didn't mean to imply anything about you and Conrad."

She shakes her head and squeezes my hands. "Flower, I know. You don't have to explain. I ask myself that same question every night." She laughs. "Three years into this marriage and I still don't have an answer. That's why I pray for Conrad's salvation."

"I pray for Amory's. But I'm running out of time, Glizzy."

She tilts her head to the side, and I take a deep breath. Now I understand why Amory confided in Conrad. I understand what he meant when he'd said he had no idea what else to do or who else to talk to. I constantly take my concerns to God, but I want to share this with my friend as well.

Gisela is the only person I've spoken to about what's really been happening in my marriage. I know I can trust her, so I get comfortable and tell her about everything that happened last night. She sits and listens quietly, not interrupting or even reacting, except to give me a mischievous grin when I awkwardly stutter over the details of Amory and I locked in that guestroom together.

When I'm finished, she takes a deep breath and reaches up to mess with her ponytail. "That's an awful lot to take in."

"And he told me to think about the consequences of loving a man like him."

"Well, that's a good word of advice. If we're being honest."

I chew my lip. "But … is it really okay to love someone like him? I mean, is it okay with God?"

"Flower," Glizzy strokes my cheek the way Melissa would have. "*God* loves him. More than you ever will. So, why on earth would He punish you for loving him, too? A man you didn't even have a choice in marrying."

I twiddle my fingers. "I don't know."

"Do you remember the story of Hosea and Gomer?" Gisela asks.

I nod.

"Hosea was a man of God, but he ended up marrying a prostitute because God told him to."

"God didn't tell me to marry or love Amory." *And* ... there was a bigger picture for Hosea. His marriage to Gomer was symbolic, representing God and His never-ending love for the Nation of Israel, even though they were unfaithful to Him.

I am not Hosea. And Amory is not Gomer.

But that doesn't mean my marriage serves no purpose to God. Father Serrano helped reveal that to me. God wants this city, and He plans to use Amory to get it. Somehow, being his wife puts me in prime position to introduce him to the Lord. I think I've failed this mission so far, but there is still time to save it.

Gisela makes a face. "You didn't have a choice in marrying Amory. So God won't blame you for loving him. Just like He didn't blame Hosea for being intimate with his wife—in fact, He expected Hosea to father children with his ungodly wife. He didn't punish him at all for sharing a bed with her or for showing her affection."

"I just feel so guilty," I admit sheepishly.

"You shouldn't," Glizzy tells me, a serious edge to her voice. "You are married. It isn't a sin to be intimate with Amory and it isn't a sin to love him." She leans forward and pokes me in the chest. "In fact, I think it's your love for him that will lead him to Christ."

"How?"

She laughs. "If a sweet little flower like you could fall for the likes of Amory Jäger, then it won't be so hard for him to believe a pure and righteous God could love him, too."

I bite my lip, replaying her words in my head.

Gisela pokes me again. "God is a *kind* Father, Rosa. Always remember that." Her arms are around me before I can protest. "It sounds like you already have an answer to Amory's question."

Can you say it back?

I shiver as his husky voice whispers into my memories, but the sound of Gisela's stomach growling ruins the moment.

"Maybe we should order lunch now," I suggest.

She giggles and pats her empty stomach. "I'll order something for myself. *You* are going home to tell your husband exactly how you feel."

"What do I say to him?"

She touches my hand. "You'll know when you see him."

During the drive home, I go over a dozen different ways to say those magic words. It shouldn't be this difficult to tell your own husband that you're in love with him, right?

It *is* difficult. In fact, I almost talk myself out of it.

Maybe I'm not in love. Maybe I'm just caught up in the moment.

Amory and I have history going back ten years, but we haven't been married for long—less than three months, actually. That hasn't seemed to bother him, he's already told me that he loves me. He ruined his chances of getting an army for this war because he loves me. But I couldn't get myself to say it back when he'd asked how I felt in turn.

I'll admit I'm attracted to Amory; I'll even admit I have feelings for him. I'm just not as sure as he is that these feelings are strong enough to call love. But its undeniable that *something* is growing between us. Despite all our hardships and fights, *something* has taken root in both our hearts—and if we're careful, I'm certain it can become love in time.

I'm sweating bullets by the time I arrive home. Part of it is because I still haven't thought of a way to tell Amy how I feel, but the other bucket of sweat rushing from my pores is because there's another car in front of my home when my driver pulls up. I stare at it as I walk to the front doors; it's a vehicle I've never seen before.

When I enter my home, there is a guard standing right beside the door. He greets me with a tense smile and then quickly steps in front of me.

I stare at him, bewildered. "Excuse me—"

"I've been instructed to escort you to your room, Mrs. Jäger."

"My room?"

He nods and holds his arm out to direct me upstairs, but I step back and start marching through the main foyer.

"Mrs. Jäger!" the guard calls, but I ignore him.

Something is wrong. Something is terribly wrong.

"Why am I to be escorted to my room?" I don't stop walking as I toss the question over my shoulder. I'm not going anywhere in particular, I'm just determined not to be taken upstairs.

"To gather your things, ma'am."

His answer threatens to stop me in my tracks. Is Amory sending me away like he'd suggested earlier? I shake my head. I won't go live with my grandfather. I'm not letting Amy lock me up in a guarded palace so he can run off and fight the Russians alone. There is no assistance I can offer him by staying, but there is no comfort in abandonment, either.

If he dies, I'll die right beside him.

It sounds like a suicide pact because it is. Marriages in this business can be that dark.

Did you forget I was raised in the mafia?

Voices draw my attention to one of the studies. Without missing a step, I fling open the doors and almost fall over dead.

Amory is sitting in a lounge chair, legs crossed, a very focused look on his face—across from him is a very beautiful woman with long legs sliding from beneath her formfitting black dress. As soon as she sees me, she pushes from her chair and glares at my husband.

"You will not insult me with her presence."

"*Excuse me?*" I snap, stepping into the room.

The guard behind me tries to apologize. "I'm sorry, Mr. Jäger. She insisted—"

"It's all right," he says calmly.

The woman exhales in anger. "You *will* get rid of her." Then she strides to the door and leaves without even acknowledging my presence.

I take another step, blood boiling. "Who is she?"

A few moments of silence scream through the room before

my husband very evenly replies, "My fiancé."

The raging boil inside me instantly freezes over.

"Amory ... How can you have a fiancé when you're already married?"

Without words, he stands and motions to the small table beside his chair. I inch closer and glance down at the stack of papers waiting for me.

"No," I whisper, stumbling backwards.

Amory catches me by the arm and pulls me close. At first, I think he's trying to hold me, but as I lean into his embrace, he shifts away and presses a fountain pen into my hand.

"All you have to do is sign."

I throw the pen across the room. "What is going on?"

"You know exactly what's going on."

"I want to hear you say it."

"We're getting a divorce."

The words pierce my heart and threaten to cleave me in two. The jolt of pain I feel inside is so real, my knees buckle. Amory catches me yet again, but I shove him away and he trips backward into the table.

"We promised!" I holler. "We promised not to give up!"

"I know." His voice is so quiet, I blink at him, momentarily unsure if he's even spoken. He's staring at the floor now, no longer able to look me in the eye. It's the first time he's shown any sign of being hurt by what he's doing.

"Look at me," I demand. "Look me in the eye and tell me you don't want me."

To my horror, he raises his eyes to meet mine and says the

words so easily, I feel a strike of lightning shoot through my heart. "I don't want you, Rosa. I want an annulment."

I laugh bitterly. "You're a good actor."

"This is for the best."

"The best for whom?"

"For both of us."

"If you're doing this for soldiers and weapons, then don't." I take a step back and unzip my dress. It falls gracelessly to the floor, pooling around my ankles. I'm left in just my pink lace panties.

Amory stares at my naked breasts and takes a slow, careful breath.

"All we have to do is consummate the marriage," I say, stepping toward him to tug at his belt. "Then everything will be fine." When my hand slips lower to brush against the firmness between his legs, he lets out a hiss.

"*Rosa.*" His large hands grab me by the wrists, and he shoves me back a step. "*Stop* it."

"Why?"

"I promised not to touch you until you wanted me to."

I try to yank my hands away. "I *want* you to touch me."

"No." He shakes his head. "You want me to stay."

My anger swells. "This is what you've been after since we got married! I don't understand why you won't take it now!"

In one swift motion, Amory yanks me toward him and wraps his arms around me. His voice is low and strained. "Because it isn't mine to take."

"But it's mine to give."

"To someone who deserves it."

"To whomever I want to have it."

"Rosa, *please*," he grates out, "don't do this."

"Don't sleep with my own husband?"

"Don't sell yourself to me."

I clutch at his shirt, gasping as painful tears sting my eyes. "I can't—"

"You're free now, don't you see?" His arms tighten around me, and I hear the wild beating of his heart against his firm chest. "You won't be tied to New York anymore. You won't be chained by this marriage."

Diamonds are just pretty shackles...

I shake my head and let out a sob so deep, Amory shudders in response.

"This will be the first and only time I break a promise between us," he whispers into my hair. "I'm so sorry."

With strength I didn't know I have, I shove him away and stand there with tears streaming down my cheeks, hands balled into tight fists. I have only one word for him, and I hope it stings like poison.

"*Coward.*"

A flicker of emotion fills his eyes before its blinked away and replaced by the calm demeanor he wears so well. Like a true underboss, Amory straightens his shirt and buttons his jacket, the life and love draining from his face. His eyes seem to fill with ice.

He drifts away from me, locking me out of his heart.

"Sign the papers, Rosa."

Amory pulls another fountain pen from his jacket pocket. This time, he doesn't hand it to me, he simply drops it on top of the stack. "When you're done, one of my men will drive you to King James' Palace. I'll have your things sent over by the end of the day."

Without another word, he walks out the door.

I sway on my feet before making it to the table. My legs feel like they could give out at any moment. I don't trust myself to stand on my own. I'm not even sure how much longer I can maintain consciousness.

This can't be happening.

I had come home to tell my husband I loved him, instead I walked in on him arranging a marriage with another woman. And now I'm being put out of my own home.

This is all my fault.

If I hadn't been so stiff when we'd first gotten married. If I had gotten over my reservations before now. If I had been brave enough to love him even a day earlier, I wouldn't be staring down at papers of annulment now.

I grasp the pen in my hand and try to search for the dotted line through my teary vision. I don't want to admit it, but Amory is right. Once I sign these papers, I'll be free. I won't be tied to New York any longer. I'll be sent to live with my grandfather, but with war breaking out around us, I'm sure there will be another opportunity to slip away. I could finally get out. Like I've always wanted.

Maybe this is a gift from God. Maybe He's decided He doesn't need Amory to save this city or this country.

345

Is that what this is? I ask Him in my heart. *Are You giving me a way out?*

I'm not even sure it matters. Amory has already signed his copy of the papers. Not signing mine will hold up the process, but it won't stop this from happening. Unless we both tear up our copies, Amory and I *are* getting an annulment. We're ending our marriage.

I place a hand on the table and lean closer. The pen smoothly glides across the paper.

Once the deed is done, a deep exhaustion settles over me. With tired limbs and red-rimmed eyes, I gather my dress from the floor and head for the door.

The chains have been cut loose. I have been set free. But only in mind and body. My heart is still shackled to Amy.

It always will be.

Continue the series...

Clipping Thorns
Starting Over (Fall 2022)

More books by Valicity Elaine & TRC Publishing!

Christian Fantasy

Cross Academy
The End of the World series
The Scribe

Christian Science Fiction

I AM MAN series

Christian Romance

The Living Water
The Woof Pack (Coming Soon)

Christian Children's Fiction

Too Young

ACKNOWLEDGEMENTS

If you've made it this far, you are awesome. Writing this book was a challenge and a joy. I hope you enjoyed reading it as much as I enjoyed writing it. There was a lot of prayer, a lot of planning, and even a lot of research involved in this project. Fun fact, I'm *so* not a fan of romance XD This book was my attempt to write something I would enjoy reading and seeing more of in the Christian romance market. I can only hope and pray, right?

I fell in love with Amory and his struggles. I lost myself in Rosa and her dependence on God. I look forward to continuing their journey together in the next installment, *Clipping Thorns*. In the meantime, feel free to busy yourself with some of my other books! Like I said, I don't enjoy romance, so here are a few Christian fantasy adventures for you enjoy.

<u>Cross Academy</u>
<u>I AM MAN</u>

Sign up for my monthly newsletter at therebelchristian.com to stay updated on new releases, sales, and updates! See you soon.

The Rebel Christian Publishing

We are an independent Christian publishing company focused on fantasy, science fiction, and YA reads. Visit therebelchristian.com to check out our books or click the titles below!

  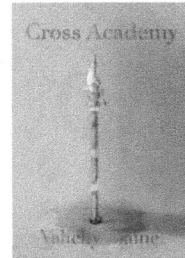 

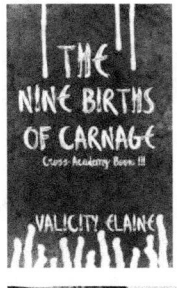   

   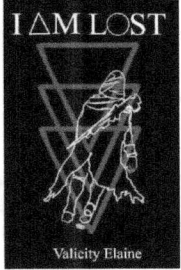

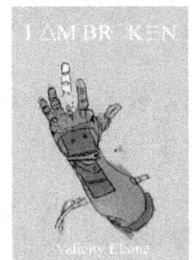

I AM BROKEN

Valicity Elaine

I AM FREE

Valicity Elaine

I AM COMPLETE

Valicity Elaine

THE LIVING WATER

A. BEAN

PATCHES

Valicity Elaine

The I Word

Valicity Elaine

Original Author's Notes

This book was originally published as an episodic story on the Kindle Vella platform. Please enjoy the original author's notes below.

Chapter One

I'm so excited to be able to write this story. I feel like this task is a gift from God. I truly hope you enjoy this book; I know it is unique in the fact that it is a Christian mafia romance, but hey, what is Christian fiction if we can't imagine the wildest of stories? On a serious note, I pray the Lord uses Rosa's story to inspire and encourage women who feel trapped in darkness to depend on Him for escape.

Chapter Two

It was hard for me to write this chapter because of what happened to Minnie, but please don't worry!
SPOILER
She is not dead.
I hope you enjoyed this chapter, I'll see you in the next one!

Chapter Three

I have to be honest, it is a little hard to write about men in the mafia. Can you imagine trying to tap into the head of someone like Amory Jager? As a Christian, writing from his POV worried me a little, but God blessed; I think it was a dark but intriguing character introduction. Don't worry, it won't always be this grim.

Chapter Four

Fun fact! My parents lived in Germany for five years before I was born. They loved it so much, I grew up hearing amazing stories about this wonderful, adventurous-sounding country. I have the utmost respect for every culture used in this story but my heart lies with Germany! It was so much fun doing research on the food and the language. My mom taught me some German phrases but I had to really sit down and study to make sure I was using certain words correctly. I hope you enjoyed it.

Chapter Five

I honestly worried that I waited too long to introduce the characters to each other, haha. It's only chapter five but for a romantic suspense novel, that may as well be an eternity. I hope the wait was worth it, there will certainly be more romance from this point on.

Chapter Six

I just want to say that King James is one of my favorite characters.

Chapter Seven

My little sister really enjoyed Rosa's connection with Arthur. In many ways, he is her strength, but I think Rosa draws strength from nearly everyone in her life. She loves Minnie and Melissa and God, too! I hope you can see her faith and dependence on God.

Chapter Eight

Diamonds are just pretty shackles... Thoughts?

Chapter Nine

I was really hesitant when writing this chapter. I battled with just how dark I should allow Amory to be. I understand he is a mafioso, but I'm still a Christian author so I didn't want to cross certain lines with his behavior. I hope I was able to maintain a balance between his position as a hardened mafia underboss and a man who wants to change for the better.

Chapter Ten

Things just got a lot more complicated XD

Chapter Eleven

My little sister is such a sensitive person, haha. She told me her heart was broken when Amory hissed to Rosa, 'You promised.' Does this mean he was hurt by her betrayal? Is he starting to change or develop feelings for Rosa? We shall see ;-)

Chapter Twelve

Hmm... This may be the beginning of change.

Chapter Thirteen

Rosa's strength lies in her faith, I couldn't wait to write this chapter just to demonstrate her relationship with God and how it affects every area of her life.

Chapter Fourteen

I just want to say I was proud of Rosa for not drinking when Amory offered her the bottle (even though I'm the one who wrote it, haha!).

Chapter Fifteen

Ahh, gotta love Mikhail Volkov, right?

Chapter Sixteen

This chapter was painful to write for so many reasons. Can you believe my little sister was actually upset that Rosa and Amory weren't intimate? haha XD Even though this couple is married, I am still a Christian author so I'm not too keen on writing detailed love scenes. We'll see what happens from here.

Chapter Seventeen

I don't exactly agree with Rosa's dilemma, but I feel like Amory's attitude kind of justifies her hesitancy. Thoughts?

Chapter Eighteen

I think Amory said it best, he's being a drama king XD

Chapter Nineteen

My sisters LOVE Gisela. I love her too. I know she is a bit gimmicky, but I made her over the top on purpose. She is meant to demonstrate how quickly some people can jump to conclusions based solely on a person's clothing. God looks at our hearts, we should learn from His example. Like Gisela said, Christians come in all shapes, sizes, and styles XD

Chapter Twenty

Sometimes Amory can be such a jerk. But he's trying to change. I promise he is. Pray for him lol

Chapter Twenty-One

I feel like nothing ever goes Amory's way--just more evidence that he needs Christ in his life XD

Chapter Twenty-Two

Ehh... I am not looking forward to the next few chapters.

Chapter Twenty-Three

There was a lot of internal debate when writing this chapter, and previous ones like it. Even though Amory and Rosa are married, I do believe there is still a line I should not cross as a Christian author. But it does beg the question, how far is too far? Where exactly is the line when the couple I'm portraying is married? Everyone is different. Some scenes may be too steamy for certain readers while others may have no problems whatsoever. I can only pray the Lord led me to find the right balance. See you in the next chapter.

Chapter Twenty-Four

Whelp... This can either end really well or really badly. Haha, we'll see. One thing I want to say is that I'm proud of Amory for continuing to dive into the Word of God even though he doesn't completely understand it. Is he on his way to salvation? Only time will tell.

Chapter Twenty-Five

Ohhhhh this ending was so bittersweet! I hated writing it! BUT it isn't the end. I hope you enjoyed this story--I can't believe you stuck around until the last chapter! Things will continue in Book II, Clipping Thorns, so keep your eyes peeled. It will be here sooner than you think!